I0678780

A Quiver Full, Or How Mr. Darcy will Not Sit on that Sofa Again!

Jenifer Hanen

Published by Jenifer Hanen, 2024.

This is a work of fiction. Similarities to real people, places, or events are entirely coincidental.

A QUIVER FULL, OR HOW MR. DARCY WILL NOT SIT ON THAT SOFA AGAIN!

First edition. September 15, 2024.

Copyright © 2024 Jenifer Hanen.

ISBN: 979-8991469210

Written by Jenifer Hanen.

A Quiver Full is with a full, happy heart dedicated to all the lovely folks at AHA who kindly encouraged me to take my 2016 AQF short story and turn it into a book. Big hugs to the whole of the Jane Austen Fan Fiction community. Y'all Rock!

Many thanks to Kate the Beta, Elaine C, FJ, Erika, my family, Megan M for encouraging me to write and publish. And thanks to AHA / Meryton.com for the space to spread my wings safely.

Chapter 0 - A Small Preface

Really this is an Author's Note, from me - Jenifer Hanen - to you, the Reader.

Yes, yes, before you ask there will be Happily Ever Afters (HEAs) for everyone, or very near everyone. At the very least, HEAs for all the usual suspects and a few unusual suspects.

Rating: Not very salacious, although more than slightly vulgar in Mr. Fitzwilliam Darcy's opinion, he will not sit on that sofa again but Mr. Bennet will. If you are a Clean and Sweet reader, there are only mentions of kissing but please note that while the law of the story is pretty clean, the spirit is on a madcap romp around Regency England.

Warning: If you love Canon accurate Jane Austen Fan Fiction (JAFF) stories, please click on your back button now. This is a humor story where I explore the consequences of several main characters actions which will cause plot and characters to diverge/grow in a different direction from Canon.

Alternate Universe Notes: This book is an AU, aka Alternate Universe, What-if of Jane Austen's Pride and Prejudice.

This is a story occurs in a Regency England one or two universe instances parallel to our own historical universe. The biggest difference is that in the AQF universe there are two colleges granting Bachelor's degrees to young ladies open in England in response to Mary Wollestonecraft's 1792 book *On the Vindication of the Rights of Women*: Matlock College at Cambridge and Lorien College at Oxford.

While nearly 20 years has passed in A Quiver Full since the 1793 Ladies Education Bill, society at large is still not quite ready for a several hundred upper class and upper middle class women with university degrees. While many men in the upper classes and upper trade classes will want educated wives as a status symbol or help with their businesses, most of these women will still not be able to contribute to society as similarly educated men do. Reactionaries will push back at the Lorien and Matlock College ladies labeling them bluestockings and worse. The consequences of being a pioneer at a ladies college is a sub-plot that will affect the Bennet ladies in this story.

For folks who have followed the history of universities in our own historical UK time, in 1800 there was a revamping of the education, exams, and courses offered at Oxford and Cambridge Universities moving away from the Medieval Quadrivium and Trivium education that young men seeking to join the Church or the Academy would undertake starting in their early teens and graduate with a Ph.D. in their twenties. By 1810 or so, current modern system of lectures, tutors, and exams had been instituted at Oxford and Cambridge. In this story, at both Matlock and Oxford Colleges for ladies will be providing the new modern style of education and granting Bachelor's degrees in the Quadrivium and Trivium, as well as the modern subjects of Literature, History, Natural Philosophy (the natural sciences), etc. In this AU, a few very determined and brave souls will be pushing for and obtaining their Ph.Ds and then returning as Fellows and eventually Professors at Matlock and Lorien.

As you can imagine from the names of the Ladies Colleges, the Fitzwilliam and Darcy families in AQF are very pro-ladies Colleges.

To this end, I dedicate this AU to my 4th great-grandmother who was the first woman in our family to earn a bachelors degree in the 1830s. Here is to all the pioneering women!

Chapter 1 : The 1780s were a very Different Time...

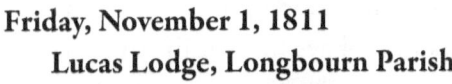

"Lo, children are an heritage of the LORD: and the fruit of the womb is his reward. As arrows are in the hand of a mighty man; so are children of the youth. Happy is the man that hath his quiver full of them..."
- Psalm 127:3-5, KJV

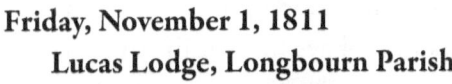

Friday, November 1, 1811
   Lucas Lodge, Longbourn Parish
   Meryton, Hertfordshire
   Across the ancient, great hall of Lucas Lodge, a man with his cousin Lewis's countenance raised an inquiring eyebrow at Mr. Fitzwilliam Darcy's intent gaze. *That must be Aunt Catherine's cicisbeo of long standing.* Darcy shook his head to clear out the invading thought, but it crept back in. *Good Lord, she boldly admitted that her lover of many years fathered both Anne and Lewis! And here he is in Hertfordshire...*
   "I can guess the subject of your reverie," Miss Bingley, who in her court shoes was almost taller than Mr. Darcy, whispered into his ear. Darcy jumped forward as she accosted him from behind. He noticed with some irritation that the man leaning against the fireplace mantle was watching with amusement. Darcy wondered, with a shudder, if Miss Bingley was going to bite his earlobe or lick the soft skin just behind his ear.
   "I should imagine not," Mr. Darcy said as he stepped a full stride away from Miss Bingley. She did not take any hints and continued to move forward towards him.

"You are considering how insupportable it would be to pass many evenings in this manner, in such society; and indeed I am quite of your opinion." Miss Bingley licked her lips. "I was never more annoyed! The insipidity and yet the noise. Look at the youngest Bennet girl, she is a hoyden!"

Mr. Darcy looked at the youngest Bennet, a Miss Lydia, who for all of her height and womanly curves could be the sister of his cousin Anne de Bourgh. While his cousin's hair was a dark coffee color and Miss Lydia's was a light auburn, the shape of Lydia's face, her nose, her eyebrows and how they arched, her chin, and the curve of her cheeks - it was his cousin Anne - exactly. The more he looked at Miss Lydia, the more disconcerted he became, as her eyes were the same bright green as his disgraced childhood friend - George Wickham's eyes. However could Miss Lydia have his cousin Anne's countenance with George Wickham's eyes? What manner of witchcraft was abroad here in dreary Hertfordshire?

Aunt Catherine called him the great love of her life. How could she so casually dismiss that they were both married at various times to others? Darcy's thoughts intruded over Miss Bingley's speech as his mind drifted back to an unpleasant conversation two weeks previous. *My Aunt dismissed that objection with a wave of her hand and sigh, claiming that his family's comedown in the world due to his brother's profligacy prevented any public attachment.*

Mon, Oct. 14, 1811
   Lady Catherine's sitting room
   The de Bourgh Townhouse
   Mayfair, London
"Nephew, you must apprehend that my cicisbeo's connections are excellent. His mother is from the cadet branch of the Manners family and his grandmother was a Howard. In fact, she is the aunt

of your aunt Matlock! His eldest sister, as you well know, is Lady
Beauchamp. His father's line is ancient and they were the largest
landholder in Hertfordshire before his brother's gambling destroyed
their wealth. My Thomas has worked hard these past five and twenty
years to restore his family's fortunes and consequence."

Lady Catherine pinned him with her piercing gaze. "I have called
you to attend me today, as your help in a matter related to this is necessary."

Darcy raised an eyebrow at this preposterous statement and sat
down on a rather passé gilded shell sofa. He wondered when his aunt
would have the sofa upholstered anew in a modern fabric, though a
new elegant fabric could not remedy the gilded shell ornamentation.

"It is a shame his heir is an idiot! As Lewis, Anne, and I well
know, the man is a toad eater of the..."

"Aunt?"

"My parson. I am speaking of my parson, who is the heir to the
entail on the last remaining portion of what was once the greatest
estate in Hertfordshire. Indeed, the estate was granted to Thomas's
many times great-grandfather as a favor from King Henry III for exemplary service. Nearly 600 years in the same family, Nephew, 600
years! It is a crime that my illiterate, low born parson, Mr. Collins,
will inherit!"

"Your parson attended university and cannot truly be illiterate.
Do you mean that he does not like to read or that he is not well
read?"

Lady Catherine ignored his questions. "It is more than a shame!
Thomas kindly provided two heirs for my departed Sir Lewis..."

"Aunt!"

"My dearly departed Lewis was incapable... Oh, Darcy, stop
pulling such a face, one would think you were a prudish old maid!
As I was saying, Sir Lewis' staff of life had not enough water of life..."

"AUNT!!!"

"Attend to my words, Nephew. Hope to heaven that it never happens to you! Sir Lewis could not increase any lady, not even his mistress of..."

"Aunt Catherine, please desist!"

Per her usual wont, Lady Catherine did not.

"In the year 1784, I had been married nearly thirteen years. I was six and thirty and despairing of ever giving birth to an heir. My dear departed husband suggested that Kympton's Reverend Thomas Bennet - the very same parson who christened you - was the right man to do the job. Now seven and twenty years later, Rosings and the de Bourgh fortunes are secure."

Darcy struggled to keep an implacable countenance as he considered the horrifying implications. *Mr. Bennet, the beloved parson who taught me to read, was my aunt's lover and my cousin's...* Darcy, thoroughly appalled, became restless on the shell sofa.

"Nephew, attend my words carefully. My Thomas will speak to you after you have arrived in Hertfordshire to help teach that tradesman friend of yours how to be a gentleman and manage an estate."

Before he could protest that Mr. Bingley was not in trade, she skewered him with one of her trademarked stares, "Nonetheless, you will listen to Thomas and help us. It is the least you can do since you have not married Anne and she has found another to marry."

Lady Catherine required no reply before she continued, this time with less force.

"The 1780s were a different time, truly." With a fond smile and a lovely soft sigh, Lady Catherine ceased speaking and stared off dreamily to some point below Darcy's right shoulder.

Lounging on a modern Egyptian themed sofa opposite the golden shell sofa, Darcy's cousin, the new Sir Lewis de Bourgh, the seventh of that name, sardonically raised an eyebrow and shrugged his shoulders at his mother's revelations, not saying a word.

Friday, November 1, 1811
   Lucas Lodge, Longbourn Parish
   Meryton, Hertfordshire

Miss Bingley continued to move towards him as she droned on, "...the nothingness and yet the self-importance of all these people! What would I give to hear your strictures on them!"

"Your conjecture is wrong, I assure you."

With that statement, Mr. Darcy stalked off in search of the punch bowl and hoped beyond hope that someone had poured some decent brandy into the punch. He reached the punch bowl, leaned in, sniffed, and determined that the brandy in the punch was weak and of no vintage, when the man from the fireplace approached from the other direction and pulled out a silver, engraved flask from his waistcoat.

Mr. Darcy spied the engraved initials on the flask - CdB.

"Mr. Darcy, would you like a bit of '99 Armagnac to add to your punch? A dear friend buys it from a reputable and exemplary smuggler, or so she claims." Mr. Bennet's dear friend had an estate in Kent and made it her business to always get the best Armagnac, Cognac, and Port, no matter the state of the war or blockade. Mr. Bennet greatly appreciated his friend.

Mr. Darcy picked up an empty punch glass and held it up to Mr. Bennet. "Armagnac, straight - please."

"Well, well, a young man of taste and distinction."

Mr. Darcy raised his punch glass in a salute to the older man, sniffed the fiery liquid, sighed with happiness, and took a sip. "It tastes like the excellent French brandy my aunt procures."

Mr. Bennet raised an eyebrow. "Lady Catherine de Bourgh, I presume?"

Darcy raised an eyebrow back at Mr. Bennet as his answer.

"The very same. Please, Mr. Darcy, why don't you join me in a quieter space where the echoes of this old hall won't reach us, such as the alcove beyond the fireplace? I have a few things I would like to speak to you about. The Armagnac will come with us. Indeed, I have more if necessary." Mr. Bennet held the current flask and patted the right side of his waistcoat.

Darcy surveyed the various groupings of people in the hall - Miss Bingley was being detained by the ever loquacious Sir William Lucas, many of the younger persons were dancing as the fine eyed Miss Elizabeth Bennet - Mr. Bennet's second eldest - played the pianoforte, his friend Charles Bingley was ensconced on a love seat with the eldest Miss Bennet, as the vulgar Mrs. Bennet was cackling with a few matrons, and others were conversing with militia officers or playing cards.

"Indeed, Mr. Bennet, as long as there is enough fine brandy in your flask for two more glasses, let us proceed."

Ensconced in the alcove beyond the fireplace, Mr. Bennet poured them both a dram. "Mr. Darcy, you may remember, or possibly not, that I was the rector with the living at Kympton for some few years before your birth and some few years after."

"Yes, Mr. Bennet, I do remember that you taught me to read. I could not have been more than three or four."

"You were three and a very fast learner. Your Uncle de Bourgh bet that even I could not teach the brightest young lad of three to read. I must share the earnings of twenty pounds with you, as it was a joint endeavor."

Darcy relaxed and laughed. "No need, Mr. Bennet, no need. Lady Catherine intimated that you left the rectory to help your family."

"Indeed, the troubles commenced in the late 1770s when my elder brother, while I was at Oxford, sowed his wild oats long and deep through London society and nearly bankrupted the whole of the Bennets to the tune of nearly one hundred thousand pounds.

My esteemed grandfather and father, much to the horror of the family and our connections, decided to sell two-thirds of Longbourn's acreage, as well as the townhouse in London. Once the debts were paid, my grandfather put an entail on the remaining property to keep my brother's gambling from mortgaging it further."

"In 1779, I finished reading mathematics and theology at Oxford. The next year when I reached five and twenty, my sister's husband, Lord Beauchamp secured the living at Kympton for me. The following seven years were the best of my life - the society of most clever persons, illuminating conversation, and friendships worth more than gold. I met the love of my life at that time and was able to help several friends in need. It all came crashing down in late 1787, when my brother passed away from his excesses and I was called home as the new heir to a very reduced Longbourn."

Mr. Darcy nodded and held up his now empty small punch glass. Mr. Bennet attended to his alcove hosting duties pouring them both another dram of the brandy.

"During the Kympton years, I was able to earn a good amount of ready cash through a few good deeds and I put it into funds. When I returned to Longbourn in late 1787 my grandmother, the Lady Margaret Howard Bennet, confessed that she had secretly purchased the Longbourn Old Rectory and adjacent farmland with monies from her dowry trust, and that it would be mine separate and free of the entail when she passed. I used a portion of the monies from selling the Kympton living to one of Beauchamp's cousins to purchase additional acres of good farmland. I have invested the rents from the farmland and the Rectory into the funds and a few ventures." Mr. Bennet paused to take a breath and a sip of brandy before continuing on, to Darcy's amusement. How very like his Aunt Catherine, Mr. Bennet was in these long historical discourses!

"Reading maths at university can be rewarding in life when one utilizes the magics of compound interest and keeping the knowledge of said income investments secret from one's spendthrift wife. I have nearly earned back all the funds my brother lost these thirty years ago, of which I will use for my daughters' dowries and to the Chancery Court to break the entail."

Mr. Bennet held up his hand to halt any questions. "Let me get to the crux of the matter. I must break the entail before I die. While my health is good and I do not expect to expire soon, I cannot in good conscience allow the estate of Longbourn to fall out of the hands of the Bennets and into the hands of my grandfather's cousin's grandson. If your aunt is to be believed, Mr. Collins, who I have not yet had the pleasure of meeting, has even less understanding than his illiterate father."

"By illiterate, do you mean to say that Mr. Collins cannot read or that he does not like to read or does not read well?" Mr. Darcy asked.

"The father could not read and your aunt states the younger Mr. Collins is of mean understanding and does not apprehend very well what he has read." Mr. Bennet took another sip and started patting his waistcoat to locate another flask. "The original entail was to keep my very wayward brother from completely wasting his inheritance, but the second part is my fault and must be mine to remedy."

Darcy scanned the hall again to make sure no one was listening and to assess Miss Bingley's whereabouts. To his great fortune, the oldest Lucas son was happily conversing with Miss Bingley's bosom due to the height of her court shoes' heels, her natural stature, and his lack thereof.

Mr. Bennet pressed on. "In early 1788, the scheming Miss Gardiner, now Mrs. Bennet, decided that she was no longer content being the daughter of a country solicitor. She was determined to become the wife of the heir of the local prominent estate. I was dazed with the details of everything I needed to learn to run the estate and she compromised me. My family, particularly my grandfather, was horrified and insisted that Gardiner send his wanton hussy of a daughter off to the far reaches of Scotland, or at least Cumbria. After much to-do, I found myself married and my angry grandfather added the codicil to his will and the entail to make Mr. Collins the heir to Longbourn if I was unable to produce a legitimate living male heir of my body."

Mr. Darcy waited.

"The key word here is legitimate. After Lydia was born, my disgust for my wife had grown to the point where my... umm... well... ((cough)) ... I was unable to grow and remain stiff, if you understand me, and I have been unable to father an heir with my wife."

Darcy continued to wait.

"This is where you come in."

"Pardon?"

"Mrs. Bennet was just sixteen when she accosted me. She is not yet nine and thirty, there is still time for her, as my legal wife, to increase and birth a male heir of my body."

"I will not. I cannot. And I SHALL NOT!"

"No, no, no, not you! You are not a male heir of my body. Please, do not trouble yourself." Mr. Bennet uncorked the second flask and poured both of them another dram of vintage '99 brandy. "I cannot ask Lewis, who is a male of my body, as I like and respect him too much. Also, your Aunt Catherine would have none of it and told me not to even consider such an idea. Thus, I must locate the other young man I sired in the '80s. From what your Aunt has told me, he may be in dire enough straits to accept my proposal."

Darcy was astonished and appalled. "I must insist that I do not see how I can help either you or my Aunt in this endeavor. I thank you very kindly for the brandy, but..."

"Wickham. I must find George Wickham. Catherine's men have been unable to track him down in his usual environs after the unfortunate incident in Ramsgate. She thought you might be having him followed. Do you know his whereabouts?"

Anger welled up in Darcy's breast at the mention of George Wickham; it chased out the appalling astonishment of Mr. Bennet's tale, who was this man to... The image of Miss Lydia Bennet's bright green eyes came to him. "You are George Wickham's sire?"

"Yes, he was the first stud fee I earned." At this flippant reply from Mr. Bennet, Darcy remembered a conversation from the last month of his father's life wherein his esteemed father explained a few oddities in Pemberley's books.

"I may have been aware of something to that effect, but I was not informed who did the deed."

"It was I." At this, Mr. Bennet pulled out from his coat pocket a miniature of his brother Andrew painted in 1785. "Does George Wickham look like this man?"

"Indeed! Truly." Darcy's anger receded as astonishment came to the forefront, other than the white wig in the '80s fashion, George Wickham was peering up at him from the small painting. "The George Wickham I know is tall, slender, has dark sandy blonde hair, bright green eyes such as Miss Lydia's eye color, and a very straight nose very much like this gentleman."

"From what Lady Catherine has confided in me, it sounds like Mr. Wickham has inherited my brother's tastes and gambling along with his looks, and thus might be desperate and willing to do anything to make some ready money."

"How is your brother the father of George Wickham?"

"He is not. I am. Are you aware that Mr. Ernest Wickham, as fine a man as you will find anywhere, was unable to complete his marital duties with his lovely young wife? He had no problems with tupping several of Pemberley's grooms and the blacksmith in Lambton, but he could not and would not with a lady. He was completely unable to worship at the altar of Venus, it was Mars or nothing for him. Your father knew how much old Mr. Wickham desired a family, so he paid me to do the deed as I was from a good family, clever, educated, etc."

"My g_d! The vicarage at Kympton was a busy place!"

"No, the gilded shell sofa in the alcove of the library at Pemberley was a busy place. The housekeeper at the vicarage was a gossip and a busybody, but your father ran a tight ship at Pemberley and no gossip leaked out about Mrs. Wickham nor your Aunt Catherine." Mr. Bennet giggled a bit drunkenly. "A great deal of wonderful memories were made on that sofa. I was glad to see your father gave it to Lady Catherine for her sitting room in London."

The silly grin on Mr. Bennet's face became a large smile. While Mr. Bennet recollected happier times, horror was the emotion that stampeded over the previous astonishment in Darcy's mind, bafflement followed close behind.

"How ever can the reprobate, profligate George Wickham help you end the entail?"

"Can you not apprehend? George Wickham, who I sired at the request of your father and his father, looks like my brother's twin. Thus, if I can locate him and pay him, as I was paid to sire Wickham and various de Bourghs, no one can doubt that the male heirs of Mrs. Bennet's body as my wife are of my get!"

"Look over there at Mrs. Bennet," Mr. Bennet indicated to his wife in a loud gaggle of matrons. "She is as handsome as any of the young ladies and is a rival in looks to my Jane, who is the belle of Hertfordshire. It will be no feat at all for Mrs. Bennet to incite lust in a known rake. For money and a case of French brandy, not the '99 mind you, he can be quiet about the job and ignore her vulgarity which unmans me. When a male heir is born, it will be in truth a male heir of my body, thus we can break the entail."

A quiet and taciturn man by nature, by now all words had fled from Mr. Darcy. His jaw worked up and down a few times with nary a squeak emitting from his vocal cords.

"The entail codicil making Collins heir is my fault for falling into Mrs. Bennet's trap, as it is my responsibility to finish restoring the

Bennet wealth and holdings, so must the remedy to end the entail be mine. It is imperative I find Wickham."

Darcy drained his glass of the last finger of brandy. "I will write to my cousin Colonel Fitzwilliam and see if he can have more luck than my Aunt's men at locating Mr. Wickham in his usual haunts."

"We thank you. Another pour?"

"No, thank you. Please do not mention this to anyone else, nor of my involvement. I will not inform the Colonel why I am looking for Wickham."

Darcy changed his mind. He was on the verge of tipsy and decided to tip on over. He held out his glass to Mr. Bennet. "However did the young, studious rector at Kympton get involved in the stud business?"

"Mind you, the 1780s were a very different time, not quite so many strictures as now and quite a bit more fun to be had, I was eight and twenty and had been in my living for three and a half years. The good Lady Anne Darcy was increasing with you and Mr. Ernest Wickham had recently married the young and handsome Miss Lavinia Hinton of Mayfield Rectory, Staffordshire. Pemberley was a happy place with the best library north of Oxford and a very comfortable gilded sofa..."

When it was time to depart the Lucas's soiree, Darcy wobbled to the Bingley carriage declaring to his new best friend, Mr. Thomas Bennet, "I understand how you started, but after all these years why do you still visit with my aunt? Is it to see my cousins?"

"Lady Cat is like riding a tiger, being on top is the most invigorating, exhilarating activity in the world, but falling under her claws is most fearsome! Fearsome!" Mr. Bennet made claw shapes with his hands, as he let out a big growl and shook his head from side to side, dislodging his spectacles in the process. "Grrrrrrrr!"

A QUIVER FULL, OR HOW MR. DARCY WILL NOT SIT ON THAT SOFA AGAIN!

15

Miss Elizabeth Bennet exited Lucas Lodge rapidly walking toward her father, with Mr. Bingley and a concerned Miss Jane Bennet following behind. "Papa! Oh no, the brandy..."

"Grrrrrrrr! Tigersh! Tigersh clawsh!"

Miss Elizabeth gently took her father's elbow and steered him away. "Papa, our carriage is over here."

Mr. Hurst poked his head out of the Bingley carriage. "Whatever have you been drinking and where is my portion?"

Mr. Darcy leaned on the side of the carriage, as he tried to smile and wave at Miss Elizabeth Bennet and her fine eyes. It took effort.

Mr. Bennet stopped, disentangled his elbow from his daughter's hands, reached into his waistcoat and handed Mr. Hurst a flask. " '02, Cognac..."

"Thank you, kind sir!"

Darcy attempted to mount the carriage steps and turned back to Mr. Bennet. "I will never sit on that gilded shell sofa again! Do you know that she refuses to get it re-upholstered?"

Mr. Bennet weaved about as he proclaimed, "The 1780s were very good years, my friend, very good yearsh! Comfortable gilded shell shofas most of all!"

Chapter 2 - The Intrigue Deepens, Part I

─────── ⟋⟍ ───────

Just a bit after 8:00 am
   Sat. Nov. 2, 1811
   Longbourn Manor
   Meryton, Hertfordshire

The morning after the gathering at Lucas Lodge, as the sun rose between the clouds, Miss Elizabeth Bennet walked downstairs muting her steps to look for her new heavy silk pelisse without bothering Mrs. Hill or one of the maids to fetch it for her. The late autumn morning appeared to be a bit damp outside but the sun was shining and Elizabeth did not want to waste a moment, as at this time of year one never knew when it would rain.

After inspecting the hall and the closet under the stairway for her pelisse to no avail, Elizabeth walked down the hall to the kitchen where she could hear Mrs. Hill's voice speaking to Cook. Opening the door, Elizabeth greeted all in the kitchen. "Good morning. Mrs. Hill, have you seen my new pelisse? It is not in the hall closet nor the one under the stairs."

"I do believe that Miss Bennet took it up to her room last night after the family returned from Lucas Lodge."

"Oh, dear. Thank you, Mrs. Hill." Elizabeth nodded at Cook and the scullery maid as she shut the door and started back towards the stairs. *Dear Lord, please do not let Jane have stitched a battle scene onto my new Chinese silk pelisse. Please.*

Knocking on Jane's door, Elizabeth heard a faint "Come in." Upon entering the room, she saw a rumpled bed, clothing and cloth strewn on the floor, while Jane was sitting by the eastern window with drapes fully open as the morning sun streamed in. Jane's sewing basket was at her feet and there were two burnt out candles on the table next to her chair.

Jane was releasing Elizabeth's pelisse from her embroidery frame as she looked up. "There you are, Lizzy. I tried to finish stitching as fast as possible so that you would have your pelisse for your morning walk."

Rather than expressing anger or bursting into tears at the wanton destruction of her beautiful new pelisse, Elizabeth's concern for her sister's sleepless state was more pressing. "Jane, how long have you been up?"

Smoothing the wrinkles out with her hand, Jane lifted the pelisse up and showed it to Elizabeth. "I woke up after a few hours and could not go back to sleep. I decided that your new pelisse would look quite jaunty with an Agincourt knight embroidered vertically down the front on each side of the frog enclosures."

"Jane, the silk and frogs are Chinese in pattern."

"Yes, now the embroidery is English. I made sure that I did not pierce the interior quilting nor the silk lining. It is a lovely decoration, look - I stitched the knights to historical accuracy."

"Oh, Jane." Elizabeth blinked rapidly.

Jane looked down at the two burnt out candles and shrugged her shoulders. "I know it is your new pelisse gifted from our Aunt Beauchamp. Lizzy, please understand."

Jane jumped up and opened her trousseau trunk which was at the foot of her bed. She pulled out a long length of hemmed fine linen cloth. "I can hardly bear being here at Longbourn, especially after the freedom we had at Lorien College and in the City of Oxford; as the close society of Meryton, the petty arguing, Mama's nerves, Lydia's wildness, Papa's ignoring of it all and hiding in his study as if he were a badger defending its den - I just want to leave and return to London."

Jane walked back with the fabric to her window side chair and
pulled a larger embroidery frame out of her basket, put the edge of
the linen in the frame, secured it taut, picked up her pencil, and
chose a new roll of silk floss in a light blue to thread through her needle.

"Jane, Jane, Jane." Leaning on the bedpost, Elizabeth looked at
the portion of the 15th century English knight in full plate armor
on the front of her pelisse as she considered her next words. "We are
to return to our Aunt Beauchamp and the Gardiners in Town at the
beginning of December - it is merely a month away. Just after Easter,
we will be presented at court and have our Season. There is plenty of
time."

"You say that, Lizzy, but what did we go to University for if only
to marry? For what, Lizzy? Society is not ready for the new modern
educated lady, however few of us there are. What are we to do with
all of our knowledge and with our four years of freedom? Here I am
in a small market town stitching a trousseau for a non-existent suitor.
Lizzy, I am nearly four and twenty. I feel trapped."

Elizabeth started to speak, but Jane cut her off and said, "You as
a mathematics graduate can audit my uncle's books and that of his
fellow tradesmen for a good fee. You can help others formulate investment plans. No one is willing to pay me to discuss how Randúlfr
Eikenskaldi helped turn the Battle of Hastings in favor of the Nor-
mans. No one, Lizzy."

"Jane..."

"I do not wish to return to Oxford as a fellow nor to one of the
girl's preparatory schools to teach nor do I wish to remain trapped
here in Meryton. I must marry. I must marry a man that I can love,
who in turn will love me and who will understand me. I must get out
of here soon." Jane picked up her pencil and started to lightly sketch
guidelines on the taut linen. "It is just eight in the morning, go now

on your walk before it rains and our mother starts demanding our presence in the sitting room."

"Jane..."

"Lizzy, go walk. Leave me to my stitching." Seeing that Elizabeth was not moving, Jane tried another tack. "Did you know that Mr. Bingley read medieval history at Cambridge? His favorite battle is Agincourt."

"Oh, Jane."

Jane held up the frame to the window light and added a few more lines before picking up her needle and thread. "Go for your walk, Lizzy. I will rest later, I promise."

Seeing that Elizabeth was still hesitating, Jane added. "Truly, Lizzy, I am well. Go."

With that command, Elizabeth silently walked over to her sister, kissed her cheek, and then walked out of the room. She ran down the stairs, barely touching the steps, and out the front door to the freedom of the paths about Longbourn manor.

The sun was rising higher. The autumn air was cool and crisp, and raindrops glistened on newly bare tree branches. Some oak trees still held on to their orange and rust colored leaves. The footpath was strewn with brightly colored leaves as Elizabeth strode out on her favorite walk. The beauty of the morning held her lightly, as Elizabeth mused about Jane, her father, and Mr. Darcy waving to her last night as they departed. *I thought he disliked me? Why would he flirt and wave? Was it the drink my father plied him with? Something is afoot. What is Papa's newest scheme?*

10:00am, the very same day
Netherfield Park
Meryton, Hertfordshire

As Miss Caroline Bingley entered the breakfast parlor at Netherfield Park, the estate that her brother was leasing, she espied only her older sister and her brother at the table. "Charles. Louisa. Where are Mr. Darcy and Mr. Hurst?"

Mr. Charles Bingley smiled as he put another rasher of bacon on his already full plate. "Both are taking breakfast in their rooms. We are to go shooting later this afternoon."

"You mean that they are recovering in their rooms from last night's overindulgences. I will admit to being quite astonished at Mr. Darcy's drinking to the point of tipsy. I have never seen him drunk in all of our acquaintance!"

Mrs. Louisa Hurst took a sip of her tea and raised her eyebrow at her younger sister. "Caroline, judge not, lest you be judged."

"Sister! Are you quoting Scripture at me?"

"Yes, Sister, when appropriate. Do not try to tell me that you have never stayed in your room past breakfast with an aching head and a sour stomach from too much wine. Let me remind you of..."

"No, do not." Caroline sat down and motioned for the servant to bring her tea. "Whatever was Mr. Darcy thinking to spend the whole evening in a corner drinking with that awful Mr. Bennet?"

"Mr. Bennet is a capital chap!"

"Charles, do not defend the man merely because he is a good shot, he carries flasks of brandy in his waistcoat, and his eldest daughter is a very sweet girl." Caroline motioned for the servant to bring her the tray of cakes and pastries.

Cutting his food into bite sized pieces, with a spark in his eyes Charles replied, "Sweet? Nay, she is truly the most beautiful angel."

After picking out a pastry for the servant to place on her plate, Caroline looked up at her brother. "Oh, Charles, not again. Not another angel. I implore you to fall in love with an heiress angel, not a penniless country angel."

Looking at the full smile and sparkling, dreamy eyes of her brother, Caroline could feel a headache coming on, one that had nothing to do with overindulgence.

11:00 am, the same day
Longbourn Manor

After a quiet and sedate breakfast wherein Mrs. Bennet remained upstairs in her chamber, Mr. Bennet requested that his youngest daughter Lydia attend him in his book room. Before she could protest, he ushered her into his study, shut the door and indicated that she should sit in the seat in front of his desk.

Lydia flounced onto the chair. "Papa, what do you need to speak to me about that cannot be said in front of Jane and Lizzy?"

Mr. Bennet leaned back in his chair and lowered his reading spectacles so he could see his most recalcitrant and disobedient child clearly. "Lydia, you cannot be in suspense of my reasons for this interview."

"Lord, not this again!"

"Lydia, you will return to school before the month is out. To be expelled from school for outrageous and inappropriate behavior is not acceptable for a Bennet. We discussed this last summer, but I will remind you again of it." Mr. Bennet rapped his desk at each point. "You will have no dowry other than one thousand pounds at your mother's death unless you finish school. If you finish school with honors, pass the examinations to enter university, attend university without any trouble, and graduate with a degree like your two eldest sisters, then you will have a very good dowry upon your presentation in London that will recommend you to a good marriage. If you do not..."

"And be a spinster stitching her trousseau at three and twenty with no prospects? No, I will not." Lydia laughed at this statement as her fingers played with a curl near her cheek. "I will be the first of my sisters to marry. How well that sounds, to be married at fifteen to an officer..."

"What will you and this penniless Militia officer live on? Air? The mites and fleas in his red coat? You and your mother are greatly fooled if you think that a daughter of mine who runs off with an officer before she completes her education will get one penny more than what is written in your mother's settlement. It is time for you to return to school and complete your full studies; if you do not, you will be a stranger to this house."

Lydia shifted in her seat, eyed her father. "Papa, you reprimand me for being expelled from school, for having high spirits, and for being the silliest girl in England; but you drink too much, hide away in this room, and are mean-spirited - verging on caustic!"

"I am not mean-spirited!"

"Yes, you are! To my mother and at times even to me!"

"She is vulgar and of mean understanding. Her head is filled with lace and silly schemes to marry you girls off to unsuitable young men of no consequence in the world."

Lydia smiled at her father. "If you expect me to go to school to be educated, to become a lady, then why did you not teach Mama to be a lady?"

Mr. Bennet took his spectacles off, laid them down on the desk and leaned forward. "She was already a lost cause when she came to me."

"She was only sixteen! The same as I am now."

"You are fifteen and four months, hardly sixteen."

"Am I a lost cause then?"

"No, you are not and you will not be when you complete your schooling, which you will return to as soon as can be. You have no choice in this matter."

"I am her daughter and nearly the same age that you declared her a lost cause. It does not follow, Papa. Either I am her daughter and should languish in the vulgarity of my fate here in Meryton or both of us can learn to be ladies and I can return to school. It is your choice." Lydia stood up and walked to the door of the study without looking back at her father.

In the west facing sitting room, Elizabeth and Jane could hear their Father and Lydia's raised voices arguing two rooms away. Pulling an embroidery thread into a knot, Jane sighed, "It is really too bad that ladies cannot train for the law, as Lydia would make an excellent barrister."

"Truly." Looking up from the letter she was writing to her cousin, Elizabeth wished to revisit their earlier conversation that morning, "Jane, I do hope whoever you marry has as great of a passion for the major battles of English history as you."

Jane smiled and lifted up her embroidery hoop. "I am stitching the beginning of the battle of Agincourt on this sheet and pillow set; at the very least he will need to know his Shakespeare."

"Agincourt? Is that not what you were discussing with Mr. Bingley on the Lucas' sofa last night?" Elizabeth teased her sister.

"Oh, Lizzy, Mr. Bingley is everything a young man ought to be: amiable, handsome, and he read History at Cambridge. His interests are later in the medieval era than mine - Agincourt to Bosworth - but we were able to converse some time on Agincourt and he was quite interested in my thesis. He wishes to read it."

"Mr. Bingley will read your magnum opus on Randulfr Eikenskaldi's role in the Battle of Hastings and immediately fall to his knees to propose marriage!"

"How quickly your mind jumps from a mutual academic interest to matrimony!"

Elizabeth laughed. "At the very least he will be able to appreciate that your trousseau linens are all stitched with scenes from Hastings to Agincourt..."

"Oh, Lizzy, I do not wish to be disappointed if Mr. Bingley turns out to be a mere acquaintance."

"Oh, Jane, Mr. Bingley is very much on the way to being in love with you. Besides, how could anyone object to my Jane? You are everything lovely and accomplished. You are a true modern lady: a Bachelor's degree from Lorien College, Oxford, a true gentlewoman, and the handsomest lady in Hertfordshire."

"Lizzy!"

"Please do not interrupt my praising of my beloved sister! Now where was I? Oh yes, a lady in every way that matters, and to hear our Father and his friend Lady Catherine de Bourgh speak, impeccable connections and a fine dowry, however much it is."

"Lizzy! Stop your teasing! I am three and twenty and have had my share of disappointments, I do not wish for another. I will be four and twenty next Season for my presentation." Jane picked up a small pencil and finished a tracing of a small knight on the linen in her hoop as a smile graced her face, "Though, I do very much like Mr. Bingley."

"Jane, like? That is too paltry of a sentiment. How could Mr. Bingley not love you?" Elizabeth had put her letter away and walked over to the window to assess the state of the weather as the morning's damp sunshine had turned to rain. "Besides, it is not uncommon these past ten or fifteen years for young ladies to wait to be presented until after they graduate from Lorien or Matlock Colleges; it does not make us bluestockings or old maids."

Jane raised an eyebrow. Elizabeth laughed. "Very well, then, it does not make you a bluestocking, for all of your historical battle scene stitching! My writing of mathematics papers with Cambridge fellow, Miss Anne de Bourgh - Lady Catherine de Bourgh's daughter

A QUIVER FULL, OR HOW MR. DARCY WILL NOT SIT ON THAT SOFA AGAIN!

25

- to present to the Royal Society, well, I might very well be accused of being a bluestocking."

"Lizzy, do you not think it is odd that in countenance Miss de Bourgh and our sister Lydia look to be sisters, twins even?" Jane held up her needle, and re-threaded it, pleased at successfully diverting the conversation away from Mr. Bingley. "This may be an old discussion, but I do wonder about Papa's claim that the great families of England have intermarried so often for such a long time that even people who aren't closely related appear to be so."

"Miss Anne and the young Sir Lewis de Bourgh are the first cousins of our second cousins once removed."

"But it does not make them our blood relations."

"Papa once told me that old Sir Lewis de Bourgh had relations in the Manners family as well. His mother was a Manners, a cousin to our Grandmother Bennet, which then makes Miss de Bourgh our third or fourth cousin."

"That does not explain why..." As Jane attempted to pursue this line of reasoning, the dispute in the other room got louder and Lydia burst into the sitting room with her father directly behind her.

"You WILL return to school. You WILL attend university. You WILL graduate with a bachelor's degree like your sisters Jane and Elizabeth."

Lydia flounced onto the sofa during her father's pronouncements and then jumped back up, gesticulating with her hands. "To do what? Spend another two and a half years in school and then three or four at university, to sit in a parlor and stitch my trousseau for a non-existent suitor like a well mannered spinster? Why should I when the militia are here now in Meryton and there is so much to be merry about?"

Jane gasped.

Elizabeth glared at Lydia.

Both Jane and Elizabeth got up, picked up their various stitchings and letters, and left the sitting room.

"Lydia!" Mr. Bennet looked at his youngest daughter up and down with a surprisingly stern visage. "There will be no more arguments or negotiations, until you return to school you are now restricted to this house and are no longer out in society, no matter what your mother may say on the matter. Please return to your chamber to think on your words and how you will apologize to your sisters."

Mr. Bennet escorted a shocked Lydia to the stairs. He watched as she ascended and waited for her door to slam. He asked Mrs. Hill to make sure that all the servants were to inform him immediately if Lydia attempted to leave the house. Mr. Bennet returned to his study to write a letter to his cousin Colonel Fitzwilliam and send inquiries to a few schools who could take Lydia before the end of the month.

Chapter 3 - Further Inquiries, or how Sir Thurston Hurst the first will have his say in this conversation

---

Early afternoon
    Sat. Nov. 2, 1811
    Longbourn Manor
    Meryton, Hertfordshire

Upon arriving back in his book room, Mr. Bennet found on top of the stack of the day's mail a letter from his cousin, Sir Thurston Hurst. Rather than leaving the letter to languish a few days as was his usual wont with personal correspondence, he pulled his letter opener out of the desk drawer and separated the wax seal from the paper.

As he scanned the letter, the long-awaited good news had arrived as Sir Thurston Hurst was announcing the birth of his son, Thurston Hurst III, born on the 24th of October. *A son? Excellent! I shall use the stud fees I earned on Hurst's heir to pay for the Colonel to search out Wickham and hopefully the rest will be paid out to Wickham this upcoming autumn on the birth of Mrs. Bennet's son who will then break the Longbourn entail.*

Rubbing his hands with the letter opener between them, he then pulled out a new sheet of paper, picked up his quill, and filled the nib with ink to begin a letter to his Fitzwilliam cousin - the good Colonel. He wrote inquiring if the man had time a week Monday to meet with him at Lady Catherine's townhouse in Mayfair on a matter of business that would be beneficial to the both of them. He smiled to himself, as he would lure the Colonel in with the implication the meeting would be about the Colonel's desire for permission to court Elizabeth. *Hopefully, Darcy will have forgotten that I asked him last night to write the Colonel about Wickham.*

Mr. Bennet then wrote a letter congratulating Sir Thurston and Lady Lavinia Hurst on the birth of their happy bundle of masculine joy, as well as inquiring if they had time Thursday or Friday for him to call on Sir Thurston.

His next set of letters did not give him pleasure to compose, but write them he must. He pulled out the list of schools that educated and prepared young ladies to take the Lorien College entrance exams. He wrote letters to the heads of the three very reputable schools Lydia had not been expelled from to inquire if they had room to admit a third year student at the end of the month. He praised her intelligence; strength in debate and rhetoric while carefully avoiding any comment regarding which schools she had already attended.

As he sealed each letter, he said a small prayer to any deity that would listen that one of them would take his most rebellious daughter. If they did not, then a long line of Bennets attending a college at Oxford would be broken. The only options after these were the Cambridge preparatory ladies' schools that would equip her to take the exams to enter Matlock College in Cambridge. *Hmmph! I do not care if my cousin Lady Phoebe married the man who founded and funded the College, we Bennets attend and graduate from Oxford.*

Regardless of her accusations this morning, Mr. Bennet was not ready to give up on Lydia nor was he willing to let her feigned ignorance and high animal spirits ruin his four oldest daughters' chances for excellent marriages and opportunities. He was not going to allow his youngest daughter's wild behavior at her last school to mar Jane and Elizabeth's upcoming presentation to the Queen and Season in town with his sister, Lady Beauchamp, even if Lydia's last cruel words had marred this morning for Jane and Elizabeth.

After Mr. Bennet folded, addressed, and sealed all of the letters, he rang for Hill and asked them to be delivered to the Post as soon as may be. With those tasks done, with great delight Mr. Bennet opened his newly arrived book, *Undine*, by Fouqué.

Later afternoon
> **Sat. Nov. 2, 1811**
> **In the vicinity of some hedgerows**
> **Netherfield Park, Hertfordshire**

"'Tis the start of pheasant season and a glorious day now that the rain has stopped." Mr. Charles Bingley strode through a shorn field towards a row of hedges that would hopefully contain some birds, humming to himself.

Mr. Frederick Hurst's head still hurt from his late night binge with Mr. Bennet's fine brandy but he was determined to make the most of their first day of shooting. "Bingley, please tell me that you posted the notice in the papers and are properly deputized for the liberty of the manor? I do not wish to shoot a brace and be arrested as a poacher."

Bingley turned to his brother-in-law. "Did you not see the notice in the papers this last week in preparation for the first of November?"

"You know as well as I that I only pretend to read the papers in the morning to avoid your sisters' conversation."

"Which one?"

"Both of them."

Mr. Fitzwilliam Darcy's pointing dogs followed closely behind him, as careful and muted in their actions as their master. Netherfield's gamekeeper and a footman, who was acting as a beater, followed farther behind in quiet conversation about what hedgerows might have the most birds.

Ignoring the other conversations about him, Darcy walked through the field thinking about last night's amusing but appalling conversation with Mr. Bennet. He was glad that he felt few lasting effects of his overindulgence as his valet had kindly allowed him to sleep off most of the ill effects and had provided him with willow bark tea upon waking up. By one o'clock in the afternoon after a restoring bath and hearty breakfast in his chamber, he not only felt human but was ready to walk the fields and focus on pheasant hunting.

It was now nearly three o'clock and they had a bit more than an hour and a half left before sunset. The pheasants would be out foraging in that last hour before sunset, which gave the hunting party sufficient time to find the best hedges.

Darcy still could not believe that Bennet truly intended to go through with his plan for having Mr. George Wickham sire an heir for Longbourn. The plan was fraught with too many traps. *I tried to explain to Bennet that Wickham would not just do it for the money but would most likely blackmail him afterwards.* He shook his head at the memory of Bennet's sly smile and confidence that his plan would work. *He doesn't know Wickham like I do...*

Hurst stopped bickering with Bingley and turned his attention to Darcy. "I would like a full accounting of why you and Mr. Bennet hid in an alcove and drank brandy all night? Why ever did you not save me from faking slumber on a sofa and invite me to join you?"

"What would have stopped Miss Bingley from following you into the alcove?" Darcy asked dryly.

Bingley arrived at a hedge that separated a harvested grain field from a pasture and turned to his gamekeeper. "Parker, shall we stop here to shoot?"

"No, sir, we should make a left here and walk through a wood lot to the pasture on the far side of the next, as that is where I sighted and heard the most birds this morning at dawn."

With this information and direction, Bingley turned to Darcy. "Speaking of Caroline, she was gravely disappointed that neither of you came to breakfast."

Hurst snorted out a laugh. "You mean to say that she was gravely disappointed that Darcy remained above stairs."

"She also objects to my angel. How one could object to Miss Bennet is beyond my comprehension. Miss Bennet is truly the best woman I have ever become acquainted with..."

"This week." Hurst rejoined.

"I object to that statement. Miss Bennet is truly everything I have ever wanted in a lady. She is lovely beyond compare, with eyes of the deepest..."

"Don't quote bad poetry, Chaz." Hurst smirked.

Bingley hated the pet name 'Chaz' and firmly ignored his brother-in-law. "Miss Bennet is more than poetry made flesh, she is intelligent and accomplished! She read medieval history at Lorien College and wrote her thesis on the Battle of Hastings. We discussed the Battle of Agincourt most of the night. She has a very well developed sense of not only the strategies used by the commanders..."

"Fustian!" Hurst stopped walking and put up his hand to indicate Bingley should stop speaking and listen. "Do I hear the calls of the Lesser Ring-necked Bingley? Is it the bleating noises of a Charles trapped in the ensnaring net of a golden haired, blue eyed, big bosomed, educated angel?"

Before Bingley could protest, Parker directed them to a path through a coppiced woodlot. "Sirs, if we go this way, it will take us to the far pasture."

Hurst turned to Darcy. "What Charles has not told us but my wife did is that Caroline refuses to believe that Miss Bennet is connected to the Manners and Howard Families, regardless of any evidence to the contrary. Both Louisa and Caroline are quite against college girls, they think it is a waste of time when one should be out in society."

"I know that Mr. Bennet's grandmother is Lady Fitzwilliam's aunt on the Howard side. Lady Fitzwilliam is sister to the Duke of _____." Darcy ducked around a particularly unruly growth of coppiced branches. "As for the Manners side, I have it on the firm authority of my aunt Lady Catherine that Mr. Bennet is the second cousin of her deceased husband via the Manners family - the cadet branch of the former Earls - not the primary branch of the Dukes of _____."

Hurst interjected, "Bingley, I also know that Mr. Bennet is the third or fourth cousin of my grandfather, Sir Thurston Hurst, through another branch of the Manners family. I brought this up to both Louisa and Caroline, but they dismissed it as an insignificant connection."

Bingley laughed. "With the implication being that your connection to the Manners family is insignificant?"

"Precisely. I then pointed out to my wife that my connections were sufficient enough for her upon our marriage. Apparently, my being the direct heir, at the time, to a baronetcy sweetened the prospect." Hurst reached the edge of the wood lot. "Parker, which way are we to walk now?"

"This way, sir." The gamekeeper pointed to a path along a hedge that would take them to the far side of the long pasture.

"Bingley, the material point here, whether your sisters like it or not, is that Miss Bennet is a very good match for you - she is connected to two Dukes and one Baron. Mr. Bennet's sister is Lady Beauchamp, who is to present Miss Bennet and Miss Elizabeth at St. James this upcoming season." Darcy looked at his friend and stated firmly but not unkindly, "Miss Bingley, who has not yet found a sponsor to present her at court nor received vouchers to Almack's,

A QUIVER FULL, OR HOW MR. DARCY WILL NOT SIT ON THAT SOFA AGAIN!

33

ought to be overjoyed to have her family's status so raised if you were able to receive consent to marry Miss Bennet."

Darcy chuckled. *Let us not forget the Bennets' very close connection to the ancient de Bourgh family.*

Hurst's attention snapped up. "What is the humor there?"

When he received no reply, Hurst said, "Even if the connection to my family is not good enough for the Bingley sisters, my grandfather and his new wife - the former Mrs. Lavinia Wickham - are quite closely acquainted with Mr. Bennet."

At this Bingley smiled. "Oh yes, Sir Thurston Hurst, a man so full of vigor that we all ought to aspire to be - aged nine and eighty and his new wife just delivered a son to him! Have you ever heard of such a thing? Now, that is a man."

Bingley's teasing hit much too close to home. Mr. Hurst had stayed up to nearly four in the morning nursing his late night flask of brandy and re-reading his grandfather's most recent letter announcing his dethronement as heir to the Hurst estate, townhouse, and baronetcy. The very same letter that lectured him for drinking too much, eating too many rich foods, being lazy, and the lack of an heir with Louisa after four years of marriage. According to the letter, one of many, his grandfather was thus forced to re-marry and sire a new heir to the Hurst line. The brandy and letter re-reading came after his wife again denied him entrance to her chamber.

Grumpy was the mere beginning of the discontent that Mr. Hurst was experiencing.

Before Hurst could lash out at Bingley, Darcy's dogs began pointing at a hedge just ahead of them. The gentlemen took their guns and pointed them above the hedge as the beater thwacked a switch on the side of the hedge, two pheasants flew upwards, and the guns discharged. The birds flew off to safety as Bingley shot wide, Hurst did not lift his gun high enough and Darcy was silently chuckling rather than sighting his shot.

The dogs did not point again at any of the nearby hedges but heeled.

"Sirs, we are not yet halfway down to the spot that I found birds feeding earlier, and I believe that we will find several braces of birds and ground with more stable footing at the other end of this pasture or the field by the river." All three gentlemen began walking in the direction the gamekeeper indicated after they repacked their guns with shot and powder.

At the Fashionable Hour
Sat. Nov. 2, 1811
Hurst House
Mayfair, London

"Dear Lady Hurst, your son is truly a handsome baby." Lady Catherine de Bourgh bent over the cradle and trailed a finger across Thurston Hurst III's downy cheek as his eyes reposed in sleep. "While he is not yet two weeks old, little Thurston does not look like a shriveled maggot as so many newborns do."

Lady Lavinia Hinton Wickham Hurst did her best not to laugh, as she was only nine days into her post-natal confinement and most of her laughing muscles still hurt - badly. Giving birth at age three and forty was not for the weak. She gave birth to her first son at eighteen years of age and her second son just a week and a half ago.

"Lavinia, my dear, I think he will have the green eyes of..."

"Do not say it, Lady Catherine, we must continue..."

"Yes, yes, yes, with the fiction that your husband is..." For once in the whole of her life, Lady Catherine de Bourgh lowered her voice to a slice of a whisper so that the infant's nurse in the dressing room would not be able to hear her words.

"Truly, Lavinia, we have known each other these seven and twenty years - since you were only seventeen - you know me well, I think

I may be in love." At this statement, Lady Catherine leaned down to press a light kiss on the infant's forehead and whispered, "Dear Father in Heaven, let this precious life grow strong to manhood and be a blessing to his family and his country." She placed another kiss on his right cheek. "Please, dear Jesus our Savior, a long and fruitful life for this little one that he may learn to love you with his whole heart." And a third kiss on his left cheek. "Sophia, the blessed Spirit, do hear me and bless this little one with your wisdom, grace, and knowledge."

"Lady Catherine, you have always had a soft spot for newborns of every stripe." Lady Hurst smiled at her old acquaintance, who had managed to direct most of the major events in Lavinia's life from her first marriage to Mr. Ernest Wickham, to arranging the conception of her first born, as well as the suggestion that she marry Sir Thurston Hurst just over a year ago, and then conception of this final precious child at the grand and miraculous old age of three and forty. Lady Catherine was attentive to even the smallest details in the lives of so many - be they family, friends, acquaintances, tenants, and many others - even if they lived many counties away.

Lady Catherine lifted her eyes up from the cradle to the woman reclining on the chaise lounge nearby and smiled mistily, "Lavinia, I do. I love any infant be it a human baby, a puppy, a calf, a kitten, a chick, or a foal. It is the downy, soft perfection of the newborn, not to mention the potential for greatness if guided with a firm hand by a proficient in the art of formation, decision, and command."

At this Lady Hurst tested her body's healing as waves of laughter struck her. "Oh, Lady Catherine, please do not make me laugh, it hurts mightily!"

A bit after Meryton's Fashionable hour
   Sat. Nov. 2, 1811
   Longbourn Manor, Hertfordshire

Miss Jane Bennet tried to take a rest after Lydia's insults, but to no avail. One would think that after so little sleep she should have been able to take a small nap, but her mind raced hither and yon, not stopping on any one thought for long. Rather than work herself into a fine case of nerves which would lead to more stitching, she rose from her bed and decided to clear out the remaining stalks of asters, Michaelmas daisies, and coneflowers from the flower garden. While it was not quite time to prune the roses, perhaps the activity of turning over the soil and preparing it for its winter's rest would calm her thoughts. On Monday, she would ask a stable hand to put old hay on the flower beds.

In the still room Jane donned her gardening apron and gloves and put her flower shears in a wide basket. She walked to the flower garden, taking a big breath of cool air, and delighted in the clouds flitting across the sky. While the air was cold and still damp, it was not overly so and once she started working amongst the flowers she ceased to notice the weather or the time.

When Miss Charlotte Lucas entered through the flower garden's gate, her appearance startled Jane. "Oh! Charlotte, you have come!"

"Yes, I had hoped to find you and Eliza at home." Charlotte smiled at Jane. "Clearing up the last of the autumn flowers are you?"

"Yes, the final burst of coneflowers and daisies faded over a week ago and I did not wish to see dead stalks from my window as I was stitching."

"Did you enjoy the evening at Lucas Lodge last evening?" Charlotte sat on a bench near where Jane was working. "I was very pleased to see Mr. Bingley paid attention to you quite exclusively."

At this proclamation, Jane blushed and lowered her eyes. "I did enjoy the evening, Charlotte, very much."

"Jane, we have been friends for many years, so I will cut to the chase. Do you return Mr. Bingley's regard?"

"Yes, most definitely! Mr. Bingley is everything that a young man should be if he possibly can."

"Do you wish to secure him?"

"Charlotte! How can you ask such a thing? You are as bad as Lizzy!"

"Do you?"

Jane's modesty and long held ideas of propriety were in conflict with her desire to shout to the world her regard for Mr. Bingley. Demurely she replied, "I cannot possibly admit that, even to a particular friend, after only knowing the gentleman for less than a fortnight."

"If you wish to secure him, you must show more than you feel - even the most confident amongst us have difficulty falling in love without some encouragement. For a gentleman as modest as Mr. Bingley, he will need encouragement."

Jane gasped and her lack of sleep conspired against her normal serene countenance as tears gathered in her eyes. In a low, hurt voice Jane said, "Charlotte, that is a bold statement. How can you say such a thing?"

"Jane, you have protected your sweet, tender heart with a strong cloak of serenity and a gentle smile in all situations against the gossips of Meryton in the face of your Mother and sister Lydia's brashness and improprieties. How is Mr. Bingley to apprehend that you return his affection if you do not show even a minute portion of your affectionate feelings? You do not have to be brash like Lydia, there are other ways of letting a young man know."

Jane took off her gardening gloves and reached into her apron's pocket for a handkerchief. After dabbing at the corner of her eyes, she gathered her shears and the dead stalks for the compost pile into the basket. "Let me put these things away in the still room and then we shall find a quiet room to take tea - just the two of us - to discuss this. I do need a strategy, but you must promise that this is confidential between just ourselves. Lizzy is not yet one and twenty and she simply cannot comprehend my feelings in this regard."

Charlotte raised her eyebrow, cocked her head, and smiled. "You need not ask for my secrecy, you have it. While we are at it, we must plot for my future marital felicity. We must band together in this regard."

Jane nodded in agreement and smiled wide. She led the way to the still room at the back of the house.

Just before sunset
  Sat. Nov. 2, 1811
  In the vicinity of some hedgerows in the far pasture
  Netherfield Park, Hertfordshire
"Darcy, since you spent all of the evening in conversation with Mr. Bennet, what do you know of the man and his family? From my grandfather's letter, I learned that Mr. Bennet rarely comes to town but when he does he stays with your Aunt." Mr. Hurst asked.

Darcy attempted to cough but lost the battle and started to speak before he found himself laughing. "Mr. Bennet and my aunt, Lady Catherine de Bourgh, are acquaintances of long standing - some thirty odd years or so. They originally met through her husband, Sir Lewis de Bourgh, who was his cousin and have retained their friendship long after my uncle passed away."

"Ah, to have such a long and true friend; at least they are discreet." Hurst smiled. "Is it true that he will be buying back Netherfield? I heard that rumor the night of the assembly."

"I believe that he is seeing to his daughters' dowries first, before he purchases back more of the land that his brother and great-grandfather lost." Darcy's dogs remained alert but did not sense any birds in this section of hedges.

"My wife and her sister have this odd idea that the Bennet girls' dowries are pinned to their educational achievement."

"This rumor is true, as Mr. Bennet explained it to me last night. Mrs. Bennet is too fond of spending money and he has rightly put her on a strict budget. She has even less interest in education for women than the Bingley sisters; allegedly she did not even want a governess for her girls, let alone to attend school and continue on to university." Darcy's countenance reflected the disdain he had for this mistaken notion. "To provide the best for his daughters and force his wife's hand, Bennet decided to prorate the dowries to levels of education accomplished. Miss Bennet and Miss Elizabeth will receive the maximum amount as they both have graduated from Oxford. Miss Mary, the third daughter, is on track to receive her bachelors in theology and philosophy in two years..."

Bingley perked up at this last statement. "A lady parson? Would not that be delightful! What ever will they think of next?"

Darcy, determined to complete his point, continued. "The fourth daughter is in her final year of school in London and will not take the exams for college, but will instead continue with masters in London in painting and drawing. The fifth daughter is currently on a break from school and we have met her..."

"One could not help but hear Miss Lydia and Mrs. Bennet wherever they go, even when one is diligently feigning sleep as is my wont." Hurst laughed at his own joke. "What I want to know is where is Bennet getting the capital? The local gossips have his income pegged at a bit less than two thousand a year."

"I do believe that he keeps his real income secret as to not excite interest..."

"As you do."

"... and to keep his wife from imprudently spending it all and fortune hunters importuning his daughters."

"How much farther do we have to walk in search of the elusive birds of Netherfield Park?" Bingley stopped walking at a large mud spot created by the churning of hooves on the edge of a stream in front of them. He was weary of this conversation and of the lack of pheasants. The sun was soon to set and Bingley wanted to have a brace of birds to take back to Cook.

The gamekeeper wisely said nothing and pointed to a small ford over the stream so they might reach the hedges nearby. As Hurst crossed the ford, his gun accidentally discharged into the stream, which caused nearby birds to flush. The other two gentlemen and the gamekeeper groaned.

When he finished cursing at his gun, Hurst stated, "I have yet to hear of a woman gaining a bachelors in Theology. If Miss Mary Bennet is as pretty as her sisters, Charles would very much like a lady parson. He might even attend services with some regularity."

"Yes, yes, I would. I would be much more faithful in my attendance if a lovely angel was in the pulpit preaching rather than a dry, dull old man," Bingley stated fervently. "I suppose lady parsons and curates would bring many young men back regularly on Sunday mornings. I think educated ladies should be able to join all of the professions, although maybe not the military. On further thought maybe they should, as Miss Bennet would make an excellent military strategist."

Hurst, ignoring Bingley, looked like he was turning a great weight over and over again in his mind. His countenance darkened. "Darcy, as we both know, Bennet's Fitzwilliam-Howard connection and Manners' connection are verified. Why did he not marry equal to or higher rank? How then did he fall into the trap of a scheming small town solicitor's daughter who does not believe in educating women? That woman is vulgar, loud, and of mean understanding."

"It could happen to any of us, which is why..." began Darcy.

Hurst snapped, "Do stop that potential lecture before you start!"

Bingley stopped walking and turned to Hurst. "What rotten piece of meat lodged itself in your craw today? Was it the letter from your grandfather that arrived yesterday?"

"Yes! The man is nine and eighty years old and his wife of a year just had a son! My grandfather sired a new heir - the new rightful heir to the baronetcy unseating, me if I do not produce an heir before I die - and at his advanced age! He told me three years ago that if Louisa and I did not have a son by last year, he would marry again and assure succession himself. I cannot even convince Louisa to... Never you mind that!" Hurst opened his gun to repack it with powder and shot.

"The worst part is not the birth announcement of Thurston Hurst III this past week - my departed father was the second - but the lecture that came with it. My grandfather's letter reminded me to reduce my brandy and port consumption, to eat only roasted fowl and fish with no sauce, to eat more vegetables than meat, and to eat fresh fruit every day; otherwise I will die like my father and my grandmother before I turn eight and thirty. Who can swallow roasted meat with no sauce? Bah!"

Darcy's attention focused on Hurst. "Your grandfather had a son this past week? When did he marry again?"

"Oh nearly a year ago, you may know her as she is the widow of your father's old steward, Mrs. Lavinia Hinton Wickham, now Lady Lavinia Hurst."

Darcy coughed to hide the laughter bubbling up. "Let me guess, your grandfather took her on a wedding trip nine or ten months ago to London and they visited with his cousin, Mr. Bennet?"

Hurst eyed the hedgerows looking for the movement of a pheasant. "How did you know? Mr. Bennet even invited them to Lady Catherine de Bourgh's for dinner and to the Matlocks' for a card party. My grandfather talked about it in his letters for months afterwards. He said it was the most pleasant time he has ever spent in

London. He praises Bennet, calls him a real man, though I am not sure what for."

Darcy's dog pointed to a hedge 15 feet to the left of Bingley, the beater took a switch to the hedge, pheasants flew upwards, talking stopped and the shooting recommenced.

Chapter 4 : The Truth about Relations and College Girls

The Dinner Hour
Wed. Nov. 6, 1811
Netherfield Park, Hertfordshire

Mr. Charles Bingley sat at the head of the dinner table at Netherfield Park on this dark, cold, and rainy Wednesday evening feeling a great deal of felicity and pride. The pride that his father wished for him to have: pride of place - an estate of his own, albeit leased, pride of his family arrayed in great finery, and pride of the two brace of roasted pheasants arrayed in their feathers and autumn mushroom sauce to pour over them. Mr. Bingley felt all the contentment of his situation.

"Charles," said Caroline, Mr. Bingley's youngest sister. "We must speak about this infatuation of yours."

Mr. Bingley was quite diverted that Caroline was arrayed in an assortment of feathers jutting out from the back of her silk turban not unlike the pheasants' tail feathers.

Mrs. Louisa Hurst looked across the table at her younger sister and pointedly looked at Mr. Darcy before looking back at her sister. "Must we?

"Yes, we must." Caroline looked pointedly back at her sister and then at her sister's husband, Mr. Hurst.

"Caroline, please let us not discuss this at the dinner table."

"Louisa, our brother is about to bring great embarrassment to our family with Miss Bennet's low connections."

More pointed looks were exchanged between the sisters. The gentlemen watched while sipping their wine. Charles asked Mr.

Hurst, "Would you like to carve the birds you shot yesterday or should I?"

"As Lord of the Manor, I believe that it is your place to carve." Hurst winked at his brother-in-law as he tossed down the rest of the wine in his glass and indicated to a footman that he would like more.

Miss Bingley glared at both of them. "This is not to be taken lightly. Who are Miss Bennet's relations? Do not tell me of the Duke of _____, nor the Countess of Matlock, nor the cadet branch of the Manners family. No, I ask about that tradesman brother of Mrs. Bennet!" Miss Bingley sat ramrod straight and glared at her brother. "A tradesman who lives near Cheapside, no less."

Louisa raised her glass in salute to the gentlemen and retorted, "Of which said tradesman is our second cousin!"

"Never!"

"Our grandmother Louisa Bailey Bingley's oldest sister married Mr. Jonathan Gardiner, the son of a baronet, not an Irish tinker...

Caroline, to the whole of the table's great surprise and a great boon to the local servant's gossip chain, smashed her wine glass against the table sending wine and glass shards in every direction. "We have no grandfather. Our father has no father!"

"Sister of mine, our father's mother had a very respectable rector's family and her oldest sister married a Gardiner. Your namesake Caroline Bailey Gardiner's son married and had three children: Mrs. Bennet, Mrs. Philips, and Mr. Edmund Gardiner of Gracechurch Street. Our second cousins!"

"Absolutely not! It shall not be!" Caroline stood up, upended her plate of food, and stormed out of the dining room.

Not a breath was heard. The two footmen in attendance were aghast. Mr. Hurst drank down his third glass of wine and indicated another round for the whole table with one discreet hand gesture. The nearest footman poured for the four who remained at the table.

Bingley looked at Mr. Darcy, his sister, and Mr. Hurst, and raised his glass. "To all of my relations: dead, alive, gentry, tradesman, and most of all to traveling Irish tinker grandfathers!" The other three diners raised their glasses and said, "Hear, hear."

Bingley put down his glass and reached for the carving knife as he indicated for the footman to bring the pheasants closer to him. "Louisa, is our excellent cousin Edmund and his lovely wife family to my Miss Bennet?"

"Yes, I wrote Mrs. Gardiner this week after hearing that Mrs. Bennet and Mrs. Philips were from the Gardiner family. I received a letter from Marinda today and she confirmed that Mrs. Bennet is Mr. Gardiner's oldest sister - we knew that the oldest was married to an estate owner - and that his next sister is married to the man who took over his father's law firm. Mrs. Gardiner had a great deal of worthy praise for the accomplishments of Miss Bennet and Miss Elizabeth."

Bingley sliced each pheasant in half, as they were on the small side, and passed the trays around for serving. His smile was broad. "That makes my beautiful angel our second cousin once removed."

Louisa turned to Mr. Darcy, who was smiling at his friend's delight. "Mr. Darcy, the Gardiners are the respectable side of the family, it is the Bingleys who are more—how shall I say?"

"Mrs. Hurst, you need not defend nor defame your Bingley forefathers, as your father was a man to be much admired in his rise from the son of a traveling tinker to a man who owned four very productive factories and raised several fine children."

"How democratic of you, Darcy." Hurst smirked.

"Mr. Darcy," Louisa addressed him again, "You have met our cousin Mr. Gardiner and his wife? Not only are they very fashionable people but Mr. Gardiner is a very trusted source of investment advice. With his advice, Mr. Hurst and I have not only increased our returns on our investments but also on our capital."

Louisa smiled apologetically at the footmen and indicated that she would like more wine. "Mrs. Gardiner has become a dear friend these last two years, though I cannot allow my sister to know that." With a sigh, she took another sip of her wine. "I wish Caroline would not revile those who have worked hard to obtain what we now enjoy."

As the gentlemen started to eat the pheasant they shot the previous day on their second foray into the hedgerows - this time to greater success - Mrs. Hurst continued to sip her wine lost in her thoughts. After some time, she put her glass down and thanked her brother for his provision, wherein he demurred. "Oh Charles, do not be so modest. Do not let Caroline sour our evening, nor defame any of our relations and your accomplishments."

With a sly smile, Louisa added, "I would quite like Miss Bennet as my new sister." She took a bite of her pheasant. "This is delicious."

All four diners enjoyed the rest of their meal.

11:25am

Thurs. Nov. 7, 1811

In front of the de Bourgh Townhouse

Mayfair, London

As Mr. Thomas Bennet's carriage pulled to a stop before the de Bourgh townhouse, he reflected on the scene upon his departure this morning from Longbourn. His wife was waiting for him in the entrance hall of the manor house in her dressing gown and night cap - ready and waiting to dress him down in front of the footman and several maids. To say it was a scene worthy of a Drury Lane theatre was putting the matter mildly. *I am sure that all of Meryton now knows that I am arriving at Lady Catherine de Bourgh's today and staying for nearly a week.*

A QUIVER FULL, OR HOW MR. DARCY WILL NOT SIT ON THAT SOFA AGAIN!

47

His wife accused him of marital infidelity, then she decried the loss of her status and reputation in the face of his repeated visits to London without her. She threw out his lack of ability to produce an heir with her loudly. Furthermore, she begged to be taken to London to prove that he was proud that she was his wife. The hedgerows, her nerves, and his demise were all taken off the shelves of her worry closet and examined with great verbosity. When he climbed into the carriage, she threatened to turn him into a cuckold by starting an affair with a young militia officer. She was still a very handsome woman! How would he feel to be cuckolded and have a son to inherit Longbourn who was not of his get?

At that last salvo, he smiled at her, kissed her furiously red cheek, and said in a low tone of voice, "My dear, please do wait, as I shall arrange for that within the fortnight with a handsome new militia officer."

Mr. Bennet chuckled at the remembrance of his last witticism as he rose to exit the carriage. His footman opened the carriage's door as Lady Catherine's footman opened the front door to the townhouse. Bennet alit from the vehicle, straightened and smoothed his coat before walking up the steps to the townhouse anticipating a good week.

11:25pm
Thurs. Nov. 7, 1811
Netherfield Park, Hertfordshire

Mr. Frederick Hurst approached the inner door between his chamber and his wife's chamber and knocked tentatively. "Louisa, do let me in." Hurst waited - upon receiving no response - he knocked a little less tentatively. "Louisa, I know you can hear me. I just heard you wish your maid good night."

No response from the other side of the door. Knock. Knock. Knock. Hurst tried the door handle, but it did not give. "Louisa, Let. Me. In."

A muffled small "no" came through the door.

"Why ever not? You read my grandfather's letter, I need to produce a male heir!"

Another muffled "no" along with a mumbled "it is too late for that" came through the door. Minutes went by. Hurst huffed. Then he sighed. "Come now, Louisa. Let us be rational about this."

The door between their chambers opened a hair and he could see one of his wife's eyes peering at him. "Frederick, did you brush your teeth?"

"Hades forbid that I ever touch a tooth brush and that horrid Trotter's Dentifrice tooth powder to my teeth, gums and mouth. I swished my mouth with my mint and brandy concoction!"

"When? Three days ago? I can still smell your rotting gum abscess from a room away." Louisa started to close the door, when she stuck her nose in the crack and took a sniff. "When did you last bathe in a bathtub with soap and hot water?"

"Last week! What does that have to do with getting with child?"

"Everything!" The door snapped closed and the lock firmly latched.

With a loud humph, Hurst sat down with a plop on the stuffed chair next to the fireplace and stared at the fire. *That woman has no idea of the efforts I have made to conform to her ridiculously high standards of hygiene! 'Cleanliness is next to Godliness'... Bah!* He picked up his glass of brandy with smashed mint leaves in it from the side table. He drank it down rather than swishing it about his mouth. *Bathing more than once a week is positively unhealthy - I don't care if Brummell made daily bathing fashionable - it leaches out a man's life force.*

Hurst stared at the now empty glass and wondered if the brandy and mint would be improved with the addition of some citrus juice and sugar.

10:22am
Fri. Nov. 8, 1811
The Family Dining Room
Longbourn Manor, Hertfordshire

Longbourn manor's ostentatious gilded interior ornamentation of Mr. Bennet's father and grandfather's era, so dearly loved by the current Mrs. Bennet, had been sold off years ago to help cover the family's debts. Mr. Bennet had recently, much to Mrs. Bennet's horror allowed his daughters Miss Elizabeth and Miss Kitty to redesign and rearrange the furniture, paintings, draperies, and wall coverings in the formal and family rooms on the ground floor to bring out the best in the Palladian influenced Restoration architecture of the manor house. The family dining and sitting rooms were now light, elegant, and comfortable to the pleasure of most of the family and all of the servants.

At this moment, the morning sun was streaming through the draperies and dancing on the pale striped walls of the family dining room where Miss Elizabeth and Miss Lydia had settled in to break their fast. Mr. Hill, Longbourn's butler, had entered to deliver the morning's post to Miss Elizabeth when a fracas erupted out of Miss Lydia. Mr. Hill sighed.

"Give me that letter!" Lydia demanded of her sister as Elizabeth read off the names of who sent the letter and who they were addressed to while sorting the correspondence into small piles. Mr. Hill continued to hold the salver that he had brought the post in on.

"No, Lydia, it is for Papa. You must wait until he returns home from London and he chooses to tell you what is in the letter; you cannot open his letters!" Elizabeth started to hand the letter from the Lincolnshire Friends School for Young Ladies back to Mr. Hill when Lydia snatched it away from her. Elizabeth quickly grabbed it before Lydia could use her superior height and reach as leverage and asked, "Mr. Hill, can you please lock this and any other letters for my father in his desk drawer away from prying eyes?" Mr. Hill bowed and exited with the Master's correspondence.

Lydia stood up from her seat, disrupting her tea on to her ham and muffin, to lean over Elizabeth, "Miss Always Right, you have no right to take the letter that will decide my future away from me, even if it is addressed to Papa!"

Elizabeth stood up and looked up at her youngest sister, "I have every right to protect our father's privacy." As Elizabeth made this pronouncement, Jane walked in to join them for breakfast.

"Whatever are you quarreling about? I could hear you from the second floor. Mama is still sleeping, do lower your voices." Jane sat at her seat and requested that the tea be passed to her as well as the basket of breads and the pear compote.

Elizabeth sat back down and passed Jane the requested items around the small breakfast table, while glaring at Lydia.

Lydia plopped back down into her seat. "Lud, I am ready to return to school, perhaps the Quaker school will have handsome footmen. Being restricted to Longbourn has grown so very dull." Lydia poured more tea and looked slyly at her sisters. "Do tell me about college - how many Oxford men did you kiss?"

"Lydia!" Elizabeth exclaimed to no effect while Jane blushed a bright red and looked down at the muffin and compote on her plate.

"Well, well, well, did sweet, sweet Jane kiss some handsome sons of the gentry and nobility whilst at Lorien College, Oxford?" Lydia was highly intrigued that her ever so good eldest sister may not be so very good after all. Jane said nothing and buttered her muffin.

Elizabeth was incensed. "Lydia, do not ascribe your morals and motivations to others, especially not to Jane, of whom, I am certain, is waiting for her first kiss to be on her wedding day with her husband as I am."

Lydia lifted with her fork and licked the tea off a slice of ham before returning it to her plate to slice it. "Miss Goody Two Shoes, not all of us desire to have only kissed one man for the whole of our lives. My mother encouraged me to kiss as many boys and young gentlemen as could be while I was at school. She said I may very well find a husband that way."

"I do not like your way of getting husbands," Elizabeth huffed.

Lydia then picked up the second slice of ham with her fork, licked it all over the while casting come hither looks at Chalmers the footman who stood near the door. "I did quite a bit more than kiss, however do you think I got sent down from school? I did everything but let the school's footman put his yard in me..."

Elizabeth choked on her tea and sputtered in astonishment at Lydia's crude words and even more improper claims! Jane got up to pat Elizabeth on the back and then turned to the footman, "Chalmers, can you please ask Cook for more pastries and fresh hot water for the tea?"

Elizabeth regained her breath. "Lydia, how could you? Do you wish to bring scandal down on us all? Have care!" With this statement Elizabeth folded up her napkin and placed it next to her now empty plate as she rose to depart. "Please excuse me, I have proofs for a math theorem to finish before I send out a letter to Miss de Bourgh in the afternoon post."

As she passed through the door, she turned back to her sisters. "Do not mock me, Lydia. I do intend on saving my first kiss for my husband on our wedding day."

As the footman was still in the kitchen and Elizabeth gone, Lydia leaned forward and in a low voice meant to inspire confidence, asked

Jane, "Come now, Jane, do tell. You liked kissing those Oxford boys, did you not? You liked the power you had over them, did you not?"

Jane reached for the dish of shirred eggs to her left and placed one on a piece of toast on her plate. As she daintily ate the egg and toast, her cheeks and neck remained a rather alarming shade of red. "Oh Lydia, it is not proper to talk of such things."

"Oh Jane, I know you kissed some college men. Were they handsome? Were they rich? Did they light a fire in your nether regions?"

"Lydia!"

"Did you let one of them put his mouth on you? It feels divine!"

"No, Lydia, I did not! How can you do such a thing with a man you are not married to?"

The footman returned with the pastries and hot water to refresh the tea pot. After he placed both on the table, Jane dismissed him all the while thanking him. "Contrary to the German book of folk tales that Papa has in his library, kissing frogs - be they gentry frogs or noble frogs - does not turn them into human princes."

"Jane, that is a very prim way of saying that you kissed quite a few young men at college."

Jane leaned forward putting her finger to her lips in a silencing fashion. Lydia nodded and crossed her arms over her heart at their old signal to keep a secret. In a whisper Jane said, "I couldn't say no."

"What?!?!?" Lydia nearly tipped her tea onto her plate.

"I was very conflicted with Mama's instructions to catch a husband versus what I know to be proper and right behavior for a young Christian gentlewoman."

Lydia snorted and laughed.

"Mama pushed me out into Meryton's society at fifteen and encouraged me to show blatant affections for suitable and unsuitable young men much as she has with you. Papa tried to protect me by sending me off to school and furthermore to college with Lizzy and...

Well, Lydia, I did not have the constitution to say no to nice gentlemen even though I knew my actions to be very wrong."

Lydia was truly astonished. "You liked kissing them did you not?"

Jane demurred, "Some, maybe. The wet kissers, no, definitely not. A few were lovely kissers and lovely young gentlemen..."

"So, you let them go a bit farther?"

Quite primly, at complete odds with the confidences being shared, Jane said, "One or two of the best gentlemen were allowed to touch me with all clothes on from the waist up. I did not say no or make a fuss, as I didn't want any gossip. I do not have Lizzy's strength of principle and I have a very hard time saying no to nice men who beseech me with clever words." At this last confidence Jane's color returned to normal but she looked quite worried and as if she were to start crying. "I do hate to make anyone disappointed with me."

Lydia was rather aghast that Jane did not comprehend the power she could have had over these gentlemen. Instead of showing her true feelings, she smirked at her sister.

"Lydia, you must know there are rumors that college girls are only one step up from the demi-monde! Do not think that this behavior is acceptable, because it is not. I dread my future husband finding out any of what I did with other young men at college."

"Well then, sweet Jane, we must find you a husband before he hears of any rumors in Town!" Lydia started to line the remains of her breakfast up in a neat little pattern on her plate with a rather predatory look on her countenance. "You do like Mr. Bingley, do you not? He shall do quite nicely, as he also has a hard time saying no. We need to make a plan to get you alone with Mr. Bingley, preferably in a dark place..."

"Lydia, I must concur with Lizzy, I do not like your way of getting husbands! If Mr. Bingley wishes to court me, then he shall - without you and I making a plan." Jane rose from the table and refrained from telling her brash, improper youngest sister that she and Charlotte Lucas had already made a plan. A plan that did not rely on seduction.

Left alone in the sunlit dining room, Lydia leaned back in her chair while she inspected the pastry selection. In the distance, she could hear her mother calling for Mrs. Hill. *Lud! Is Mama incapable of ringing the bell for Hill? Longbourn and my sisters are so very dull. I must convince Papa to let me out of the house before I return to school... Or maybe I can convince Chalmers to have a little fun. Now there is a happy thought.*

2:37pm
  Sat. Nov. 9, 1811
  The de Bourgh Townhouse
  Mayfair, London

It truly was a shame that Mr. Bennet had not brought Mrs. Bennet to London, as the de Bourgh townhouse would have been exactly to her tastes in gilded moldings, ceilings, wall fixtures, and ornate furniture; not to mention the antique rugs and tapestries shot with silver and gold threading.

A few weeks in the de Bourgh townhouse would have set Mrs. Bennet up for a very long time. Whereupon she would have a multitude of ideas for decorating Longbourn manor, thus illustrating one of several excellent reasons why Mr. Bennet kept her from London which also included frivolous expenditures, shopping and, of course, a clash of personalities between Mrs. Bennet and Lady Catherine.

On occasion, he diverted himself to the point of chuckling in public at the idea of Mrs. Bennet and Lady Catherine in the same room. At the very moment that he was imagining such a meeting and laughing quite noisily to himself in the library, his cousin, Colonel Fitzwilliam, was announced.

"Fitzwilliam, it is a pleasure to see you. Thank you for calling on me." The two gentlemen bowed to each other and Mr. Bennet indicated with a sweep of his hand that they should sit in the wingback chairs near the fireplace.

"Bennet, it is good to see you. My mother has been in transports over the new Hurst heir. Apparently my aunt took my mother with her on one of her daily visits this week. It may be your fault that I am now expected to produce a grandchild."

"My fault? Do tell." Bennet held up a decanter of brandy and raised an eyebrow at the good colonel.

"Yes, please." As Bennet poured two fingers of brandy into two fine crystal tumblers for both himself and his cousin, the colonel smirked. "Let me recount the chain of actions: You are friends with your cousin Sir Thurston Hurst and introduced my aunt to the Hursts, Lady Hurst has a baby, my aunt visits her daily and takes my mother with her on a visit, my mother has no grandchildren as of yet, now she wants some - thus your fault."

Bennet lifted his glass in a toast. "To the health of the little lad."

"Here, here." The colonel sipped his brandy, sighed happily at the fine vintage, and settled into his chair. "I take it that you barely descended from your carriage when my Aunt whisked you off to meet London's newest resident, where she has been kissing the baby and giving childrearing advice to Lady Hurst."

Bennet laughed. "Actually, she let me rest a full two and a half hours before we descended upon the Hursts; she made the visit to the confined Lady Hurst and the infant while I enjoyed port and good conversation with Sir Thurston. Since then, I have had a meeting with my bankers, dinner yesterday eve with the de Bourghs and Beauforts, and this evening Catherine and I will go to the theatre with your parents and to supper afterwards. Quite a full schedule for a man who has been in town for a scant two days. I will be glad for the respite of sabbath on the morrow and a fine nap with my eyes open at St. George's in the morning will set me up for the day."

Fitzwilliam laughed. "Truly the best way to deal with the long sermons at St. George's! Now about your request that we meet today. Have you reconsidered my request that you raise my lovely cousin Elizabeth's dowry and thus will grant me permission to court her?"

Mr. Bennet looked over the rim of his brandy glass piercing the colonel with his stare. "Tell me again your minimum amount of dowry required for a bride?"

The Colonel smiled. "Not a pound short of thirty thousand, cousin, not even for the lovely, bright Miss Elizabeth Bennet." Seeing his jest had not produced the desired effect, he leaned forward and spoke earnestly. "Cousin Bennet, I jest. Can you not raise Miss Elizabeth's dowry even by ten thousand pounds? I can economize and she can do wonders with investing the capital."

"Is that all you see my daughter as, a beautiful gold making machine?"

"No, that is not the case, I simply cannot live on the interest from ten thousand pounds."

Bennet prevaricated. "Try five thousand pounds."

The colonel gasped. "I must withdraw my suit. I cannot retrench and economize to live on the annual proceeds of five thousand. No, I must withdraw from the field."

Bennet stifled the smile at the success of his lie. *Under no circumstances is the Colonel to know that Elizabeth has a twenty thousand pound dowry. Amiable and loyal as my cousin may be, he is not clever enough nor does he have the strength of character to make a good marriage with my Lizzy. She would not be happy to rule over a man. She must respect her husband and be respected in turn.*

Bennet leaned forward. "I am sorry to hear of this. However, would you like to make a few hundred pounds this week while you are on leave?"

Fitzwilliam sat up straight and presented his empty glass for a refill. "Indeed, I would."

Bennet poured another two fingers of brandy for himself and his cousin. "I need your research and tracking skills to find a one George Wickham..."

"What has that bounder done now!" The colonel leaped to his feet in agitation nearly disrupting the brandy pouring operation.

"Nothing yet. Here, have your brandy, sit down and listen to me." Fitzwilliam sat back down stiffly and gruffly received his tumbler. Bennet continued his rehearsed pitch. "For reasons of my own, I need to have Mr. George Wickham, formerly of Derbyshire, located and convinced, if not bribed, to join the _____shire militia that is currently quartered in Meryton. I will give you a total of five hundred pounds to cover your expenses to locate Wickham and money to purchase his commission and uniform. I need him in Meryton and in uniform no later than a week Tuesday."

"You will pay me five hundred pounds to excavate George Wickham from whatever sewer he has mired himself in, purchase his commission, and make sure he has reported to Colonel Forster? I know Forster and he is a good military man who does not deserve such filth in his command!" The Colonel's countenance was rigid. "To top off this indignity, I am to accomplish all of this in ten days?"

"Yes."

"It will take nearly five hundred pounds to buy the commission if he is to enter at the officer rank his inflated sense of privilege believes he should have. Thus, five hundred pounds to locate George, purchase his commission, and escort him to his new post - as I do believe I may have to bribe him on top of paying for the commission. And an additional five hundred pounds to recompense my labors in dealing with that scum whilst I am on leave. You can pay my five hundred half on deposit and half on delivery, but I will need the five hundred for George's commission and bribe up front."

Bennet would not haggle with Colonel Fitzwilliam on such an important matter as siring his future heir, or the fact that the militia did not require a commission, instead he extended his hand.

"Deal." The two men shook hands.

Bennet could not resist adding, "Moreover, for the immense total of one thousand pounds to complete this task you will sign a contract that states all of the monies will be owed back to me if Wickham does not of his own free will report to duty to Colonel Forster by eight o'clock in the evening on Tuesday, the Nineteenth of November of this year."

Colonel Fitzwilliam shook Mr. Bennet's hand again firmly. "Deal."

"Very well, cousin, meet me at my solicitor's office on Monday morning at eleven o'clock. I will have a contract for you to sign and the money to start the project. I trust you will be very discreet about my part in this scheme and will not allow Mr. Wickham to know who is paying for his commission."

"I will let him think that my cousin Darcy is wishing to promote his career." The Colonel smiled in anticipation of the hunt. *Bennet said nothing about Wickham arriving in tip top shape, just that he will arrive of his own free will. Capital!*

"Now, cousin Bennet, can I not convince you to raise lovely and clever Miss Elizabeth's dowry another fifteen thousand pounds..."

Chapter 5: Off to Netherfield They Go

---❧---

10:28am
   Wed. Nov 13, 1811
   Second Floor, Guest Wing
   Netherfield Park, Hertfordshire

When Elizabeth donned her pelisse, gloves, and bonnet in Long-bourn's entrance hall, her mother pronounced that no one died of a trifling cold and that it was Elizabeth's job to keep Jane at Nether-field for as long as could be. Mrs. Bennet said all of this with a few winks and a knowing stare. It was to ascertain Jane's actual condition that had led Elizabeth to run nearly the whole of the three miles between her home and Mr. Bingley's. Elizabeth arrived much to, alternately, the horror or admiration of the Netherfield party glowing and breathless with her hems six inches deep in mud.

Mr. Bingley escorted her to Jane's rooms and assured her that he had already sent for Mr. Jones, the local apothecary. Elizabeth felt a bit less like an interloper after Mr. Bingley further assured her that both she and Jane were very welcome to remain at Netherfield as long as it was necessary and even longer if they wished. Mr. Bingley's amiable enthusiasm was a balm that laid to rest any concerns that Elizabeth had about imposing on his hospitality.

In parting, Mr. Bingley left her at the door to the chamber. "Miss Elizabeth, the housemaid who is sitting with Miss Bennet is at your disposal for the duration of Miss Bennet's stay." At this Miss Elizabeth smiled and nodded, as Mr. Bingley said, "Mr. Darcy, Mr. Hurst, and I will be going shooting this morning for a few hours, but we will be close by if you have need of me. Please excuse me while I have a

servant check on when Mr. Jones will arrive." Bingley bowed in parting.

After thanking Mr. Bingley, Elizabeth walked into the finely ap-
pointed guest chamber wherein her sister Jane lay asleep. Upon a
quick perusal of the room, she doubted her mother's nonchalance
as Jane looked very ill indeed. She saw that the housemaid in attendance was sitting at the window stitching plain work. Elizabeth
walked to the bedside and gently laid her hand on Jane's brow; Jane's
face was red and hot with fever. To Elizabeth's ears, Jane did not appear to sound overly congested, which was a great relief.

After making sure that her beloved sister was comfortable and
the covers were tucked in nicely against any drafts, Elizabeth whispered to the housemaid to remove to the adjacent dressing room so
that they could converse more freely.

Once in the other room, Elizabeth asked for the girl's name,
which was Letty, and said, "My sister's breathing is not too labored.
Hopefully, the fever will be of a short duration, as long as a putrid
throat or a heavy cough does not set in Jane should recover within a
few days. Letty, do you know how all of this came about?"

Letty described Jane's arrival the previous day soaked through
and shivering from her horseback ride in the freezing rain and sleet.
"Whoever let Miss Bennet leave Longbourn with the weather so
close to freezing and a storm due in?"

Elizabeth said nothing, as the answer was her mother. Letty continued to say that Miss Bennet had dined with Mrs. Hurst but in the
hours after dinner during the tea service it was evident that Miss Bennet had not warmed up and that her shivering had increased. "Mrs.
Hurst was very kind and would not hear of Miss Bennet returning to
Longbourn in the rain, even if in a carriage. Instead she brought her
up to this chamber with a good fire and stayed with her until bedtime." Letty then recounted all that she and Mrs. Hurst had done for
Jane, no mention was made of Miss Bingley at all.

"Miss Elizabeth, I am sure that the family is glad that you have come."

"Has Miss Bennet woken up yet this morning?" Elizabeth asked. Letty nodded. "Has she eaten this morning?"

"No, ma'am, she has not."

"I left Longbourn before breakfast was served. Would it be possible to request a breakfast tray with tea, as well as some restorative broth?"

"Yes, ma'am, the family is still at breakfast, so I will bring a tray up as soon as may be." The young maid curtseyed and departed the room.

10:41, Same day
Breakfast parlor
Netherfield Park

Eyeing the last bite of ham on his plate, Mr. Frederick Hurst wondered if he should eat another ham slice or two to fill up the corners in his stomach. Upon further reflection, he decided not to as the gentlemen were to go shooting this morning. An overly full stomach would be uncomfortable as they rambled over the hills and through the hedges in search of game birds. Hurst was impatient to leave breakfast and commence shooting but he was for the nonce awaiting Bingley to return from escorting Miss Elizabeth Bennet, whose sudden appearance at breakfast had surprised the entire party, to her sister's rooms.

Miss Caroline Bingley had spent the subsequent ten minutes ridiculing Miss Elizabeth to whoever would listen; given that Mr. Darcy was diligently reading his newspaper, Hurst applying himself to his ham, and Mrs. Hurst was inspecting her bracelets and pushing the food on her plate around, it was only the two attending footmen,

Homme and Hughes, who mostly followed the whole of Miss Bingley's diatribe.

Both Mr. Hurst and Mr. Darcy had attended quite closely to the arrival of Miss Elizabeth. Hurst imagined that Bingley had admired Miss Elizabeth's filial loyalty to his sick angel and that Mr. Darcy admired Miss Elizabeth's dewy complexion and fine eyes. Hurst himself marveled at her small waist and heaving bosom. He further surmised with all of that walking that Miss Elizabeth would have a fine, firm haunch which further led him to consider if he should have another slice of ham.

Sensing that the storm named Caroline was brewing into a tempest across the breakfast table from his person, Mr. Hurst abstained from the remaining ham slices and rose from his seat without excusing himself. He walked to Mr. Bingley, who was standing in the doorway of the breakfast room. "Charles, shall we go shooting directly?"

As mutterings about hems six inches deep in mud and a conceited sort of independence grew louder, the rest of the table continued ignoring Miss Bingley's invective. Indeed, since her dinner party tantrum, the party had been inured to Miss Bingley's vitriol in the particularly delightful manner of a long married couple who appeared to be attending each other's words but had no idea of what was uttered at all.

"Ladies, please excuse me," Darcy said as he put his newspaper down and rose from his seat. Walking the entrance to the room, he said to Bingley and Hurst, "I shall meet you in the gun room in a quarter of an hour. Will we be taking a beater with us or just the dogs?"

"Muddy hems! Are any of you attending?" The tempest sputtered from the other side of the breakfast table. "Ignore me by all means, but do not ignore that Miss Eliza's hems were six inches deep in mud. It shows a complete lack of country-town decorum! Miss Eliza is unfit for..."

Hurst and Darcy walked out of the breakfast parlor and mounted the stairs to the guest chambers, whereupon Bingley called out, "Indeed, we shall meet in a quarter of an hour in the gunroom and we shall take Homme and Hughes here as our beaters."

Bingley winked at the two footmen, waved them off from their post at the breakfast parlor, and walked to the gunroom to make sure all was in order.

In less than a half an hour later, the housemaid returned to Miss Bennet's room with a breakfast tray. She also brought the good tidings that Mr. Jones would be arriving within the hour and that Mrs. Hurst would come as soon as she had settled her sister's nerves.

Jane's eyes fluttered open as Elizabeth poured the tea and buttered a piece of warm bread for her own belated breakfast. "Oh Lizzy, you have come."

"Jane, I could not remain at home all the while knowing you were here ill." Elizabeth tried to make a joke of her haste to arrive at Netherfield Park by showing Jane her muddy petticoats. "I spared no puddle in my haste to arrive at your side."

Jane rose slightly to look and then laid back down on the heap of pillows. "Please tell me that the housekeeper or a footman escorted you here directly and that you did not greet Miss Bingley in that state."

Elizabeth did not answer but took the tea and breakfast dishes from the tray and put them on the little table near the window. She placed the cup of broth on the tray. "Jane, the maid brought up some breakfast and broth. I do believe you should drink some broth to regain your strength." Jane gave her sister a steady look at her evasion and gratefully acquiesced.

Elizabeth helped Jane to sit up and once she was settled, she placed the breakfast tray with the broth on Jane's lap. Jane smiled. "I can take the broth myself. Why do you not sit and eat your breakfast?"

After drinking some broth, Jane asked, "May I have a cup of tea and a piece of buttered bread with ham? My throat is not so very bad that I cannot swallow some bread and ham softened with tea."

As Elizabeth prepared the tea and bread, she said, "Your head feels quite feverish. How do you feel otherwise?"

"Yesterday morning, I felt a scratching in my throat and had a slight headache before I departed for Netherfield. I should have declined the invitation to dine with Mrs. Hurst, as the carriage was still in town with our Father and the temperature had dropped so precipitously. Our mother would not hear me staying home and I was foolish to ride out in the freezing rain on old Nellie." Jane finished her broth and began to apply herself to the ham and bread, chewing carefully and taking sips of tea before swallowing. She flushed a deep red. "Lizzy, I know you wanted me to stay home yesterday, but I did so look forward to dining with Mrs. Hurst."

The maid had stepped out of the room to get more hot water for the tea. Elizabeth lowered her voice to a whisper, "Jane, what are you about?"

"I am not so very ill," Jane said just as she sneezed violently four times and upset her tray of food. Elizabeth jumped up to catch the tray and did so before the dishes fell off onto the floor.

"Jane..."

"May I have more tea and buttered bread? And a fresh handkerchief?"

"Jane..." Elizabeth passed the requested items to Jane and sat back down with her own tea.

After daintily wiping her nose, Jane asked, "Has our father returned home from London?"

Jane enjoyed her tea and buttered bread as Elizabeth recounted their father's return last evening; a few highlights of his trip to Lon-

don, the great mutterings and flutterings as their mother angrily refused to acknowledge their father's return. All this as well as this
morning's row between Lydia and their father over the Quaker
School she would be attending and the amusing letter announcing
the impending arrival of their distant cousin and the Longbourn
heir, a Mr. Collins. Elizabeth noticed that Jane did not laugh at Mr.
Collins' intentions of marrying one of the Bennet girls as an olive
branch to heal the breach in the family.

Horrified Jane gasped, "I will not be the olive branch. You must
promise me you will not either." Jane sat up straighter and stabbed
her handkerchief with an angry motion towards the direction of
Longbourn. "I have done everything that Papa asked us to do: I left
my home and family to go to preparatory school, I attended Lorien
College and graduated with honors. I will have my promised season
in Town and a good dowry."

"Indeed, Jane, we will marry for the deepest of love as we have always promised each other. I read the letter after Papa read it aloud;
our cousin is ridiculous and a fool. You know that I could never marry a fool." Elizabeth laughed and then reached out to take her sister's
hand. "Neither shall you marry a fool. Do take comfort that we have
met all the goals that our father has set for accomplished, educated
young ladies. We will have our season in London and there is nothing our mother can do to ruin that for us. Even if we do not marry
straight away, we have good dowries and I can invest them such that
we will not need to marry in fear or panic about hedgerows."

"Lizzy, I do wish to marry for love." Jane's face flushed an even
deeper red and she smiled hesitantly. "I do believe I am in a fair way
to falling in love with Mr. Bingley."

A knock was heard at the door. Elizabeth rose to greet the
apothecary as he entered the room with Mrs. Hurst. Mr. Jones examined Jane and determined that she was suffering from a fever and a
cold. He gave Elizabeth and Mrs. Hurst instructions for Miss Bennet

to remain in bed in a warm room, to drink broth and tea, and most of all to sleep to avoid the fever from entering her lungs. He said it was not necessary to bleed Miss Bennet, much to everyone's relief. As he departed, he promised to send a packet of herbs for tea if any congestion started in her chest.

Mrs. Hurst kindly stayed with Jane and Elizabeth for another half hour entertaining them with humorous stories of Town until Jane fell back asleep. "Miss Elizabeth, please do feel at home here. If you wish to remain with your sister, I will send for your trunk. I would be pleased to see dear Jane so well cared for."

"Mrs. Hurst, if it is no bother to you, I would very much like to stay with Jane until she is well enough to return home."

"You and Miss Bennet are welcome to stay even after she has returned to full health." Mrs. Hurst smiled warmly. She hesitated a moment and then said, "I am not sure if you are aware of this, but we are second cousins once removed. My grandmother Louisa Bailey Bingley was the sister of your great-grandmother Caroline Bailey Gardiner."

Elizabeth was surprised to hear this information now after nearly four weeks of their acquaintance. "My father's preference is to remain at Longbourn with his books and equations, thus I have heard stories of my many relations but have not met all of them. I do remember that my Uncle Gardiner started in business with the help of a cousin from the north of the country. Was it your father?"

"Yes, it was. In fact, since my marriage I have become quite close with your Uncle and Aunt Gardiner. Marinda is truly a wonderful woman and has become a particular friend of mine. She sent me a letter last week confirming that the Longbourn Bennets were their Gardiner relations. I quite look forward to becoming better friends with Miss Bennet and yourself." Mrs. Hurst's smile faltered. "As with almost all of life, there is a worm in this particular apple as my sister, Caroline, is very ambitious for herself and in turn for my brother.

She denies how our father made his money and only wants to acknowledge our mother's family, the Swithenbanks - a country gentry family in Yorkshire..."

Mrs. Hurst told Elizabeth of Miss Bingley's refusal to acknowledge how the Bingley's made their wealth in trade, the Gardiner side of the family - even her namesake Caroline Bailey Gardiner - and of her sister's bad behavior of the past few weeks. "I have no doubt that she will be difficult to you and Miss Bennet. But you must know that both Charles and I sincerely wish to know your family better and we do not hold our Bingley and Gardiner relations in contempt. I must go downstairs now, but I will return before tea to see how our dear Jane is."

After Mrs. Hurst departed and as Jane slept, Elizabeth reflected on Mrs. Hurst's familial revelations and words of friendship. Elizabeth hoped that it was true that Mr. Bingley and Mrs. Hurst did desire a closer connection, particularly for Jane to join their family.

Before Dinner
> **Thurs. Nov. 14, 1811**
> **The Drawing Room**
> **Netherfield Park**

Elizabeth made sure that Jane was comfortable as she slept, before asking Letty to send for her if Jane took a turn for the worse, even if they were still dining. Then she departed for pre-dinner drinks in the drawing room. Elizabeth had remained with Jane the previous evening because Jane's fever had risen and sore throat worsened as the day progressed and she had no wish to dine with the party as she had little desire to deflect Miss Bingley's barbs. She had been quite content to take her meals with Jane yesterday and read to her sister in the evening from a book of fables found in the library.

After that morning's mortifying social call from Mrs. Bennet and Miss Lydia, Elizabeth left Jane's chamber determined to face any censure at dinner. To proclaim that this morning was mortifying was merely the beginning of the disaster that was her mother's visit. Neither Mrs. Bennet nor Lydia had inquired after Jane nor did they visit her. Instead they displayed their ill-bred, vulgar manners with speeches on the Bingley's wealth and consequence.

Miss Lydia demanded that Mr. Bingley hold a ball, of which the gentleman was too amiable to deny her. Elizabeth had been mortified and Mrs. Hurst embarrassed at the display of their mutual relations. Elizabeth could not look at Mr. Darcy, as she was sure he held all the Bennets in contempt. Miss Bingley's eyes had contained a certain glee. As for Miss Bingley, Elizabeth's courage was sure to rise at Caroline's every attempt to intimidate her.

As Elizabeth descended the grand staircase, she mused that the only solace of the last day and a half at Netherfield was Mr. Bingley's attentions to Jane this afternoon. He had waited at the door of Jane's chamber until Mrs. Hurst joined him to visit Jane. It was obvious to both Elizabeth and Mrs. Hurst that both Jane and Mr. Bingley were fair on their way to being in love with each other.

Mr. Bingley spent most of his visit hovering next to the bed. While Jane was very pleased to receive his attentions, her throat was sore enough to make talking difficult. Mr. Bingley whispered and Jane smiled. Elizabeth and Mrs. Hurst sat near the window making their own conversation and finding themselves fair on their way to a firm friendship discussing books, art exhibitions they had both seen in town, and the wonders of their mutual relations: Mr. and Mrs. Edmund Gardiner.

Elizabeth stopped before the drawing room door to gather her wits and courage. She walked into the drawing room to find the air tense and Miss Bingley pacing circle eights between the poles of her brother at the drinks table and Mr. Darcy on a sofa near the fireplace, leafing through a book.

"Ah, Miss Elizabeth, welcome! Would you like a glass of sherry? We are waiting for the Hursts to join us before proceeding into the dining room," Mr. Bingley called. He lifted the sherry decanter and poured a small glass before Elizabeth even had time to respond. He broke out of his sister's prescribed path to bring the glass to Elizabeth, who smiled in welcome.

"Thank you, Mr. Bingley." Elizabeth said as she received her sherry.

"It is a dry sherry from Jerez, Spain. Our mutual cousin, oh - I mean your uncle, my cousin, Edmund Gardiner gave me a few bottles as a gift to start out my cellar here at Netherfield. He also kindly gifted me with a bottle of real French brandy. A capital chap!"

Elizabeth sipped the fine sherry. "This is a wonderful vintage. My uncle Gardiner is quite talented at procuring brandies, port, and sherries - even through the blockade."

Mr. Darcy, also desiring to escape Miss Bingley's silent pacing, walked towards the twosome. "Miss Elizabeth, how is Miss Bennet's health this evening?"

Elizabeth smothered a smile at Mr. Darcy's attempt to escape Miss Bingley, mistaking his welcoming smile as relief. "She is still feverish and her throat sore, but she is now sleeping. Thank you for asking."

Miss Bingley stopped her pacing and turned on her heel to face Elizabeth. "Should not Miss Bennet be well by now? As we all know, your mother's purpose for her was to capture my brother in a compromise..."

"Caroline! This is simply not true!" Charles was astonished at his sister's rude conjectures. "At no point during her illness have we been unchaperoned! I went to visit Miss Bennet this afternoon with Louisa. Miss Bennet has a fever. She is not playing us false."

"How do you know that she is not putting a warm cloth on her face before you enter? Or that Miss Eliza is not aiding and abetting her in this scheme?"

"Miss Bingley," Mr. Darcy said. "I do believe you have read too many gothic novels. Perhaps you are ascribing your own possible methods to Miss Bennet."

Miss Bingley reddened and gasped. Rather than lash out at Mr. Darcy, she turned to Elizabeth. "Eliza, do tell me who your family is. Let us not talk of the alleged noble connections, rather let us talk of your mother's relations in Cheapside."

"Miss Bingley, our mutual Gardiner relations choose to live less than two blocks from the Bank of London and Coutts Bank in the City and the warehouses on the Thames river, as your own father did before his full removal to York in the latter years of his life." Elizabeth looked at Miss Bingley with her right eyebrow slightly raised in a challenge before continuing. "As you may remember from your childhood, Gracechurch Street is fashionable. And as we both know, my Uncle Gardiner got his start in business from your father rather than going into law or the Church as previous generations of the Gardiners did. You may have seen more of my uncle - your cousin - than I have."

Miss Bingley resumed her pacing in great agitation and clipped the drinks table with her hip - tipping it over much to the horror of her brother and the Hursts, who had just entered the drawing room. Mr. Bingley saved the evening by leaping forward to catch the table and the tray of decanters before they fell onto the expensive Turkish rug he purchased over the summer. Mr. Hurst rushed over to help with the drinks table and to collect a drink. Heaven forfend if they should lose the smuggled brandy and port to the carpet! Louisa stood at the entrance of the room with her arms folded across her chest and shaking her head at her sister.

Miss Bingley ignored the chaos she had created and stalked around Elizabeth. "Mr. Darcy has defended your high born relations: a duke, an earl, and Derbyshire's oldest barony. I don't believe him, for he is plainly addled by your fine eyes," Miss Bingley sneered. She fixed her gaze on Elizabeth's bosom, "and your rather full-blown allurements." Miss Bingley stood over Elizabeth and flicked a finger at said allurements as she leaned down and whispered, "Padding, I am sure."

"Miss Bingley, padding is not necessary, I assure you." Elizabeth whispered before she stepped back with her posture absolutely straight and said aloud, "Miss Bingley, did you not attend Miss Swithenbank's Seminary for Elegant Young Ladies?"

"Yes, I did. To what does this portend?"

"Did you not memorize Debrett's Peerage as a part of your young ladies education?"

A bewildered Miss Bingley nodded.

"A perusal of DeBrett's Peerage in your accomplished memory will disabuse you of any allegation that Mr. Darcy or anyone else is deceiving you. To aid your recall, my father is Thomas Claudius Bennet and his father is Andrew Cornelius Bennet." At this salvo, Elizabeth walked further away from Miss Bingley.

Before Mr. Darcy could address the insult that Miss Bingley leveled at his character, Mrs. Hurst held out her arm to her husband and suggested that they proceed into the dining room and not keep the first course waiting. Mr. Darcy offered his arm to Elizabeth and apologized in low tones to her for the ill-bred and deliberate insults leveled at her by Miss Bingley. Elizabeth whispered back as he helped her into her seat at the table, "You need not apologize for Miss Bingley, I have met her type before at school. I can defend myself."

Mr. Bingley offered his sister, Caroline, his arm and escorted her back into the recesses of the drawing room as the others were seated in the dining room.

Mr. Darcy sat next to Elizabeth after helping her in her chair leaving the empty space on her other side for Mr. Bingley. Mr. Hurst seated Louisa across from Elizabeth and motioned for Hughes to fill their wine glasses. Louisa made small talk while the soup was served to cover up the raised voices coming from the drawing room. "Please do not let your soup grow cold. We will not wait for Charles and Caroline. They will join us soon."

Through the closed doors the diners could hear Miss Bingley shout at her brother, "That woman is not my cousin. Let me repeat, Mrs. Bennet is not my cousin!" Mr. and Mrs. Hurst both coughed in unison attempting to disguise the raised voices.

Rather than let a tense silence fill the dining room, Mr. Darcy asked, "Miss Elizabeth, will you be in Hertfordshire for the Christmas season?"

"No, it has been planned for some time now that Jane and I will be departing for London at the beginning of December to stay with our Aunt Beauchamp to prepare for our presentation in the spring."

"Lady Beauchamp will be sponsoring you?" Louisa asked breathlessly.

"Yes, she is. Jane and I are quite anticipating spending the winter and the Season in London."

Before Mrs. Hurst could ask her cousin Elizabeth if she already had vouchers for Almack's, a grimly determined Charles entered the dining room and took the empty seat at the head of the table with Elizabeth to his left and Louisa to his right. Mr. Bingley said not a word and ate his soup silently.

Caroline followed some minutes later just as the soup course was being cleared. She was not repentant in the least but had a shrewd gleam in her eye as she sat in the seat at the foot of the table. "Mr. Darcy, please forgive my absence. A small task called me away."

Mr. Darcy said not a word. Miss Bingley took a surprisingly large sip of her wine, followed by another. She then asked Mr. Hurst to pass a dish or two to her, whereupon she put the tiniest amount of each dish on her plate; she arranged the samples in such a way that each food item was a minimum of two inches from the other. After exactly arranging the food on her plate but before she started to consume any of it, Caroline in a large gulp finished her wine and motioned for more.

Mr. Hurst coughed in amusement, "Homme, my good man, can you please?" He lifted his glass for a refill as well. At this display, the other diners occupied themselves with selections from the first course dishes.

A rather astonished Elizabeth did her best to not break out in peals of laughter. In an effort to keep her wits about her, she drank two or three sips of water for each sip of wine. Mr. Darcy looked at her inquiring with a lift of his brow at which she shook her head and smiled at him. He smiled back and at once she was struck with what a delightfully handsome man he was. This did not go unnoticed by Miss Bingley.

Chapter 6 : Love, Ferment, and Other Boils at Netherfield Park

At Dinner
   Thurs. Nov. 14, 1811
   The Dining Room
   Netherfield Park

Miss Bingley, after spying the secret smiles between Mr. Darcy and Miss Eliza, picked up her wine glass and took a sip before inquiring, "Now, Eliza, there is much talk about this and that noble relation and connection of the Bennets. Why then is everyone in this country town absolutely silent on the topic of your dowries and the Bennet family's wealth? The lack of gossip is very odd considering we had not been at the assembly above five minutes before the Bingley wealth and dowries were bandied about - quite accurate on the amounts to my surprise."

Elizabeth put her fork down before she replied. "Miss Bingley, my father is a very private man - to the point of eccentricity and being a recluse. You may have heard that my father's older brother had a rather disastrous gambling habit to the loss of my family's consequence." Miss Bingley nodded. Elizabeth lifted her glass of water and drank. "What is not bandied about is that my father has worked very hard these past three decades to restore our family's fortune and provide good dowries for his five daughters."

"Yes, yes, yes. I have heard all of that, but how much are your dowries? The way your mother talks, your dowries are nothing and

A QUIVER FULL, OR HOW MR. DARCY WILL NOT SIT
ON THAT SOFA AGAIN!

75

you must all be married off immediately to rich men to save her from the hedgerows."

Louisa gasped at her sister's bald remarks. "Caroline..."

Elizabeth intervened. "Have you heard of my father's dowry scheme? The reason my mother is worried is that she does not understand the contract that my sisters and I have entered into with our father; it is quite shocking - we must earn our dowries."

Even though Caroline looked to spew her wine out of her mouth at this impertinent reply, Elizabeth did not cease. "In fact, if we choose not to go to school at all, we will only have as much dowry as an equal portion of my mother's settlement at her death. If we graduate from university with a first, then we will have a dowry equal to any of the prominent debutantes entering their first season. There are, as you can imagine, levels of attainment between no school and a first at university. While we do not know the exact amounts, Jane and I trust our father to be fair."

"That is preposterous!" Before Caroline could continue, Mr. Darcy interrupted her.

"Miss Bingley, Miss Elizabeth's account is exactly what Mr. Bennet told me at Lucas Lodge and what both of my aunts have reported on the Bennet daughters' dowries - which are very good. Shall we let the matter rest?"

Caroline ignored Mr. Darcy and looked directly at Elizabeth, "You will enter the London season at two and twenty or three and twenty without knowing the amount of your own fortune? You will be laughed out of drawing rooms."

Charles ceased his silent eating. "That is hardly the case - with connections to the Matlocks, the Howards, the Manners, the Beauchamps, and the de Bourghs - Mr. Bennet is a very clever man who is protecting his daughters from fortune hunters so that they can attain their complete education. Caroline, I warned you before dinner, cease badgering Miss Elizabeth."

Caroline took a long sip of her wine. "Charles, I am not being a bother at all. I am merely trying to assess the Bennet family's condition and fitness to join our family."

Mr. Hurst laughed at this. "They are already joined to your family by dint of mutual and recent grandparents - have you forgotten your Gardiner relations? The ones you so despise in Cheapside."

Lousia rapped her husband's wrist with the butt end of her knife, "Frederick, you are not making this any easier."

"My lovely wife, would you like me to make this dinner flow with easy conversation?" She nodded. He smiled and motioned for a refill of his wine glass. He took a deep sip and smiled at the table. "Right then, let us discuss a much more important topic than family connections, wealth, and dowries: toothpowder!"

The whole of the table and the footmen attending stopped and stared at Mr. Hurst.

"How ever can any of you put that vile, chalky, poisonous tooth powder on a small brush made of boar bristles and swirl it around your mouth? Revulsion only begins to describe what I feel when I think of committing such a crime to my mouth and teeth..."

Louisa very drily remarked, "Revulsion only begins to describe what I smell because you never commit such an act to your mouth and teeth."

It was all Elizabeth could do not to dissolve into horrified giggles, so instead she found herself gripping Mr. Darcy's hand under the table. Much to her surprise, he squeezed her hand in return before letting her hand go ever so slowly trailing his fingers along hers. As he let go, Elizabeth's fingers and the palm of her hand tingled. She blushed.

Caroline's voice rose. "Stop at once, both of you are being vile."

Mr. Hurst did not heed either of the two ladies' assertions, he focused on his intended audience. "In fact, Mr. Darcy and Miss Elizabeth, I believe that there are other ways to keep one's mouth clean and pure without the application of tooth powder. I will share my secret with you. A cousin of mine has land in the West Indies and has traveled to the Spanish colony of Cuba; two years ago when he returned to London he introduced me to the most delightful tonic of rum, lime, and mint leaves."

Louisa groaned at her husband's words and took up with her wine glass as he continued on. "I have a glass of this tonic every night before bed, for medicinal purposes - I assure you - I swish it around my mouth before gargling and swallowing it."

Elizabeth smothered her own smile before inquiring, "Do you advise also chewing on or consuming the lime and mint leaves?"

"No, I recommend swallowing the liquid after swishing and gargling. If one cannot obtain limes, lemon juice will do." Mr. Hurst pointed to himself. "Look at me, I am the picture of health and well-being."

Louisa could not stifle her disgust. "I will dispute this alleged health and well-being, particularly of..."

Caroline's countenance took on colors that were not natural to her complexion. From the other end of the table, Mr. Bingley interceded before dinner dissolved into a shouting match between siblings and a spouse.

"Miss Elizabeth, I have spoken at length with Miss Bennet on the topic of our mutual passion for medieval military history, but we have yet to speak on the experience of attending Oxford versus Cambridge. I have many fond memories of Cambridge."

"I cannot speak of Cambridge, but I did enjoy Oxford and not just my studies in mathematics and astronomy at Lorien College. Oxford is a lovely city. The buildings, ancient and modern, are mostly of local sandstone and glow in the sunlight. The spires of the college towers are much praised, but I was more fond of the individual college libraries when I could obtain permission to venture beyond the Bodleian and Lorien libraries."

"Ah, libraries... I was thinking more of college life: punting on the Cam - I think you had the Isis - dinners with your college fellows, the nights at the local public house..." As Mr. Bingley reminisced on the glories of student life at Cambridge, his sister Caroline drank deeply of her wine and ate little on her plate.

Mr. Darcy interjected, "From discussions with my cousin Anne, the ladies at Matlock and Lorien colleges did not have quite the same liberties that we had."

"To say the least!" Elizabeth laughed. "We had vertible dragons of chaperones at Lorien who curtailed any liberties that would result in the lowering of our reputations or the reputation of the college. Though the Bear Inn near Christ Church College kindly hosted a Lorien ladies evening once a month with small glasses of sherry and our chaperones guarding the doors to keep all gentlemen out."

"What about sport?" Louisa asked with genuine curiosity.

"Sport was a matter of great debate while I was at Lorien. Many families did not want their daughters to participate in any games nor any sport more rigorous..."

Caroline took a last, long draught to the last drip and put her wine glass down rather forcefully. "Nor should they! No gently bred lady should participate in sport. A small walk around the garden, even a little flower gardening, possibly some archery or punting on a pond at a picnic, but sport? No, it is not to be conceived of."

"Miss Bingley has much the same opinions of a few of the college trustees. We were allowed to ride horses - though no riding to the hunt whilst at college, walk in the Port Meadow in groups or with a chaperone, punt on the Isis, as well as archery and occasional informal cricket games. As you all know, I am a walker - thus Oxford and its riverside meadows were a delight. Given my love for the calculus of the trajectories of arrows and balls moving through the air, I do enjoy a good archery match and I have been known to bowl in a game of cricket." Elizabeth did take a sip of her wine and requested that a vegetable dish be passed.

Charles, recovered, entered back into the fray. "I have heard that there is talk of establishing a match of games between Lorien and Matlock colleges."

"It was much talked about this past year and a half, but the debate on whether the games should include more than distance walking and archery became acrimonious. I see nothing wrong with a ladies cricket match between the two colleges."

"Nor do I." Charles opined in agreement.

"I do." Caroline was not to be repressed nor cut out of her share of the conversation. With more than a touch of a sneer in her voice, she pronounced, "With all due respect, gently bred ladies should not attend college at all. It is a disgrace to our reputation as a nation to have university educated women. What is next, a gentlewoman living as a man or - heaven forfend - working as a man in a profession? It is a disgrace, I tell you! A lady should only have attained schooling to the seminary level where she learns the accomplishments of elegance and refinement such as embroidery, netting, designing a table, the modern languages, how to be a mistress of an estate, and the arts of drawing and music."

"Forget not to add the memorization of the pages of the Peerage for purposes of hunting and stalking of prime game," a very impish Mr. Hurst added. Both Mr. Darcy and Mr. Bingley visibly shuddered in repressed laughter.

By Elizabeth's count, Miss Bingley had consumed very little food and at least four or five glasses of wine. Dinner was nearly at the end and it was time for the ladies to move into the drawing room while leaving the gentlemen to their after dinner drinks.

Louisa looked ready to stand but Caroline did not relent, she requested more wine from the footman Hughes and continued to expound. "In fact, I consider it a greater disgrace not that a woman is learning a man's education but that the college ladies are waiting three, four, even five years to come out in society and are marrying so very late. A well-bred young lady ought to be out and presented by or before her eighteenth birthday, not waiting until she is two and twenty or even three and twenty." She stared at Elizabeth.

"I am not yet one and twenty." Elizabeth was quite ready to leave the dining room and the company, as Miss Bingley was also insulting Jane who was not present.

Mr. Hurst snorted inelegantly, fixed his attention on his sister-in-law whilst ignoring Elizabeth's quiet interjection. "Quite right, sister. And by what age ought this paragon of accomplished, barely educated femininity to be married by? No later than the end of her first season at eighteen, I am sure. Certainly to be unmarried at one and twenty when one has been out since seventeen is a disgrace by your own measure is it not?" Hurst's gaze was pointed at Miss Bingley.

Dinner was at an end by Elizabeth's measure. Before a very red faced, tipsy, sputtering Caroline could belie her alleged elegant seminary education by screaming at her equally tipsy brother-in-law, Elizabeth rose to excuse herself from the table. "Mrs. Hurst, the dinner was everything lovely and delicious. Please excuse me, I must attend my sister Jane."

Elizabeth smiled, curtsied to the whole of the party, nodded at Mr. Darcy, and departed the dining room before any further tumult could erupt.

Mr. Darcy waited for Miss Elizabeth's footsteps to fade away, but Miss Bingley did not. It was obvious to the whole of the dining room that Miss Bingley was not sober, even if it was not yet obvious to the rather wobbly Miss Bingley. In her haste to make sharp remarks about the Bennets she forgot to dress down Hurst for his cutting re-

marks to her. As she cut Miss Eliza with her words she poorly divided
the food on her plate into further parcels of smeared, former edibles.

"As I was shaying..." Caroline lost control of her knife and it clat-
tered to the floor. Mr. Darcy laid his silverware down on his plate to
indicate that he was finished eating.

"Cease, Miss Bingley." Mr. Darcy asserted. "You may have all the
opinions in the world about women's education and place in society,
but the truth of the matter is that speaking ill of Miss Bennet and
Miss Elizabeth will only sully your own reputation." Caroline opened
her mouth to refute this when he pushed his chair back and stood
up.

"What should be material to you, Miss Bingley, is that you have
yet to be sponsored to court and presented to the Queen, even
though you have been out in London society for four years. Your sister, Mrs. Hurst, was presented upon her marriage to Mr. Hurst, but
you have not yet been to court. Furthermore, you do not have vouchers to Almack's, nor does your sister or brother. Given your ambitions for yourself and your family, why would you antagonize members of the powerful Beauchamp and Matlock families? Do beware
of crossing the Ladies Beauchamp and Matlock; not only are they
both very influential, but they will be sponsoring the Misses Bennet
this upcoming season."

"That is immaterial." Miss Bingley swayed in her seat as she attempted bat her eyelashes at Mr. Darcy. "My husband will have me
presented and I will then also be admitted to every drawing room in
London as Mrs. Dar-Darsh."

This was too much for Mr. Darcy. He completely ignored Miss
Bingley and instead addressed the others. "Mrs. Hurst, thank you for
the lovely dinner. Charles, Hurst, and Mrs. Hurst, please excuse me
for the rest of the evening, I will not be joining the party in the drawing room."

Darcy bowed and exited the dining room. As he walked through the large and ornate foyer to ascend the grand stairway, he could hear Hurst laughing at his sister-in-law calling her every type of fool and Charles berating his sister's bad manners and drunken behavior. As he reached the second floor, all of their voices of protest had faded to a murmur; he nodded to the footman on duty in the guest wing as he entered his chambers. He locked his door and informed his valet that he was in for the rest of the evening.

Darcy sat in the comfortable wing chair near the fireplace, he started to pick up his book but the hand that held Elizabeth's faintly tingled in remembrance. He put the book back down to gaze at the flames and muse on a pair of fine eyes in the face of a lovely woman who he would so dearly like to kiss.

Thurs. Nov. 14, 1811
  After everyone has retired for the night
  The Family Wing, Netherfield Park

As Mr. Frederick Hurst undressed for the night, he rubbed his jaw and neck to relieve the pressure where it had been constricted by his high collar and overly tight, but oh so fashionable cravat. He stopped rubbing at his jaw and neck when the pain of a rather large boil just below his jaw bone and above the starched collar became too much and the pain was shooting up his neck and down his arms.

After he had changed into his nightshirt and performed his wife's required nightly ablutions and toothbrushing along with a follow-up of his Cuban mouth rinse, nee minty limey nightcap, he knocked on the door connecting his chambers with those of Mrs. Hurst. There was no answer and so he knocked again.

"Louisa, please open the door."

"No, Frederick, I will not. You are drunk."

Mr. Hurst leaned against the door. "No, Louisa, I am not drunk. I have done everything you have asked me to do. I diverted your sister's tirade at dinner with a funny story, I have brushed my teeth with that vile toothpowder, and I have rinsed it with my mint concoction. Please let me in."

He heard something that sounded like a head or a forehead softly hit the other side of the door. He knew how this would end, but he wanted to make a last try. A try for his dignity, an attempt for an heir, but really it was a last crack at saving the heart of their marriage. His legs gave out and his back slid down the doorway. He fell to the floor with an 'Oomph' and then leaned back against the door.

"Louisa, you loved me once. I loved you. What happened to us?" He could hear her breathing, it was slow and erratic.

"Frederick, you have a boil on the side of your neck." Came the muffled reply from the other side of the door.

"That is not an answer to my question. Has our mutual neglect gutted our marriage? Is there no hope for me with you?"

"Frederick, I don't know. I truly have not the answer." He thought he could hear muffled sobs.

"Louisa, just let me in. At the very least, we can lie down on the bed together and discuss this." All he heard was a sigh. "If not tonight, then let us go away, far away from your sister and the concerns of life, and mend our marriage."

He heard a hiccup. "Frederick, going away just you and me will not mend what lies between us. We made a bad match with each other. We do not fit together."

"We did once, Louisa. We did once, not that long ago." He heard her leave the doorway and walk across the room. He thought he heard her blow out the candles. He wanted to cry, but could not, instead he felt a great pressure in his chest. Pain radiated down his arm and across his shoulder blade. The pain increased. He felt very tired. He slumped against the door and blacked out.

Fri. Nov. 15, 1811
   In the afternoon
   The Gardens at Netherfield Park
   As soon as Darcy spied Miss Elizabeth venturing out for a walk, he grabbed his coat, gloves, and hat to follow her out into the cold, blustery afternoon. He told himself that he needed to get out and walk around, but if he examined his motives closely he would find that he desired Miss Elizabeth's company above all else. When he caught up with her on the far side of the kitchen garden, she was on the path to walk down a forested lane. He invited himself to join her and a lively discussion ensued.

   He was not sure when it happened but Miss Elizabeth had become the handsomest woman in his acquaintance; it was not her dark auburn curls, nor her heart shaped face, nor her lovely complexion with roses in her cheeks on a blustery day like today, no it was her dark sea blue eyes that seemed to change depending on the light from a deep blue to a navy blue to an obsidian color when in candlelight and with her emotions flickering through their depths. He knew she had caught him frequently staring, but he could not stop himself. He could lose himself in those eyes.

   He was lost even now as they walked back on another lane, her eyes were dancing in merriment, and the urge to kiss her overwhelmed him. They had walked a good two miles down the lanes and had looped back around to Netherfield's formal gardens. Before they reached the garden gate, he pulled Miss Elizabeth into a copse of trees.

   "Miss Elizabeth, please put me out of my misery. May I kiss you?"

   Surprise flitted across her countenance and her eyes, now a dark sapphire in color, opened wide. "Kiss me? I thought I was tolerable but not handsome enough to tempt you?"

"Miss Elizabeth, I was out of sorts that evening and was an idiot. Can you please accept my apologies for uttering such an untruth. You are one of the most handsome women of my acquaintance." He moved closer to her and could feel the air crackle between them.

Her eyebrow raised in disbelief. "I am waiting for my first kiss to be with my husband."

"I am as well."

"Who do you plan for your first husband to be, Mr. Darcy?" Miss Elizabeth's laughter tinkled about him like pixie dust, enchanting him thoroughly. His deep laughter followed hers. They smiled at each other, eyes dancing.

They both moved closer towards each other until there was less than a finger's breadth betwixt them. She raised up her face to his and he lowered his in anticipation, when...

"Louisa! I cannot fathom why you forced me out of doors for a walk in the lane on the other side of the garden! It is cold and windy, quite horrible to be out of doors and away from the fireplace in my room. I have such a head!"

"Caroline, your headache is your own fault, if you would only drink less and eat more at dinner you would not have such a head. The fresh air will help clear it out. Let us continue to walk."

Both Darcy and Miss Elizabeth jumped away from each other in great surprise at the sound of Miss Bingley and Mrs. Hurst's voices and each hid behind a large ash tree trunk that could not be seen from the garden gate nor the lane. After Louisa and Caroline continued down the lane and when they were out of sight and sound Darcy and Elizabeth moved out from behind the tree trunks.

The moment was gone in an instant. Miss Elizabeth turned to him, "Thank you for joining me on my walk, I must return to the house now to check on Jane."

Rather than pressing the point, he smiled at her and offered his arm. He asked after Miss Bennet's health and was glad to hear that

she was recovering apace. Miss Elizabeth surmised that Miss Bennet may even be able to join dinner on the morrow. Once in the house and having given their outwear over, Mr. Darcy bowed to Miss Elizabeth and went to the library. His book took second place to gazing into the fire and dreaming of kissing Miss Elizabeth.

Other than her rather outrageous and vulgar family members, Miss Elizabeth was everything that he desired in a wife: an improved mind with a seeking intellect, lively even prone to whimsy on occasion, lovely, and... the list went on as the fire crackled.

Sat. Nov. 16, 1811
In the afternoon
Netherfield Park

No one in the Netherfield party noticed that Mr. Hurst had taken ill for over a day and a half. Friday morning Charles and Louisa assumed that both Hurst and Caroline were suffering the ill effects of too many glasses of wine from the night before, although neither thought to check on Hurst when Caroline appeared after one o'clock. By Saturday afternoon, Louisa became concerned when her husband was still abed, she inquired to his valet and was assured that he was merely sleeping off a cold. As she departed to return downstairs, Mrs. Nichols alerted her that Hurst's valet had requested two pots of foxglove tisane over the past two days.

Since Miss Jane Bennet was to come down for dinner and the evening's entertainment in the drawing room, Mr. Bingley had become completely distracted in anticipation and Louisa was not able to gain his attention long enough to ask after Hurst. She was not about to approach Caroline with her questions and concerns, instead she went into the library to see if there were any medical texts to tell her what foxglove tisane would be used for, as she remembered being told as a child that foxglove was poisonous.

In the library, Louisa found Miss Elizabeth and Mr. Darcy sitting in opposite chairs near the windows and reading quietly.

"I am very sorry to break the silence, but have either of you seen any medical texts in Charles' collection?"

Miss Elizabeth greeted Louisa and replied, "I have not. May I ask what it is you seek?"

Louisa's shoulders drooped and she decided to confide in Miss Elizabeth and Mr. Darcy. "I think that Mr. Hurst has had a health incident - well, more than just his habitual overindulging in drink. He has been abed since Thursday night and his valet will not let me in to see him. Mrs. Nichols just informed me that she has made two pots of foxglove tisane in the last two days for Mr. Hurst. Is foxglove not poisonous?"

Mr. Darcy said, "Foxglove, while poisonous in strength, has been used for heart ailments these past thirty years. My father took an extract of foxglove during the last three months of his life. Has a physician been called?"

"No, not that I know of. My husband's father and his grandmother died young of heart ailments." Louisa began to twist her dress fabric in her hands. "Mr. Darcy, will you please go up and see if you can talk to Mr. Hurst? Charles is currently too distracted to be of any use."

Both Darcy and Elizabeth put down their books and accompanied Louisa upstairs. Elizabeth and Louisa waited in her chambers while Mr. Darcy spoke with Mr. Hurst's valet and eventually Hurst himself. It was nearly time to dress for dinner when Mr. Darcy knocked on the door of Mrs. Hurst's sitting room.

"Mrs. Hurst, your husband remains ill and he is resting. Although we discussed it at length, he does not wish to see a physician this evening - he wishes to rest. He claims that he is no longer having any chest pains. He believes that the foxglove tisane is doing its job as recommended by a doctor in Bath," Darcy said. "His color is quite gray and if he is unable to get out of bed tomorrow, I will send an express to my father's physician in Town before we go to church."

Louisa nodded and smiled at Mr. Darcy's account, all the while her eyes appeared as if she had been crying. "Thank you, Mr. Darcy, for checking my husband's situation so thoroughly. Thank you, cousin Elizabeth, for waiting with me. I do believe it is time to prepare for dinner. Please excuse me." As she departed for her bedroom, Mr. Darcy and Elizabeth could hear her crying.

"Are you certain that the physician should not be called for now? Even Mr. Jones', the apothecary, could come this evening." Elizabeth asked Darcy. "It would be a great relief to Mrs. Hurst to have a doctor examine her husband."

"I quizzed Hurst's valet quite thoroughly and then spoke to Hurst. He visited a reputable physician in Bath last year who gave him a receipt for foxglove tisane when he has pains. I wish to respect his request to wait until tomorrow. If it is his heart, there is not much one can do other than rest and take the medicine. He is very young, not more than four years older than me." Mr. Darcy walked to the window and stared out at the last light of the late afternoon. "Miss Elizabeth, there is naught we can do right now other than prepare for dinner and make sure Mrs. Nichols has some foxglove extract on hand. I have asked Hurst's valet to alert me if he has another incident."

Elizabeth nodded and thanked him for his help in the matter. She then departed to check on Jane's preparations to go downstairs for dinner. She arrived in Jane's chamber to find her aflutter and unable to decide what to wear. Elizabeth sat her down and attended to her dress and hair to calm her down. Elizabeth smiled to herself thinking of Mr. Bingley's state this afternoon and Jane's, as they were both in such a state of anticipation to see the other.

———— ◦⟨∾⟩◦ ————

Sun. Nov. 17, 1811
 Late in the evening
 The Family Wing, Netherfield Park
Ever since Frederick Hurst felt the pain and pressure in his chest
and fell asleep at the door to his wife's chamber on Thursday night,
he had slept quite a bit. The pain in his chest had not returned with
the same intensity; he asked Mrs. Nichols to make him a tisane of
foxglove as his heart was beating faster than usual. The medicated tea
had been recommended by a physician in Bath as a preventative after
hearing of how his father and grandmother had died so quickly of a
heart attack before they had seen their respective fortieth birthdays.

While his wife did not seem to notice his inactivity or even his
absence - or at least his valet claimed that she had not come in -
Mr. Darcy had come to visit him yesterday and this morning. Before
church this morning, Mr. Darcy insisted on sending for his physician
from Town. The man arrived just before dinner and examined Hurst
at length. He agreed that Hurst was having heart symptoms and may
have had a mild heart incident on Thursday night. He wrote a script
for extract of foxglove to be kept on his person in a small vial and
taken at the first signs of further pain or pressure in his chest.

After the doctor departed to give his report to the rest of the party and take dinner with them, Hurst wrote letters to his grandfather,
his mother, a well-loved aunt on his mother's side, and a few friends
to inform them of his diagnosis and his wish to see them soon before
it was too late. He asked his mother and her particular friend Lady
Fitzhugh to spend Christmastide with him in London. To say he felt
melancholy was to say the least, as he was only one and thirty!

After a late supper was over, Louisa knocked on the door. Hurst
had finished his letters, had eaten a bit of soup, and was drinking his
nightcap. He chewed on the mint leaves ever so slowly.

"Come in, Louisa." His wife walked in, wearing her nightdress and a robe. Hurst's eyebrows rose upon viewing her attire. "This is a surprise."

"Frederick, I spoke to the physician at length after dinner. I wish to make amends for my recent behavior towards you."

Hurst rose from his writing desk and walked towards his wife. "Truly? We can try for our heir?"

"Ah, no." Louisa walked up to him and fiddled with the lapels of his dressing robe, all the while smoothing her hands over his chest. "The doctor did not recommend that type of exercise for the time being. But..." She smiled at him and lightly kissed his cheek. "I do think that we should share a bed while you are recuperating so that I might be available to administer the foxglove extract if you take a turn for the worse."

Louisa walked towards the bed and climbed in under the turned down bed clothes. Hurst smiled and walked around to blow out the candles before getting into bed.

Chapter 7 - The Truth, the Whole Truth, and Nothing but Most of the Truth

Sun. Nov. 17, 1811
   Early evening
   The Family Sitting Room
   Longbourn Manor

While neither Jane nor Mr. Bingley noticed a thing other than each other over the course of their last full evening at Netherfield, the whole of the evening had been rather baffling for Elizabeth - it was a long night of mostly watching Jane and Mr. Bingley court by the fire. Mrs. Hurst was weepy but did not wish to be consoled as Mr. Hurst remained upstairs, Mr. Darcy sat by himself to read, and Miss Bingley ignored them all with the exception of attempting to catch Mr. Darcy's attention. Elizabeth had the good sense to retrieve the book she had been reading earlier in the day from the library.

Elizabeth was pleased to have escaped Netherfield after church this morning and returned home to Longbourn. She was wearied by her stay at Netherfield. It was not just the nursing of her beloved sister back to health, nor was it the high tension of dealing with an angry and erratic Miss Bingley, nor helping Mrs. Hurst with her fears about her husband's health. No, it was the effort of trying to figure out Mr. Darcy that had been the final straw. She could not sketch the man's character.

For the first two days of her stay at Netherfield, while somewhat distant in manner, the man defended her and her family in the face of Miss Bingley's attacks. On Friday, Mr. Darcy was quite friendly to the point where Elizabeth was quite certain he was going to kiss her! Then yesterday he returned to his previous aloof and forbidding demeanor. This morning he sat next to her in church and touched her fingers as he shared the songbook and the common book of prayer. When Mr. Bingley's carriage arrived to take Elizabeth and her sister Jane home to Longbourn, Mr. Darcy lingered to help her into the carriage without a word and then watched them depart down the drive. If she was tolerable but not handsome enough to tempt him, then why did he try to kiss her and touch her hands. What ever was that man about?

Elizabeth was glad to come home, even if it meant listening to Lydia complain. Jane smiled as she worked on her embroidery and their father sat near fire as he read his newspaper. Their mother was in her rooms complaining to Hill about her flutterings, as faint murmurings drifted down the grand staircase to the open door of the sitting room. Elizabeth found she even missed Mary and Kitty, who were both away at school.

"Lawd! There is nothing to do here, not only on a Sunday night but everyday and night. It is so dull." Lydia stood up and flopped back down on to the settee. "Papa will not even tell me when I might walk into Meryton again! Papa, if this is how it is to be at Longbourn, I am ready to return to school. Even that dreadful Quaker school you found for me!"

Mr. Bennet, Miss Bennet, and Miss Elizabeth all merely smiled at Lydia.

"Soon enough, my dear, soon enough," Mr. Bennet peered at Lydia over his newspaper. "You would not wish to miss the ball you convinced Mr. Bingley to hold, would you?"

"Oh, Papa! May I truly attend Mr. Bingley's ball?" Lydia lurched towards her father and embraced him, newspaper and all. "How I dearly love to dance!" Mr. Bennet's spectacles fell to the floor in the ensuing melee of embraces from his youngest daughter.

—— ◦◦◦ ——

Late Evening
Sun Nov. 7, 1811
A dark corner table, The George Inn
Southwark, London

Mr. Horatio Theophilus Denny was more than somewhat bewildered why his father's patron's son wished to meet him here at this dark, old Thames-side public house when they could easily meet at any number of coffee houses near Whitehall or Mayfair. As the sixth son of a distracted, scholarly, albeit prolific, country parson who had his living from the Earl of Matlock, Denny was quite used to waiting on members of the Fitzwilliam family. At three and twenty, with five older brothers and two sisters younger than him, Denny was hungry for an opportunity to prove himself, not only to his father's patron, but also to the world at large. He wanted a great deal more than to live a small, quiet life in the country - he wanted to see the world.

Most of all, Denny wanted out of his lieutenant rank in the _____shire militia and to transfer into the Regulars as a Captain. As a Captain in a time of war, he would most definitely see more of the world and possibly gain a promotion through heroic action on the battlefield, rather than drinking another round of free small beer in a public house in Meryton, Hertfordshire with the motley, scruffy band of junior officers in the _____shire militia.

Denny was within one hundred and twenty pounds and some odd shillings away from purchasing his commission as a Captain in the Regulars. He had a promise from the Earl of Matlock to match whatever he was able to save. Saving for a Captain's commission while on a militia's lieutenant pay was hard and tested every ounce of discipline he possessed: no drinking other than Act of Parliament small beer, no dallying with the ladies, and definitely no gaming whatsoever. Denny could make it easy on himself and merely transfer from the Militia to the Regulars at the same rank for fourteen pounds, but he rarely made anything easy on himself - he wished to be Captain Denny of the Light Dragoons or the Hussars.

To fulfill that wish, he was sitting in this rather rough waterside pub drinking a strong ale and listening to his father's patron's second son, a Colonel in the Light Guards. At this very moment, Denny was more than astonished, he was angry. "Colonel Fitzwilliam, let me understand you correctly, you will pay me the rest of the funds I need - which is one hundred and twenty pounds - and write my letter of recommendation to the Horse Guards, if I can convince that execrable excuse for a human being - George Wickham - to return with me to Meryton, join the _____shire Militia and have signed his recruitment papers with Colonel Forester by 8pm this Tuesday? And to top it off, you do not wish for Wickham to know of your involvement at all."

The good Colonel nodded and smiled a fierce, tight little smile.

Denny leaned forward. "To be clear, you mean George Wickham, the dissolute rake, who was given opportunities to advance himself at Cambridge and the Courts of the Inner Temple where he allegedly studied to be a barrister - opportunity to raise himself from the lot of a son of a steward to that of a gentleman - and he pissed it all away? That George Wickham?"

Lowering his voice so as to not be overheard, Denny ground out, "The very man who ruined my youngest sister when she was not yet sixteen years old? I would rather tie him down, slather his whore pipe in suet and meat drippings, and release a pack of starving wild dogs on him than turn him loose on the good people of Meryton and their daughters." Denny stood up and in a normal tone of voice said, "Please excuse me, Colonel, but I must take myself back to my lodgings. I pray you have a safe journey back to yours."

Colonel Fitzwilliam jumped up and used both his arms to stop him. "Denny, sit back down and listen to my plan in full. Mr. Wickham is to be managed, never you worry, and if all goes as planned this Tuesday - you will be far from Meryton in your new regiment..."

Denny sighed and reluctantly sat back down to listen to the Colonel. As the plan unfolded, Denny's astonishment and disbelief increased. In the end, he only agreed when the Colonel guaranteed him one hundred and fifty pounds as well that Wickham would be watched and kept from the young ladies of Meryton. After they shook on the deal, the Colonel ordered another round of ale and told stories of heroic derring-do in the battlegrounds of the Peninsula.

4:20pm, Mon. Nov. 18, 1811
   The Formal Drawing Room
   Longbourn Manor

After arriving promptly at 4:00 in the afternoon and being guided into the drawing room for tea, Mr. Bennet's second once removed (or was it third?) cousin, Mr. William Collins had not ceased talking for the whole of the last twenty minutes. In a state of mild horror, Jane wondered if he would stop long enough to take a breath or if he would expire from a lack of air before the tea and cake service. Jane furtively wrote a short note to Charlotte Lucas while their cousin prattled on about olive branches, the beauty of the Bennet daughters, his surprise at the size and fineness of Longbourn, his patroness the Lady Catherine de Bourgh, her desire to see him married before the new year, the chimney pieces and the superior glazing of window panes at Rosings Park, of all things. Every time he fulsomely praised his patroness by name, Jane watched her mother twitch and clamp her lips together rather forcefully.

Not even from the most dull lecturer at university had Jane heard so many words that contained so little sense when strung together all in a row. It was rather extraordinary. She supposed it was best he was a parson, as a little sleeping in church on a Sunday morning could be quite restorative for the whole of his congregation.

Just this morning, after reading Mr. Collins' letter to the assembled family at the breakfast table, her father stated that his distant cousin's writing style appeared to be a mix of servility and self-importance that promised well for a diverting visit from said cousin, of whom they had never before met and who stood to inherit Longbourn after Mr. Bennet's death. After less than a quarter of an hour with Mr. Collins, Jane was convinced that his visit did not bode well at all - other than possibly for Charlotte Lucas' matrimony plans. Jane folded her note, rose and slipped the note to the attending footman outside of the drawing room with a request to have it delivered to Lucas Lodge immediately. She returned to the drawing room as the tea service arrived.

Mr. Collins, a tall, grave, stately, and heavyset young man of five and twenty jumped up, clapped his hands together, and squealed rather like a pig in anticipation of particularly good slop in its trough. He rushed over to the tea and cake before the maid could set it down. Jane dared not laugh, as Lydia did, but gazed at her father and Elizabeth in startled astonishment. The only person who appeared well pleased was Mrs. Bennet, who encouraged Mr. Collins to have as much cake as he wished.

Mr. Collins perched on one of Grandmother Bennet's fine, silk damask Chippendale chairs as he ploughed through a large slice of cake, crumbs falling out of his mouth on to the carpet in his haste to eat. Lydia ceased laughing and was as astounded as Jane and Elizabeth. Mr. Collins finished the last bite of his cake before anyone else had yet been served - there was a dreadful silence in the absence of Lydia's laughter and his torrent of words. Jane was hopeful now that he had been fed perhaps some sensible conversation would be proffered. As with much of her life, Jane's hope in the goodness and better nature of her fellow creatures was to be dashed.

Mr. Collins looked up, brushed the remaining crumbs off his waistcoat, and looked at Lydia. His mouth opened wide, no sound emitted, as he stared at Lydia.

"Do I have cake crumb on my face, Mr. Collins?" Lydia challenged Mr. Collins' steady gaze.

"I am all astonishment! Miss Lydia, your countenance... it is... everything about your countenance: the shape of your face, your nose, the bow of your lips, your eyebrows - especially just now as you looked at me in derision, and your chin!" Mr. Collins sputtered and spit as he searched for words. "Miss de Bourgh is far superior to the handsomest of her sex; she is the bright jewel of the English..."

"Of the English court, where she refuses to be presented at?" Mr. Bennet supplied. "Or of Cambridge University, where she is a fellow?"

"How can it be?" Mr. Collins ignored Mr. Bennet's commentary and continued to marvel as he gaped at Lydia. "Cousin Bennet, how can it be that your youngest daughter, Miss Lydia, is the very same in looks of the shape of her countenance to Miss de Bourgh? While they are not the same in their height, form, nor coloring, their countenances are as if they are sisters. It cannot be possible..."

"Mr. Collins, you may not be aware of the connection but the departed Sir Lewis de Bourgh is a cousin of mine on my mother's side of the family - thus the slight family resemblance." Mr. Bennet asserted. "Now that you are finished with your cake, perhaps you would like to be shown to your guest chamber so that you can get rid of the travel dust and dress for dinner."

Mr. Bennet, making a great show of ignoring his cousin's reply, stood, bowed, and departed to ready himself. An uncomfortable Lydia and Elizabeth hastily followed their father out of the drawing room, leaving Jane on one side of the large formal drawing room with her mother and Mr. Collins on the other. Jane sipped her tea as she listened to her mother and cousin discuss the entail and his proposed matrimonial olive branch.

Mrs. Bennet smiled at Mr. Collins who described the felicity of his situation and the glories of the parsonage at Hunsford as he ate another large slice of cake; she stopped smiling when Mr. Collins described the raptures of serving his patroness the Lady Catherine de Bourgh. Mrs. Bennet switched the subject back to her daughters, describing each in glowing terms. Jane smiled at her mother's love of their family until she noticed Mr. Collins sizing her up and grinning at her as crumbs fell off his face.

"Miss Bennet, to which of my cousins may I attribute the excellency of this cake?"

"Mr. Collins," Jane could feel the heat of his gaze on her bosom and she liked it not. "Longbourn can well afford to support an excellent cook and, as such, it is unnecessary for either I or my sisters to have been taught to cook. Do you have a cook at the parsonage?"

Mr. Collins coughed a bit and did not cover his mouth, thus a few more cake crumbs were expelled. "Well, I, that is to say - my housekeeper and the maid of all work does help in the kitchen but the parsonage's mistress will need to know how to bake."

Mrs. Bennet apprehended the line of his sight and corrected him immediately, she told him quite firmly that Miss Bennet was nearly betrothed to a fine young gentleman, that Miss Mary and Miss Kitty - who were not present - were still at school, and Miss Lydia would be returning to school at the end of the month, which left only Miss Elizabeth available to be married at this time. To Jane's relief and then distress for her sister, he reluctantly took his eyes off of her and exclaimed he would be quite happy indeed to extend his olive branch to Miss Elizabeth as she was next in precedence and beauty to Miss Bennet. He simpered and bowed to both ladies before leaving to refresh himself.

A QUIVER FULL, OR HOW MR. DARCY WILL NOT SIT ON THAT SOFA AGAIN!

99

Before Mrs. Bennet could erupt into raptures of delight about a daughter nearly betrothed to Longbourn's heir, the footman entered to hand Jane a note. Upon reading the note she informed her mother that Charlotte Lucas would be joining them for dinner and to please excuse her to prepare herself. Before her mother could erupt into descants of disgust about those artful Lucases, Jane left the drawing room to inform Mrs. Hill that Charlotte would be joining them for dinner.

Now if she and Elizabeth could sit as far away from Mr. Collins as possible and arrange for Charlotte to sit next to him, dinner would be delightful - particularly after she and Elizabeth praised Charlotte's baking abilities to Mr. Collins.

2:10pm
Tues. Nov. 19, 1811
Mr. Bennet's Bookroom
Longbourn Manor

To Mr. Bennet's intense delight, he was in receipt of a note from Mr. Denny, signed by Colonel Forester and stamped with the Colonel's seal, stating that a George Hinton Wickham had signed his official recruitment papers and had purchased a commission as a lieutenant in the ____shire Militia on this very day, the year of our Lord Eighteen Hundred and Eleven. Bennet had also received an express from his cousin, Colonel Fitzwilliam, before breakfast this morning stating that Mr. Denny would be delivering Mr. Wickham to Colonel Forester this morning. Now it was so.

Mr. Bennet leaned back in his seat and laughed heartily. He stopped himself just as he started as he did not want to count his chickens before they hatched. If Wickham would not do the job, then maybe Denny would. Meryton gossip had it that Denny was saving up to purchase a commission in the Hussars. Not only was he in need of hundreds of - if not a couple of thousand - pounds, but as the son of the most prolific parson in Derbyshire, Mr. Samuel Waltheof Denny of Matlock Rectory, young Denny should be good for a few sons.

This scheme must succeed and my wife must fall pregnant with a son, as my cousin is a right fool and would ruin everything that I have built back up these past twenty some years. I will not lose Longbourn to that pompous, servile... An explosion of noise in the foyer that signaled the return of his daughters, most particularly Lydia, from their walk to Meryton which stopped Mr. Bennet's dark thoughts from ruining his buoyant mood. He decided to join them to see what the news from Meryton was.

"How was your walk to Meryton?" Mr. Bennet asked as his daughters took off their pelisses and hats in the great foyer. A sweating, red faced Mr. Collins was just then huffing and puffing into the house. Bennet wondered how his cousin young Collins could be sweating from a walk in the chill of a November afternoon when the temperature could not be more than ten degrees above freezing outside.

"Papa! Meryton was divine! Thank you for letting me walk out with my sisters, I indeed needed the company of friends and new friends!" Lydia was aglow with rosy cheeks and her eyes were shining. "Papa! We met the most handsome and gentleman-like new militia officer, Mr. Wickham!"

Mrs. Bennet walked down the stairs and encouraged her daughters and Mr. Collins to join her in the family sitting room for some tea, Mr. Bennet followed. Mrs. Bennet asked for a full accounting of their walk.

"Mama, Jane and Elizabeth let me stop in at the Lucas's to ask Charlotte and Maria to join us on our walk. It was lovely, but cold and Charlotte kept Mr. Collins company - even though he is tall, he is a very slow walker." Lydia made a face at her cousin. "Mr. Collins, perhaps less cake and more walks and you would not have such a time keeping up."

"Lydia, mind your manners." Jane agreed with her sister, but it was quite rude to say that in the man's company.

"As I was saying," Lydia turned to Jane and pulled a sour face. "Maria and I walked ahead and met up with Mr. Denny in town and he, la di da, introduced us to his childhood friend, a Mr. George Wickham - who is ever so handsome." At this statement Lydia flung herself on the sofa and giggled happily. "I invited them to our Aunt Philips' card party tomorrow evening, I do hope that I can dance with Mr. Wickham at the ball next week." Sighs, giggles, and happy little murmurs of sound erupted out of Lydia.

Mr. Bennet raised his eyebrow at his youngest daughter and hoped he was a good enough actor to appear as if he were censuring her with a stern demeanor, but he himself would love to fling himself onto the sofa and erupt into giggles and happy little murmurs of sighs. "Thank you, Lydia, for your account. Are you quite sure that Mr. Wickham has signed up for the Militia or is he just visiting to see if he wishes to join?"

Lydia continued to giggle and talk of dancing at the ball, but Elizabeth fell right in and answered his real question. "Papa, Mr. Denny assured us that Mr. Wickham had signed his papers with Colonel Forester and bought his commission this morning. Mr. Denny was giving him a tour of Meryton. Mr. Denny looked none too happy about it."

Mr. Bennet was delighted at Mr. Denny's assurances but sensed that Elizabeth's clever mind was tickled with more than curiosity - rather that she was disturbed by the events in Meryton - which meant she would dig until she received the truth. Before he could think on it more, tea was served and Mr. Collins startled him with a rather accurate observation.

"Cousin Bennet, this Mr. Wickham was, how shall I say it - quite peculiar, no, it is rather extraordinary in the fullest sense of the word. Mr. Wickham has the same eye shape and color as Miss Lydia!" Mr. Collins took his tea from Jane and looked about for cake, instead there were only very small oat scones with no cream and no jam. "In fact, the more I think on it, Mr. Wickham's hair and complexion color match the young Sir Lewis de Bourgh - who..." Mr. Bennet coughed quite loudly to distract his cousin, which did not work as the man was like a dog with a bone. "in his countenance looks like a younger version of you! How can it be that Mr. Wickham has Miss Lydia's eye color, a green so rare I have only seen it twice in the whole of my life. And that Mr. Wickham looks similar to..."

Elizabeth saved the whole of the party by adding three more scones to Mr. Collins' plate and encouraged him to eat them even as she shot inquiring glances at her father. "Papa, what neither Mr. Collins nor Lydia have mentioned is that after meeting Mr. Wickham, we visited with Aunt Philips who has extended an invitation to all of our party to attend a card and supper evening tomorrow at seven o'clock."

"Thank you, Elizabeth, I look forward to attending Mrs. Philips' evening." All of Mr. Bennet's daughters and his wife looked at him in some state of shock, as he rarely attended any event of Mrs. Philips as he could not abide her mean understanding and gossipy ways. "Did she invite the militia officers?"

Jane answered, "Yes, Papa, she did. Mr. Denny accepted for them. Mr. Wickham was quite complimentary on the hospitality of Meryton."

Mr. Collins had eagerly dispatched his scones and wanted his share of the conversation. "Much to my amazement, the nephew of my patroness, Lady Catherine de Bourgh,..."

"Yes, Mr. Collins," said a now impatient Mr. Bennet. "Mr. Darcy of Pemberley, Derbyshire, the nephew of Lady Catherine de Bourgh is staying at Netherfield and if I may guess correctly you met the man in Meryton."

Lydia flopped back up into an upright sitting position, "La! Mr. Collins was not introduced to Mr. Darcy at all, he just saw him briefly. Mr. Darcy and Mr. Bingley were riding through town and, of course Mr. Bingley had to stop to greet his beloved Jane!" A further giggle eruption occurred before Lydia could finish her story. "Mr. Darcy upon seeing Mr. Wickham turned quite red in the face and Mr. Wickham upon spying Mr. Darcy turned very white. Whatever could be between them? Well, never you mind, I will find out tomorrow evening."

"Lydia, it is not lady-like nor proper to interrogate anyone, let alone a stranger in our midst, as if you were a barrister," Elizabeth said. "In fact, it is not proper at all for mere acquaintances to ask or even to offer such private information on so short an acquaintance."

"Well, Miss Prim and Proper, perhaps when I am practicing to be the first lady barrister and I will be able to ask as many nosy questions as I want!"

"Lydia, please do not argue with your sister. Since you had the privilege of walking out to Meryton, after you finish your tea, I expect you in my bookroom to review your lessons in a quarter of an hour." At Lydia's groan, Mr. Bennet made his departure, as he had the verified information he needed about Mr. Wickham's arrival and it was not necessary to remain in the company of his cousin, nor his wife, for a fraction of a minute longer.

Before returning to his bookroom, Bennet went in search of Mrs. Hill as he had a private task for her to complete before tomorrow evening. He found her below stairs in her very neat and organized office. After entering he closed the door behind him.

"Mrs. Hill, with absolute discretion and silence, I must ask you to air out the Old Rectory tomorrow. Please have the linens changed, the rugs and counterpanes beaten, the place dusted, wood in the fireplaces, and new candles put in the sconces." Mrs. Hill nodded in agreement without asking why.

"Thank you, Mrs. Hill." Mr. Bennet returned to his bookroom.

10:36pm
  Tues. Nov. 19, 1811
  Mr. Bennet's Bookroom
  Longbourn Manor

Elizabeth's evening was dreary after Charlotte departed for Lucas Lodge. By a stroke of luck, Jane had been able to convince Mr. Collins to walk Miss Lucas home after dinner. Their mother proceeded to angrily denounce Jane and Elizabeth for conspiring to throw her and any unmarried daughters into the hedgerows after their father's death. How could they let Mr. Collins walk out with Charlotte? Why that was nearly courting her to walk her home in the dark without a chaperone! Why would not Elizabeth obey her mother's wishes for once in the whole of her life?

It did not help to tell their mother that they had good dowries, would be able to marry well, and thus take care of their mother after their father's death - that it was not necessary for any of her daughters to marry Mr. Collins. There were the usual spasms, flutterings, and pronouncements of ungrateful, scheming daughters. After an hour of ringing a peal over Elizabeth and even her beloved Jane's heads, Mrs. Bennet succumbed to her flutterings and spasms and called for Hill to bring her sleeping tonic to her chamber.

After supper, Jane and Lydia retired and it was nearly ten o'clock when quite satisfied Mr. Collins returned from Lucas Lodge. He, unexpectedly, did not have much to say and he retired for the evening without comment. As Elizabeth sat by herself in the sitting room with only the fire to keep her company, she had time to reflect on the events of the day in Meryton. Mr. Collins' insistence that somehow

Lydia, the de Bourghs, and Mr. Wickham all looked alike in one way or another kept coming to the fore of her thoughts.

It was very improper, to be sure, for Mr. Collins to remark that Lydia looked like his patroness' daughter or that Mr. Wickham looked like Lydia and the young Sir Lewis de Bourgh. Fool Mr. Collins may be but Elizabeth was quite convinced that there was something to it. Mr Wickham's resemblance to her late uncle was uncanny; she would inspect Uncle Andrew's portrait, but it was in her father's study. There was also the moment when Mr. Denny claimed that Mr. Wickham was his childhood friend but the unhappy look in his eyes and the tone of his voice belied that proclamation.

None of this added up. Furthermore, why did her father leave his study this afternoon to inquire into the minutia of their visit to Meryton? He hardly ever wished to hear of gossip, bonnets, lace, and who met who. There was a man who could answer these questions and she would go find him in his study.

The direct approach would be best. Elizabeth did not knock on the door, she walked in and said, "Papa, I require answers. Our cousin Collins may be a fool, but perhaps he is a divine fool who is uncovering truths." She walked over to the portrait of her father's family when they were young just before Aunt Elizabeth married and Papa went to Oxford. Pointing at Uncle Andrew she stated, "This is Mr. Wickham, without Uncle Andrew's powdered wig. Do tell."

Mr. Bennet got up, walked over to his drinks cart, and poured a finger of brandy for himself and two fingers of port for Elizabeth. He handed Elizabeth her drink and told her to drink half of it and then he would explain. When she sat and drank her port, he asked, "Lizzy, are you going to be missish about this?"

"Papa! I am a miss."

"Shelve those misplaced sensibilities for a half hour while we rationally discuss this matter."

"Papa, what is the matter at hand? Is Mr. Wickham a natural son of your brother? If so, we must do something, as Lydia threw herself at the man today. Truly, tell me what is going on."

Mr. Bennet poured another round of drinks for both of them, sat back down in his chair, and he began telling his favorite and cleverest daughter a section of the truth - most of the truth.

"Lizzy, the 1780s were a very different time, not quite so many strictures as now and quite a bit more fun to be had. I was eight and twenty and had been in my living at Pemberley for three and a half years. The good Lady Anne Darcy was increasing with your Mr. Darcy and Pemberley's steward, Mr. Ernest Wickham, had recently married the young and handsome Miss Lavinia Hinton of Mayfield Rectory, Staffordshire. Pemberley was a happy place with the best library north of Oxford and a very comfortable gilded sofa..."

The small mantle clock her Grandmother Bennet had given her for her eighth birthday chimed two o'clock in the morning and Elizabeth was still sitting up in her bed in the dark deeply astonished. Her knowledge of reproductive problems of the male sex had substantially increased this evening. Even more astounding, she had three half-brothers and one half-sister - the two de Bourgh siblings she thought were distant cousins and the other two half brothers she knew nothing of until today.

Her and her sisters' substantial dowries had their foundations in her father's stud fees. The renewed Bennet wealth and consequence had its roots in her father's ability to invest and... There was no nice euphemistic way to indirectly talk about what her father did in the 1780s and again this past year. He was paid to father sons for men who could not with women he was not married to.

Mr. George Wickham - her half-brother. Miss Anne de Bourgh and Sir Lewis de Bourgh - not cousins but her half-siblings and cousins. Thurston Hurst III - half-brother. At this last thought, she wondered if her new found cousin Louisa Hurst and her husband were aware that the new Hurst baby was not actually a Hurst? Poor Mr. Hurst.

After her father told her about the four children he sired and that the original fees had accrued nearly one hundred thousand pounds in interest from his investments over the course of nearly thirty years, her father denounced Mr. Collins as the veriest fool and under no circumstances was he going to inherit Longbourn. Her father would not answer the questions of how he would solve the Mr. Collins problem nor why Mr. Wickham arrived in Meryton today, other than to say that she must trust him that it would all work out for the best. He was adamant that she could not tell anyone these secrets.

As she blew out her bedside candle and crawled under the bed covers, she took some consolation that her father promised her that Lydia would not disgrace herself with her half-brother and that Mr. Collins would not be allowed to offer for any of the Bennet girls. He did assure her that once her mother got over the disappointment of Mr. Collins not marrying any of her daughters, that her mother would be taken care of quite nicely. In fact, he said, she would be very pleased with his plans and would have no cause to repine.

As she fell asleep, she wondered if her father meant that her mother would have no cause to repine?

Chapter 8 : How Cards and Supper Turns into a Most Delicious Proposition

Evening
  Wed. Nov. 20, 1811
  The Philips' Drawing Room
  Meryton, Hertfordshire

Mr. Thomas Claudius Bennet was prepared to take care of business this evening at his sister-in-law's card and supper party. As was his wont, after he retrieved a glass of port from Mr. Philips, he secreted himself to a corner of the room where he would not be readily noticed but where he could readily observe all of the party.

Currently to his right was his daughter Lydia, Maria Lucas and his wife flirting outrageously with the militia officers near the card tables. In front of him, Jane and Elizabeth were talking quietly with Charlotte Lucas on the sofas, and to the left near the door to the foyer was his fool of a cousin bending Mrs. Philips' ear about the glories of Rosings Park. He would need more port to make this evening palatable, but first he must hunt down his quarry before numbing himself to the inanity of it all.

To Bennet's great fortune, his quarry was at this time staring at Mrs. Bennet's copious bosom arrayed in a low-cut gown with lace that provocatively led the eyes downward. Mrs. Bennet was tittering at and beckoning the man with her eyelashes. Lydia was not to be outdone by her mother, but she had much less experience at wooing men than her mother - much to his relief. Over his alive body would he allow his youngest daughter to gain more experience in this art, particularly with her own half-brother.

Before Bennet had to intervene, Mr. Wickham bowed to the ladies and sauntered over to the sofas where his other daughters sat. Mr. Wickham sat daringly close to Elizabeth and his smile oozed with slippery charm; his tongue flicking at his lips. Charlotte moved over to speak with Mr. Collins. Jane looked rather alarmed.

Bennet could imagine the love that Wickham was making to his favorite daughter and he would have none of this. He walked immediately to the back of the sofa and stood facing the group in the foyer. He was well within hearing distance of even the slightest whisper. As he pretended to be in conversation with his ninny of a cousin - who was now expounding on the details of the shelving in the closets at the parsonage to Miss Lucas - he listened closely to what Wickham was telling Elizabeth.

As he heard Mr. Wickham confide to Elizabeth that Mr. Darcy denied him the living at Kympton and did not pay out the amount stated in the late Mr. Darcy's will, Bennet rounded quickly and leaned over the back of the sofa.

In a low, stern voice, Bennet leaned into between their heads. "George Hinton Wickham, cease lying now!" He was less than six inches from Wickham's face and the gentleman fell back onto the cushions in surprise. "We both know that the current Mr. Darcy not only paid out the one thousand pounds per his father's will; he paid out three thousand pounds to further your education - which you frittered away in less than three years. Elizabeth, please leave this snake to me."

At this Elizabeth gasped and stood up. Her father rounded the couch and sat in her seat, waving both Elizabeth and Jane off. "Let me take care of this man. I have seen the proof of the canceled bank cheques that he was paid more than his fair share. Jane and Elizabeth, could you please request that your uncle provide a stronger libation than port for Mr. Wickham and myself?"

After his daughters walked over to Mr. Philips, Bennet continued to lean into Mr. Wickham. "Lady Catherine de Bourgh has had you followed these last four years, did you not know? Her investigators have kept track of you, your actions, your gambling, your petty deceits, your lies, your seductions, and your debts." Wickham's countenance was all astonishment and not a sound came forth from his previously honeyed lips.

Wickham found his voice as his face and neck had turned a bright red. "Just who are you to level these accusations at me?"

"I am Thomas Bennet, master of Longbourn. You may remember me from your earliest childhood when I had the living at the Kympton parish and the Pemberley chapel."

Wickham's face contorted ever so slightly in memory, he looked around quickly to see who could overhear them - if the ladies were still close by - and he turned a deeper red. "I will have you know that..."

Bennet looked up and saw Mr. Philips beckon him towards the door of his study. "Cease your protestations, Mr. Wickham. Come with me, I have some fine brandy and a proposal that might very well be worth your while."

In his private study, Mr. Philips poured both men a tumbler full of brandy. He informed them that the card games would be starting soon, with supper to follow, but they were both very welcome to remain there to drink their brandy in private. Mr. Philips then bowed and closed the door after himself.

Bennet could see that Wickham was in a pique, he was not sipping his brandy but gulping it and would not sit in one of the nearby chairs. Bennet placed himself on Philips' desk chair between the door and Wickham. "Mr. Wickham, thank you for indulging me."

Wickham did not respond, but only looked bewildered and worried. After taking a drink of his brandy, Wickham looked at Bennet sideways. "Is this about your wife flirting with me? If so, I have no designs on her, she is a bit old for my tastes. You need not be concerned."

Bennet merely raised his eyebrow. "Mr. Wickham, you are quite welcome to my wife. That is what I wish to speak to you of." Bennet pulled open one of the unlocked drawers in Philips' desk and pulled out a beautifully carved ebony box, from it he pulled out a miniature painting. "Do you recognize this man?"

Wickham gasped and sat down on the nearest chair. "That is me!"

"No, that was my older brother Andrew Bennet, deceased as of November 1787. As you can see, you are the very image of the man. The same bright green eyes. Did you not notice yesterday in Meryton that my daughter, Lydia, has the very same eyes - a rare eye color at that?"

Tersely, Wickham ground out, "I did."

"My cousin certainly noticed yesterday. Look more closely at this portrait of Andrew Bennet. Other than the powdered wig, this is you. You also have the same figure and stature. Have you not ever wondered who your father really was? The esteemed Ernest Wickham was not the man to do the job, I assure you."

Wickham swigged the rest of his brandy. He coughed and sputtered in the effort. "I know of that as well. I knew not who did the deed, other than the late Mr. Darcy arranged for a gentleman to father a son for my..." He could not finish, but looked into his now empty glass.

Bennet reached for the brandy decanter and poured another round. "Mr. Wickham, this is nothing to be ashamed of. The 1780s were a very different time and the late Mr. Darcy wanted to help his faithful steward, Mr. Ernest Wickham, start a family so he too could know of the felicity and contentment to be found therein."

Wickham sat up straighter and looked Bennet in the eye. "Do not think that I have not made an attempt to discover this information. I made discreet inquiries as soon as I was old enough to know what a sodomite was. This Andrew Bennet, did he not lose nearly a hundred thousand pounds at the tables?"

Bennet did not answer, he preferred - for now - to let the young man think that Bennet's deceased brother was his father.

"My mother, Lady Hurst, told me some of these secrets this past July as she was lecturing me after I ran into some trouble in Ramsgate." Bennet's eyebrow rose in censure. "I am sure you know of that misadventure as well. After my mother informed me that her new husband wanted nothing more to do with me and I was not allowed to contact them unless I completely repented and turned my life around; she attempted to explain something of my origins - though she would not give me the family's name."

Bennet waited.

Wickham looked at him. "I suppose I am damned if I do and damned if I don't. Either I am the foster son of a sodomite steward or the natural son of a wastrel gambler. There is no hope for me."

Bennet waited. Sounds of gaiety and hands of cards could be heard just outside the door.

"Furthermore, I am not sure why a man who hates the very ground I stand on for sullying his wild sister would encourage me to join the ____shire militia and would pay for my commission and uniform. I thought Denny came to challenge me to a duel a few years too late." Wickham cracked. "What do you want with me?"

Bennet stood and encouraged Wickham to do so. "Would you like to enter into an agreement that would allow you to turn your life around and make some real money while doing so? If so, come with me." Bennet opened the door to the study and walked back to his previous observation spot. A curious but subdued Wickham followed him with a refilled glass of brandy.

To the right at the card tables, Lydia was noisily claiming fish from the militia officers as she won at lottery tickets. Mrs. Bennet was drinking wine and giggling with Mrs. Forster. Most bizarrely at the whist table, Mr. Collins was clucking as he concentrated on his game with the Philipses and Lucases. Bennet did not have to look at his cards to guess that Collins was losing.

"Mr. Wickham, see the parson over there who sounds like the poultry in the barnyard as he plays whist? That is my distant cousin, Mr. William Collins, he is a dullard and the veriest simpleton. To add insult to injury, he does not read."

"Do you mean that he does not like to read or that he is not well read?"

Bennet gave him a stern, annoyed look.

Wickham grinned. "Many men, even educated ones, do not read."

"I have a beautiful library; it is not as comprehensive as Pemberley's, but it is a work of several generations. That idiot is slated to inherit it. I cannot allow this to happen."

"What am I to do of it?"

"Due to my brother's gambling losses, my grandfather had to sell off several thousand acres of Longbourn's land and he put the core of the estate that has been in the family since the 1200s into an entail. In the absence of a son from my wife, that -" Bennet waved at Mr. Collins, who was now making odd lowing sounds as he placed his cards down. " - that is my grandfather's sister's grandson who is to inherit if I do not father a son to break the entail. Obviously, my great aunt's husband and his son muddied the waters, if you will, to the point where there is no clarity of mind or intellect to be had at all."

Wickham tried to hide his amusement but could not. Bennet was not to be moved off his point. "Now look over there, that is Mrs. Jane Frances Gardiner Bennet, mother of five girls, not yet forty years old, and the handsomest woman in Hertfordshire."

Wickham dipped his head in agreement and a wicked grin spread over his countenance. "That she is. That she is."

Bennet drew near to Wickham and dropped his voice. "She compromised me not long after I left Pemberley to return to Longbourn. I was forced to marry her and after five daughters, much has soured. But you are a young man and you can do the job nicely."

"Pardon?"

"Look at her, Mr. Wickham, she is beautiful - I saw you staring at her bosom. Do not be embarrassed, most men do stare. Though after some three and twenty years of marriage, I cannot do the deed to father a son. That is where you come in."

Wickham laughed outright.

"Hush! Here have more brandy." At this Bennet fished a silver flask out of his waistcoat - this was the good brandy he was saving for himself. He poured a smirking Wickham another round. "Listen to me and keep silent about the following proposal."

Bennet looked about and determined it was safe to speak quietly. "I need a man related to me who is not a complete idiot to father a son with my wife. She unmans me, I will not do it. She is beautiful and has already incited lust in you, it will not be a chore for you to do the deed." Before Wickham could protest, Bennet said, "I saw the leer on your face as you looked down her dress, you can have no grievance with her face and figure. More to the point, I will pay you 200 pounds to secretly tup Mrs. Bennet until she is increasing. I will then pay you 1,000 pounds at the birth of any live male child and - wait, do not speak yet, listen - and I will pay you 4,000 pounds when the said live male child reaches the age of his majority and we break the entail in the Courts of Chancery."

Wickham was astounded and could not speak. Bennet sized him up and said, "If you are able to quietly, silently, and with no gossip spreading anywhere around the country to sire a son with Mrs. Bennet, I will again pay you the same amount to sire a second son before her childbearing years are over. This is to remain absolutely secret..."

"We will sign a legal, binding contract for me to be employed in such a manner and for you to guarantee said payments, will we not?" An amazed Wickham asked. For a man whose last shilling was lost in a game of chance minutes before Denny appeared only two days ago, this scheme was heaven sent.

"Yes, we will. Stay here and let me retrieve my brother Philips, he is the solicitor here in Meryton." Bennet walked over to the whist table and asked Mr. Philips to join him and Wickham.

Philips brought his empty glass with him and upon arrival handed it wordlessly to Bennet, who in turn poured Philips a glass of the vintage French brandy from his flask. "Philips, do you have time to meet with Mr. Wickham and I about the contract we previously spoke of tomorrow in the morning?"

Philips slyly replied, "I do. Are both of you available to meet at my office at eleven o'clock in the morning?" Both men agreed and Philips returned to his card table.

Bennet leaned in and whispered once again, "Not a word of this to anyone, not only will you lose the opportunity to earn 5,200 pounds over time, but Lady Catherine de Bourgh will call in your debts."

Wickham's eyes widened and his nostrils flared. Bennet stared at the man and in a low, deadly tone said, "Additionally, flirt all you want with my wife, but stay far away from my daughters. Do not lie or tell any fables about the Darcys' during your stay in Meryton. And finally, do not make any charge with a tradesman that you cannot pay. Do you agree?"

Wickham eyed the man and nodded. At the card tables, Lydia was crowing with delight at her lottery wins. Mr. Collins was slumped in defeat, as Charlotte Lucas grinned. Mrs. Philips was organizing the maids to lay out the supper buffet. Mr. Wickham eyed the prospect and turned to Mr. Bennet offering his hand. Bennet took it and they shook on the deal.

2:23pm
Thurs. Nov. 21, 1811
Longbourn Manor
Meryton, Hertfordshire

Mr. Bennet sat in his big chair in his study, perfectly satisfied at the morning's meeting in Meryton. He and Philips sewed the contract with Mr. Wickham up right and tight. Mr. Wickham would be handsomely paid to sire a live son or two for Mr. Bennet with his wife, Mrs. Bennet, as long as Wickham stuck to the detailed requirements of the contract. Philips had written it in such a way that Wickham could not breath of word of the deal or what he was up to, other than having a bit a fun with the young-ish wife of an older man, nor could Wickham blackmail Bennet at any later date for more money without risking life in debtor prison or being transported to the penal colonies.

Philips had also written into the contract that Wickham would only be paid the initial 200 pounds after Mrs. Bennet had quickened. This led to an amusing aside where the both of the older gentlemen educated the younger on the stages of if and when a woman was increasing. Bennet chuckled at how such a profligate seducer of young women could be so ignorant of the possible results of his behavior, in fact, Wickham had nearly turned green at some of Bennet's detailed descriptions.

A codicil had been added to the contract, wherein Mr. Wickham would forfeit his monies if he flirted or wenched with any woman - young or middling or old of any rank - in Meryton other than Mrs. Bennet, if he told any tales or lies about the Darcy's, and if he garnered any debts - be it of honor or with the tradesmen in town. And under no circumstances was Wickham to flirt with or seduce any of the Bennet daughters.

Bennet and Philips were both quite surprised how eager Wickham was to sign the contract and begin his new employment. Bennet now needed to inform his wife of his scheme and set them to it. He rang for a footman and asked the man to have Mrs. Bennet attend him in the study within the quarter hour. Then he sought out Mrs. Hill to make sure the tea and Mrs. Bennet's favorite dainties would be delivered to the study before the quarter of the hour was out.

When Mrs. Bennet arrived in his study, she was in a fit of pique, wanting to know what he needed that he could not come to her or have a servant deliver in a note. Bennet encouraged her to sit as he prepared her a cup of her favorite tea - three lumps of sugar and plenty of sweet wine mixed in.

He let her exclaim on the wonders of the previous evening's entertainments and her plans for Mr. Collins to marry Elizabeth.

"Let us be clear on one thing, Mrs. Bennet, Mr. Collins may not marry any of my daughters. The man is an obsequious fool. Miss Lucas is welcome to him." Mr. Bennet made another cup of tea and sweet wine for his wife as she ate her favorite pastry, specifically baked by Cook at his request. She protested those artful Lucases and made quite a bit of noise about hedgerows.

"Let me be clear about a second thing, Mrs. Bennet, that beetle-headed Mr. Collins will not inherit this estate." Mr. Bennet crossed his arms as he leaned against his desk. He did his best to deliver a stern glare at his wife. She drank the rest of her wine with some tea in it and questioned how he planned to achieve this goal of siring an heir when he was unwilling to attend her in her rooms and, more to the point, he was unable to proceed in the act to make an heir for the estate. She then rumbled into insults on his enfeebled manhood.

"Mrs. Bennet, would you like to break the entail to assure your rightful place as my wife on this estate until your passing, as well as have some fun with a very handsome young militia officer while you conceive said heir?" Mrs. Bennet bounced in her seat and rather than ask about how that would be legal, as Elizabeth did, Mrs. Bennet instead wiggled happily and whispered about handsome soldiers to herself.

"Did you find Mr. Wickham to be a handsome man? Handsome enough to spend weeks or possibly months attempting to conceive an heir? And to try again, if the first time fails? If this is the case..." She would not let him finish his sentence as she waxed poetic on how handsome Mr. Wickham was, so very much the picture of his brother, Andrew! Before she could descend into the gutters in describing at length Mr. Wickham's form, figure, and visible attributes, Mr. Bennet cut her off.

"Indeed, he will do the job quite handsomely as he is skilled in seduction and making love to us all. Mrs. Bennet, please listen to me carefully," said Mr. Bennet as he continued with a brief description of his scheme. As his tale of the scheme unfolded, Mrs. Bennet's felicity increased.

"If you agree to this proposal, then I will have you start this very evening by meeting with Mr. Wickham at the Old Rectory, where the rendezvous will take place. I will make your excuses for you with our company that you are indisposed. Please dress in a plain hooded cloak and Mr. Hill will escort you over to the Old Rectory and back afterwards. Please do keep quiet about this."

Mrs. Bennet was in exuberant raptures of delight. She tittered and rubbed her hands together in anticipation. She poured the rest of the Madeira wine straight into her tea cup with no tea to cut it down and drank heavily of it. Whereupon she began to insult Mr. Bennet. She let Mr. Bennet know under no uncertain terms that his inability to be a man in her bed chamber these past fifteen years was a heavy slight to her beauty and their marriage. Was she not the hand-somest lady in all of the surrounding towns, even more handsome than Jane - who was at the height of her bloom? What was wrong with him? What sort of husband would plan for his wife to disgrace herself by taking a younger and far more handsome lover to sire his heir?

Mr. Bennet took her insults in stride until she insulted what she called his very small bawbles and the size of Mr. Wickham's trouser bulge - Wickham's bawbles appeared to be more than sufficient - even large in her salacious estimation.

"I will have you know, Mrs. Bennet, that my small bollocks have gotten the job done to date. You should not forget that I sired five daughters with you." She wanted a row did she? Well, as long as she completed her tasks with Mr. Wickham, he did not care in the least what she said about him or his manhood. It worked just fine when she was not around.

Mrs. Bennet could not let it be, and continued to jibe Mr. Ben-net about his alleged flaccidity and small bawbles. He rang for the footman and had the young man take the tea tray and cups away. Mr. Bennet put the sweet wine decanter out of Mrs. Bennet's reach.

"This evening at eight o'clock, be ready to depart quietly with Mr. Hill and wear a plain, dark hooded cloak. There is one in Mary's clos-et that I will have brought to your rooms."

As she stood to leave, Mr. Bennet quipped, "Let us be clear, Mrs. Bennet, that my manhood - as you have so derisively coined it - may be flaccid in your presence, but as soon as you depart the room and I can no longer hear your voice it rises to attention quite nicely even at this advanced age."

No words or utterances emitted from Mrs. Bennet as she angrily flounced out of his study. Mr. Bennet leaned back against his desk, chuckling.

11:04pm
   Thurs. Nov. 21, 1811
   The Old Rectory,
   Longbourn Village, Hertforshire
A weary Mr. Hill sat in the sitting room of the Old Rectory reading a novel loaned to him by Miss Lydia, of all people. The novel was written by a Mrs. Radcliffe, who in all of her gothic effusions could not have written the wretched frolic which was currently manifesting itself upstairs. Hill lifted his spectacles to rub his tired eyes.

Mr. Bennet had been a good master of Longbourn these past twenty some odd years and had worked hard to restore the fortunes of his family. Mr. Hill would not be here chaperoning this travesty if it was not for Mrs. Hill's imploring him to do so. Mr. Bennet had offered them an additional 200 pounds to their old age pension fund, as well as a few weeks in a cottage by the sea this upcoming summer.

Mrs. Hill had never been farther than Hertford the whole of her life and was wild to visit the seaside. She said a little sea bathing would set her up for life. He loved his wife and wished for both of them to have a comfortable retirement at their pensioner's cottage in the village at Longbourn, so he agreed to escort Mrs. Bennet to and fro in the cuckolding of her husband.

He looked around at the room and thought the Old Rectory was a lovely old house, built by the original Bennets sometime during the War of the Roses. It was a real shame that it had not been used much since old Mrs Bennet had passed away two or three years ago.

The stories this house could tell; its first two hundred years as the manor house, then another one hundred or so as the parsonage for Longbourn church before becoming the dower house. Mr. Hill loved its grand dark timbers and white-washed plaster with old mullioned windows with glass that was wavy and had a rainbow sheen to it. He thought this house was more handsome and comfortable than the grand Restoration manor house the Bennets resided in these past one hundred and thirty years.

He sighed and wished that Mrs. Bennet and her militia lieutenant would hop to it and get this business finished. Ah youth, when one could stay up all night tupping away with no real lasting effects the next day. At his age, he was greatly favored by fortune if he could last more than a quarter of an hour at the activity before falling into a sleep of the dead.

As the murmurs from upstairs turned into a crescendo to joyous screams, Mr. Hill wished he had brought some cotton batting to place in his ears. Mrs. Bennet was always the vulgar one with high animal spirits. He and Mrs. Hill were quite concerned that Miss Bennet and Miss Elizabeth would lose their gentleman suitors with Mrs. Bennet's vulgar effusions.

This very afternoon an hour before dinner, Mr. Bingley, his sister Miss Bingley, and their friend Mr. Darcy arrived to invite the Bennets to a private ball to be held at Netherfield Tuesday next. It was obvious to both the Hills that Mrs. Bennet had been sneaking into Mr. Bennet's study and drinking heavily of the sherry, as she was giggling at a high pitch and practically falling on Mr. Bingley. While no amount of overly lively behavior seemed to deter Mr. Bingley from his attachment to Miss Bennet, that did not appear to be the case with his friend.

The look of disgust on Mr. Darcy's face could not be mistaken even twenty feet across the room by Mr. Hill at the doorway. Mr. and Mrs. Hill had previously surmised that Mr. Darcy may have taken a shine to Miss Elizabeth, but with such a mother however was she to attach a man as high in the instep as Mr. Darcy? Well, it wasn't for the Hills to worry about, as the eldest two Bennet daughters would be leaving in less than two weeks to spend the winter and the Season in London with their aunt, Lady Beauchamp, where there would be gentlemen suitors aplenty.

Footsteps, whispers, and giggles on the stairway, alerted Mr. Hill away from his ruminations and with a larger sigh, he stood up to gather his outerwear and extinguish the candles.

Chapter 9 : Who's got Big Balls?

Late afternoon
  Tues. Nov. 26, 1811
  Mrs. Preece's Boarding House
  Meryton, Hertfordshire

Mr. George Wickham had just received two notes borne by two servants' from the same household within three minutes of each other. The looks of surprise on said servants faces as they passed each other through the doorway of Mr. Wickham's lodgings was worth the look of censure on Mrs. Preece's countenance. One note was from 'TCB' asking him to abstain from tonight's ball at Netherfield Park in favor of a rendezvous with 'F' at the Old Rectory. The second was from 'yours always, F.' asking him to come to Longbourn no later than nine o'clock to bless the rooms at the manor house rather than the Old Rectory. He shut his door before the sour, nosy Mrs. Preece could inquire. Wickham then shredded both notes with his pocketknife and scattered them into the fire.

Wickham was not about to lose the opportunity to make a great deal of money off the Bennets' lack of an heir to Mrs. Preece's prune-faced censure. He watched the fire, stirring carefully to make sure each strip of paper properly burned to ash and could not be reconstructed by his landlady when the ashes cooled. He supposed that it was a clever bit of revenge on Denny's part by putting Wickham up at Mrs. Preece's plain and slightly ramshackle boarding house. Most of the other Militia officers were boarding with good families or at the Inn. Only the ensigns of middling families were rooming at Mrs. Preece's. Wickham resolved to ask the other officers about any future situations before he allowed Denny to lead him, as one never knew how far Denny's possible quest for revenge might take the otherwise staid, self-righteous lieutenant.

He looked at his watch and noted that he had some hours before he would depart for Longbourn. With his official duties of the day discharged, he wished he could eat his dinner this evening at the Inn with the other lieutenants rather than Mrs. Preece's plain fare but he arrived in Meryton with not a shilling to his name. Last Thursday at their first rendezvous, the luscious Mrs. Bennet upon hearing of his destitute state had given him the crown and three sixpence from her reticule. As the past four days of rain had forced him to remain away from the Old Rectory, he had spent very nearly all of it on ale and dinner at the Inn with his fellow officers. Furthermore, Denny had been watching over him rather like an owl on a branch above a vole's hole - he dared not join the games of chance in an attempt to increase what remained of his meager funds. He sincerely hoped that Mrs. Bennet would make a regular habit of tipping him, as he would not likely see his first two hundred pounds from Mr. Bennet for some months and a militia officer's pay was next to nothing.

Wickham got up to poke and prod at the fire a bit more. He knew that he must stay the course, as this course was quite fine indeed with many delightful consolations - other than Mrs. Preece's substandard lodgings. Mr. Bennet had the right of it when he proclaimed his wife the handsomest woman in Hertfordshire; her form was luscious and her countenance a delight - every bit of Wickham's form stood at attention when her clothes were divested. If he could only figure out and patent the method to how Mrs. Bennet retained her youthful figure and countenance at the age of nine and thirty, not to mention the miracle of her indented waist after five children, he would indeed be a very wealthy man.

Mrs. Bennet's lively spirits and rather vapid, continual conversation did not flag nor weaken Mr. Wickham's admiration of her arts and allurements. Best yet, he would be paid if a child resulted from this affair of the loins. No monies were going out to pay for French envelopes or British sheep intestines. What man in his right mind would want to go to a jumped up tradesman's fine country house to dance with a bunch of rather insipid maidens when there would be delectable horizontal dancing to be embraced with Longbourn's lovely and artfully experienced mistress this very night?

Audentes Fortuna iuvat. Wickham had dared much in his pursuit of love and money, to great failure in recent years but Fortuna was smiling at him even now. His luck was turning about in a rather grand way to his relief, not even the presence of Fitzwilliam Darcy nor Lieutenant Denny in this small market town could quell his joy at his new circumstances.

The fire had now consumed all of the strips of paper and his room was quite warm. Wickham sat down to plan out his seduction strategy for the evening.

Not more than a quarter past eight
   Tues. Nov. 26, 1811
   The Entrance Hall, Netherfield Park
   Meryton, Hertfordshire
   Miss Lydia Bennet was almost too excited to be out of the house at her first private ball to stand politely in the receiving line to greet her hosts, Mr. and Miss Bingley. When she attempted to skip the line and go find her friends, with particular hopes of happening upon Mr. Wickham, her father leaned in and asked if she would like to cut her evening short and return home with the carriage. The look in his eyes told her he was quite serious. She sighed and returned to her place in line behind Elizabeth, separating Mr. Collins from his attempt to stand too close to her sister.

"Precedence, Mr. Collins, demands that I go behind Elizabeth. You may either go behind me or up in front of Jane with my father." Lydia and Elizabeth were quite relieved when Mr. Collins moved up to join their father and ingratiate himself with the Lucases who were waiting in front of the Bennets. Lydia heard Lady Lucas inquire after Mrs. Bennet and Jane's response that their mother was at home on the account of her nerves.

Lydia nearly snorted in disbelief, as her mother had not had any flutterings, spasms, or nerves for the past five days complete. Instead, Mrs. Bennet had been floating about the house smiling, laughing, and singing a ditty about who's got big balls that was fit only for a bawdy house, not the mistress of Longbourn! Lydia gasped and put her hand over her mouth in shock at her reflections of such sensible - nay, proper - opinions! Elizabeth turned and raised just one eyebrow, Lydia giggled behind her hand.

Oh, she was too full of good spirits to wait any longer! To Lydia's relief, Sir William had just finished pumping Mr. Bingley's hand up and down and Lady Lucas completed her curtsy to Miss Bingley. Charlotte and Maria were next, and then her family. Only a few more minutes, if only Mr. Collins did not make a tedious speech! Lydia shifted her weight from foot to foot as she practiced her patience. At last, Mr. Bennet and Mr. Collins were greeting the Bingleys. Now, Jane—"Look, Lizzy! Mr. Bingley just kissed Jane's hand and Papa saw him!"

"Lydia, hush. We are next." Elizabeth curtsied and made proper greetings to the Bingleys. Lydia did the same as she profusely thanked Mr. Bingley for holding a ball. She did not wait to join Lizzy or Jane but started searching the receiving rooms for Mr. Wickham.

Lydia found some of the militia officers in the corner of the ballroom sipping punch, "Mr. Denny, Colonel Forster, Mrs. Forster!" She exclaimed upon seeing her friends. "Is it not a wonderful big ball? Such a crush for Meryton!" Mr. Denny and the Colonel bowed as she inquired, "Where is Mr. Wickham? I could not find him." Lydia thought it strange that Mr. Denny's face took on a sour expression as he explained that Mr. Wickham had some business that he could not put off and would not be attending. "Oh no, who shall I dance the first set with then?" Denny bowed and offered himself, as the musicians began playing the introduction music.

Lydia, while disappointed that the handsome new officer was not in attendance, took Denny's proffered arm as he was next handsome of all the officers. Lydia determined that she would do her best to jolly him into better spirits. As they walked to form the line behind Mr. Bingley and Jane, the Hursts, Mr. Darcy and Miss Bingley, and her poor sister, Elizabeth who was stuck dancing the first with Mr. Collins, Lydia teased Mr. Denny into laughing.

"Mr. Denny, is it true you will be breaking my heart by leaving the ____shire militia to join the Horse Guards? How grand you will be!"

"Yes, I will be leaving to join the Horse Guards next week. Miss Lydia, will you not be breaking mine to return to school?" They both laughed and the dancing started in earnest as Mr. Bingley led Jane out.

Mr. Frederick Hurst danced only one dance of the set with his wife before he had to bow out of the second. His heart was racing irregularly and he was fearful of what this might portend. He made his excuses to Louisa and left the ballroom. Procuring a rather large glass of wine, Hurst took himself off to the library, which was the only room on the ground floor not invaded by guests. He sat in a wingback chair in a far, dark corner of the room and gratefully sipped his wine. If anyone entered, they would not notice him. He propped his feet up on a stool, placed his left hand over his heart and took several deep breaths in the hopes that it would stop beating so fast. *This cannot be good*, he thought.

He was nearly finished with his glass and his heart had slowed its rapid pace somewhat, when he could hear the door to the library open. He heard giggles and muffled conversation but from his chair he could not see who the intruders were. He did not wish to alert them of his presence, so he stayed quiet as they sat on the sofa near the fireplace. It must be a couple. *Please do not start any mischief or deviltry,* he groaned to himself.

Instead, to his great surprise, he heard his brother, Mr. Bingley, speak. "My dearest, loveliest Miss Bennet, you must know how much I admire and love you!"

Good G-d! Charles was going to do it, wasn't he? Well, he considered, if one was to take the leg shackle, Miss Bennet would be a lovely, demure, and sensible lady to shackle oneself to.

"Please, my dear Jane, consent to marry me and I will endeavor to treat you like the princess you are each and every day of our lives!"

Hurst could not hear her reply, but the sense of love and contentment pervaded the whole room. "Truly! You will marry me?" Then Hurst heard a series of muffled yeses and multiple I love yous. Then kissing. And then what sounded like his brother hopping about like a little boy who had to urinate.

"Jane! May I call you Jane? Call me Charles! Please, stay here, while I get your father!" More murmurs, and then Bingley left the room. Hurst looked into his glass and saw only a small remainder of wine. He sighed. He should have asked Charles to bring more wine with Mr. Bennet. Hurst knew there to be a decanter of port on the other side of the room, but he would have to reveal himself to Miss Bennet. Oh, agony.

Not long after Hurst drained his glass, Charles returned with Mr. Bennet. Hurst hoped that the business of asking for the lady's hand in marriage to her father would not take above a quarter of an hour.

The only good to come of his enforced stay on the wing back chair is that his heart had returned to its normal rhythm and speed. He sighed.

In due course, Charles enumerated all the ways he loved, respected, and admired Miss Bennet. Mr. Bennet asked Charles a few very pointed questions on his opinions on educated ladies and what his plans were for his life's work. Charles answered adequately without stuttering, although Hurst imagined that he was sweating through his waistcoat even though the fire was low and the room bordered on chilly.

Hurst held his breath as he heard Mr. Bennet ask Charles about his investments and when he would buy his own estate. When Mr. Bennet found the answers and Charles' determination to be to his liking, he informed both Charles and Miss Bennet that her dowry was twenty thousand pounds. Miss Bennet gasped and said it was too much. Her father disagreed. Charles merely said he was honored. Hurst hoped they would hurry up.

Mr. Bennet suggested that they marry before Christmas under his sister, Lady Beauchamp's, aegis and remain in Town for the Season and Jane's presentation to the Queen. Both Charles and Miss Bennet agreed. Mr. Bennet suggested that they announce the marriage to their families on the morrow and go out to enjoy the ball this evening. To Hurst's great relief, all three of them left the library together.

Hurst counted slowly to one hundred before he felt safe to leave his hiding place. As his count reached nine and ninety, his wife rushed into the room. "Oh, there you are, Frederick! I have searched all over for you. Are you well?"

He walked over to the decanter of port, poured some into his wine glass and then poured a small glass for Louisa. He handed the glass to his bewildered wife and raised a toast, "To the increased fortunes of the Bingley family and lifetime of love!" Then he whispered what had transpired to his wife, extracting a promise of silence until the morrow at the end of his tale.

"Twenty thousand pounds! And a wedding at Lady Beauchamp's? Oh, Frederick, this is very good news." The Hursts sat on the sofa, drinking their port, and after they both finished their drinks, Louisa surprised Hurst greatly by kissing him quite intently on his mouth! Hurst, never a man to let a good opportunity go, kissed his wife back for some time.

Love was in the air, or at least on the library sofa.

Captain Carter led Lydia into the supper room and seated her next to Mrs. Forster at the officer's table. While Carter was not especially favored in looks, he was a good dancer and conversationalist, thus Lydia would not repine sitting with him at dinner. She was having a divine time. The officers were so very handsome in their regimentals and Lydia had danced every dance with the officers. After dinner she had promised a dance to Mr. Darcy, of all people, John Lucas, and Mr. Collins. She hoped Mr. Collins might forget about their dance. Most surprising of all, her last dance was reserved for her father!

She should not discount her Papa, as he had not headed straight for the library or card room, but had remained the whole of the evening in the ballroom talking with Mr. Darcy and keeping a rein on Mr. Collins. Lydia did notice that he was gone for much of the second set and returned at the beginning of the third with Mr. Bingley and Jane. Both of whom were smelling of April and May. Mr. Bingley was all attention to Jane and Jane was full of blushes and whispers. Lydia surmised that there would be a wedding before Twelfth Night, or she was not Fanny Bennet's daughter!

Lydia giggled at the idea that she would turn into a matchmaker like her mother. First she would need to make her own match, but not yet as there were too many handsome officers to flirt and dance with! Mrs. Forster handed her another glass of wine and Lydia giggled some more. She wished Kitty were here, as it was a bit dull without her. In her last letter to Lydia, Kitty wrote that she would remain in London to continue with her art masters, as she desired to progress further in painting than what she learned at school.

Lydia liked Mrs. Forster, but she found her to be a bit too silly. Why, they were the same age and Harriet was already married and had never gone to school. Lydia would never admit it to her sisters or father, but she rather enjoyed learning and challenging the teachers and masters. She would admit to herself that she was ready to go back to school - did this mean she was improving her mind? She laughed at her own joke.

Mr. Denny was now telling the table about his plans to join the Horse Guards and his departure next week. He had the monies to purchase a commission as a Captain and needed to go to London next week to set everything up. Lydia admired his determination but would not really miss him. She looked back over at the table that Jane and Mr. Bingley were sitting at to see that Mr. Darcy was sitting with Elizabeth and they were deep in conversation. Lydia had been rather astonished during the dinner dance to overhear the two of them debate character and manners. Could Elizabeth not enjoy the company of a handsome man and simply flirt with him?

Lydia had finished her supper. Mrs. Forster's loud laughter at everything the officers were talking of was beginning to grate. She excused herself from the table and walked about to chat with friends and neighbors. Lydia saw that Mr. Collins was seated with Charlotte Lucas and her family. While she wanted to talk with Maria she did not want to listen to her cousin droning on. She finished her tour of the supper room by sitting next to Elizabeth, when Miss Bingley rushed over to speak to her brother.

"Charles, have you seen Louisa? I have not been able to find her these past three hours, not since the end of the second set! I have had to call the dances and make sure the servants are doing their jobs. I must find her, as she is to call the after dinner dances. And who is going to start the dinner entertainment? I cannot do everything!" Miss Bingley took a deep breath and glared at her brother as if all of this was his fault. Petulantly, she added, "I haven't even had a glass of wine yet tonight."

Lydia took the glass of wine in front of her and offered it to Miss Bingley, who looked relieved to drink it. She sat down next to Lydia and actually thanked her. Imagine that.

Mr. Bingley spoke to his sister in a low voice and that appeared to do the trick, then Miss Bingley calmly got up and walked to the piano to exhibit a couple of songs. Mr. Bingley stood and spoke, thanking everyone for attending the ball, as well as having been such welcoming neighbors, while Miss Bingley arranged herself at the pianoforte. He said that he was looking forward to many more years in the neighborhood as he looked lovingly at Jane. This set off a wave of whispers and speculations. After he finished speaking, but before Miss Bingley started playing, Mr. Collins attempted to stand and make a speech - the first words coming forth from his mouth sounded more like the bleating of a lamb. Lydia giggled at his inability to speak clearly, as her father stopped him from rising with a hand on Mr. Collins' shoulder.

Much to everyone's delight Mr. Collins did not speak and Miss Bingley played. Elizabeth was requested to play and sing a jolly song or two by Mr. Bingley after his sister finished. Lydia remained seated at the table and handed a new glass of wine to Miss Bingley when she returned to sit. Mrs. Hurst slipped into the supper room just then and sat at Elizabeth's seat.

"Where have you been?" Miss Bingley asked.

"Please forgive my absence, but Mr. Hurst's heart was racing capriciously after the first dance. I helped him get settled in his chamber and remained for some time to comfort him."

"Besides his horrid tea, what comfort did he really need that his man could not provide? Do not say wifely consolation, I will not believe it."

Lydia nearly laughed at what Miss Bingley was alluding to, she held her tongue from asking what was wrong with having a little fun with your man at a ball. From the way her mother had been talking this past week, there appeared to be more than one way to dance. Miss Bingley gave Lydia no time to inquire or joke as she reminded her wayward sister of her duties to call the dances after supper. She quizzed Mrs. Hurst on what dances she planned on calling.

Lydia looked around, most of the guests were finished with their white soup and supper. Some were listening to Lizzy sing and play, but most were talking amongst themselves. Most amusing was Mr. Darcy who heard not a word that Miss Bingley was saying as he stared intently at Lizzy. From the rather silly little smile plastered on his face, Lydia guessed that Jane was not the only Bennet sister soon to have a beau.

It was not long before Mrs. Hurst walked into the ballroom to consult with the musicians as they warmed up. Lydia, thoroughly bored of the supper room, followed Mrs. Hurst and others who were to dance the next. Mr. Collins followed Mr. Darcy telling him of the health of his relations, Lady Catherine de Bourgh and her daughter, Miss Anne de Bourgh. To Lydia's ears, every time he said the name of his patroness he cooed rather like a dove. *Oh Lord, could he not shut his mouth?*

Lydia walked over to them and said, "Mr. Darcy, I believe the next dance is ours. Could we join the line now?" He bowed at her and offered his arm, as they left Mr. Collins in mid-sentence.

"Thank you, Miss Lydia."

"La! Think nothing of it, Mr. Darcy. I told my father today that if our cousin does not quit Hertfordshire within a day or two, I wish to go back to school early. Mr. Collins is so tiresome! We have to share meals and the drawing room with him every day. I have been hiding in the library with Lizzy and my father."

Before Mr. Darcy could reply, Mrs. Hurst called a country dance and the musicians began to play "Throw Physic to the Dogs[1]". As they danced down the line and reformed, Lydia quite admired Mr. Darcy's steps and form. When the dance allowed them time and closeness of space to talk, they did.

"What school have you and your father decided on?"

"The Quaker school in Lincolnshire, I believe you recommended it to my father."

"When will you depart?"

"I was to depart next week, but the school and my father would prefer me to start at the winter term after the new year. If I attend this school, I will be prepared to enter Matlock College rather than Lorien."

They danced away from each other and when they returned, Lydia said, "My father and my three older sisters went to Oxford, but I would rather be the first Bennet to go to Cambridge. I do like to be first."

Mr. Darcy actually laughed at this. Lydia was quite proud of herself. "Please tell me about Cambridge," she requested. For the rest of the dance and the next, Mr. Darcy told her about his experiences at Cambridge and that of his cousins, Miss de Bourgh and Lady Helena Fitzwilliam, at Matlock College. When he inquired about what she desired for her future, she was honest.

"My mother wants us all to be out and married, as soon as may be. I thought I wanted to have fun and quit school, but these weeks at home studying with my father has shown me that I want more for my life. I want to be the first woman barrister in London!"

Rather than laughing at her or dismissing her, Mr. Darcy spent the rest of the set discussing with her how she would accomplish that goal. He outlined what she should focus her studies on at school and at Matlock. They discussed how she could study law before the Inns of the Court were ready to admit females. Lydia decided that while Mr. Darcy was quiet and stern, she rather liked his logical mind. *He will do quite nicely for Lizzy*, she thought, *but we must get Mama away from the idea of pairing Lizzy with Mr. Collins.*

The next two sets with John Lucas and Mr. Collins were to be endured, but the last dance surprised Lydia. It was a delight to dance the Boulanger with her father. She told him, "Papa, you are quite spry for an old man! Look over there, do you see Lizzy and Mr. Darcy imperceptibly flirting as they dance? She should be more forward with him if he is to know that her affections are engaged."

"Lydia, leave your sister and Mr. Darcy to their method of courting, even if it is much too subtle for your tastes."

"Papa, you should have seen how he stared at her at supper!"

"Lydia..." With that stern sounding admonishment, she skipped away in time with the dance, laughing.

Mr. Bennet was vastly relieved when the ball was over. It was nearly four o'clock in the morning and his old bones, jarred as they were from dancing with his three daughters and Miss Lucas, were aching to be at home in his own bed with a warming brick or two.

Rounding up Elizabeth, Lydia, and Mr. Collins to depart was quite easy; extracting Jane from Mr. Bingley's company was a larger feat. By the time Mr. Bennet was able to get Mr. Bingley to say his very last and final farewell of the night, every other family had departed Netherfield Park. The Bennet carriage awaited in a freezing drizzle and the horses were impatient to be off, as Mr. Bennet gave a hand to help his daughters in the carriage.

Mr. Collins hopped in and sat next to Elizabeth before Mr. Bennet could sit next to her. "Mr. Collins, this is a small carriage and there is not room for five grown people. Please remove yourself from this carriage and ride up with the coachman, as you did on the way to Netherfield Park."

Mr. Collins protested in a harsh bray much like an old donkey being forced to move from a much loved pasture. Lydia giggled as he stepped out of the carriage and climbed up next to the coachman.

"Thank you, Papa." Elizabeth patted his hand as she softly spoke. "Mr. Collins has become quite tiresome in his attentions. When will he return to Kent?"

"Within the day or two if I have anything to say about it. Perhaps, I might convince him to spend that time within Lucas Lodge." In the half hour it took the carriage to drive to Longbourn, all three of his daughters fell asleep with contented smiles on their faces - although Jane's smile was the greatest.

4:42am
  Wed. Nov. 27, 1811
  The Grand Staircase
  Longbourn Manor
  Meryton, Hertfordshire
As Mr. Bennet and his family, tired from the ball, ascended the staircase to their respective chambers, there was a chain of loud moans floating down from the family floor.

"I hear a ghost!" Lydia giggled and repeated her version of a ghost's moan. "Woooo!!!"

Mr. Collins, still shivering from his ride on top with the coachman, was attempting to lean on Elizabeth. Mr. Bennet assessed the situation, separated his cousin from his daughter, said goodnight to his daughters, and escorted Mr. Collins up to the top floor landing to make sure he made it to his chamber alone. A series of bangings on the wall frightened Mr. Collins, who squealed and sprinted up the final flight of stairs. Mr. Bennet watched his cousin run into his room and lock the door behind him.

Mr. Bennet would have laughed long at such a display from his usually grave and ridiculous cousin, had he not known the source of the ghostly moans and banging. As it was, Mr. Bennet marched back down the stairs to his wife's chambers and let himself in. The ghosts were not in her chambers.

He walked through their shared sitting room into his room and was greeted by the sight of his wife furiously tupping Mr. Wickham on his favorite reading chair surrounded by nearly burnt out candles and flower petals. *Flower petals in November? Whatever had they been up to? Well, other than the obvious...*

Neither paid attention to him. Bennet cleared his throat loudly. "Mrs. Bennet and Mr. Wickham, my chamber is not the master's bedroom at the Old Rectory. Please assemble yourselves and I will take Mr. Wickham out."

His wife gasped, fell off of Mr. Wickham, and onto the rug with her legs akimbo. Mr. Wickham wilted from the surprise at being interrupted in the act of violating his patron's chamber. Wickham jumped up and searched for his clothes.

Mrs. Bennet rose from the rug and swiftly robed herself. She fished into her robe's pocket and placed money in Mr. Wickham's hand. *Good Lord in heaven! Fanny just tipped Mr. Wickham with what appeared to be 2 pounds 4 shillings! Well, if she wants to spend her pin money that way, she can. But at that rate she will run out before the quarter is over. I must get them out of here.*

He hastened a now dressed Mr. Wickham down the servants stairs and out through the empty kitchen. "Mr. Wickham, I appreciate your keen dedication to your task, but it is to be employed at the Old Rectory, not in my house. If you return to Longbourn at my wife's invitation, consider the contract cancelled."

Wickham had the good grace to look embarrassed and nodded at Bennet's last statement before departing into the night. He did not apologize. Insolent man!

Bennet locked the kitchen door and turned to find an ashamed Mr. Hill awaiting him. "Hill, do not apologize - there is no taming my wife. I am sure that this was her idea. I will speak with her on the morrow. Go back to bed. I will sleep in my study. Please have my bedroom aired out and thoroughly cleaned in the morning."

Bennet let himself into his study and poured a glass of his finest, reserve French brandy. He added a log to the fire and pulled a blanket out of a lower drawer in his desk. He reclined on the sofa, took a long sip of the brandy, and started to laugh. *What a night.*

Chapter 10: The Day After and the Rest of the Truth

---❦---

5:23am
Wed. Nov. 27, 1811
The Master's Study, Longbourn Manor
Meryton, Hertfordshire

Mr. Bennet had drifted off in a half-slumber after finishing his brandy, when a knock at the door of his study roused him. "Who is it?"

"It is Lizzy, Papa."

"Come in." Mr. Bennet called as he put his brandy glass onto a side table and sat up with the blanket wrapped around him. Elizabeth walked in dressed for bed in a heavy flannel nightgown under a winter weight dressing gown with a pair of felted wool slippers peeping out and her plaited hair falling out of her flannel night cap. The elegant young lady of this evening's ball had been replaced with his little girl, albeit with a fiery glare.

"Papa, we must talk." Elizabeth walked in and shut the door. She sat down on a chair adjacent to the sofa. Mr. Bennet stood up and refilled his brandy glass, then he bypassed the ladies' sherry to pour her a small finger of the best of his reserve brandy. "Papa, brandy or no, you will not distract me from my purpose to come talk to you when we should both be asleep after such a long night at Mr. Bingley's ball."

"Elizabeth, take at least three sips - not small ones - before you ring a peal over my head."

Elizabeth dutifully sipped her brandy and composed her thoughts. She looked at her father, who was sitting on the sofa wrapped in a blanket. In the fading light of the fire he looked rather depleted, his hair was more gray than brown. His eyes were tired. She sighed.

Elizabeth rose and checked outside of both of the study doors to make sure no one was in the library nor the foyer to listen. She sat back down. "Papa, those were not ghosts. It was Mama. And if I may guess correctly from our last conversation after Aunt Philips' card party, it was also Mr. Wickham. They are lovers at your direction, are they not? If I have put all the pieces together correctly, you are paying your natural son to father a child with your wife to break the entail. You are paying Mr. Wickham to father a child, much as you were paid to father Mr. Wickham. Thus, your natural son will be the sire to your grandson who will be paraded about as your heir."

The weight of his whole scheme suddenly pressed down on Mr. Bennet. He looked at his beloved, determined, and very clever daughter - the daughter of his heart - and knew that it was now time to tell the whole truth. And tell the whole truth he did - the full reasons behind the entail in 1788, who was the true love of his life from his years at Kympton - the same woman who was even now his true love - the horrifying feeling of being trapped in a compromise by Fanny Gardiner, the weight these past years of not being able to enter his wife's chamber to father a son, and why, after working all these years to save the estate, he simply could not leave Longbourn to that idiot Mr. Collins.

"Papa, you will ruin Jane's happiness with Mr. Bingley if this affair becomes known! Mama was so loud tonight that every servant at Longbourn must know what is afoot; it is only a matter of time before the gossip spreads to Meryton. Can you not train Mr. Collins to some semblance of sense?"

"Jane told you?"

"Yes, of course. She told me the whole of the proposal as I was getting ready for bed. She is very much in love with Mr. Bingley."

"Listen to me, Lizzy. I own that my scheme appears to be mad, but I will not fail you and Jane - nor will I fail Longbourn and its people. The codicil on the will states that the entail can be broken by the heir of my body male and / or his male descendants. Thus, Mr. Wickham qualifies as a male heir of my body and any son of his can break the entail and keep Longbourn in the Bennet Family."

"Papa, we both know that you are stretching the truth mightily - as an heir is the male heir born within the marriage, not a natural son born without. Thus, Mr. Wickham's sons do not qualify."

"Lizzy, you are forgetting that once a man and wife are married, by British law, all babes birthed by the wife are children of the husband, whether he fathered them or not. As long as the husband does not sue the wife's lover for cuckolding him, then the children are of the marriage and are heirs. I will not contest any male child born to my wife."

Elizabeth stared in disbelief at her father. "While this is true and this is why Sir Lewis de Bourgh the elder recognized Sir Lewis the younger and Miss Anne de Bourgh as his children, it is still stealing from Mr. Collins who is, at current time, technically the legal heir."

"Only until a male heir is born to my wife that I recognize as my heir. Wickham is my natural son, his son is my grandson, and any son he fathers with my wife will be recognized and celebrated as my heir." As the study clock chimed 6 o'clock in the morning, Mr. Bennet rubbed his eyes and leaned forward. "Lizzy, Mr. Collins is a fool of the grandest order, he has no business being the master of an estate. He will run Longbourn into the ground in five years or less. I have not left my life that I loved in Derbyshire as a rector of a very good living adjacent to the best library outside of Oxford to save an estate these past twenty-four years only to have the entailed portion of the estate be destroyed after my death."

"Papa, it is morally fraught. The whole scheme could go astray in a variety of ways exposing the whole of the family to the censure of society. Please think of Jane's felicity with Mr. Bingley."

"Lizzy, you must see that I am thinking of all of our felicities and futures. You will come out and have your season in the spring as planned. Your mother is the happiest and the quietest she has ever been - well, with the exception of this past few hours. Jane will marry Mr. Bingley before Christmas and his sisters can be quite pleased to gain our connections. I will even come to town in the second week of December to make sure that all introductions are made and that the Bingley sisters would not want to give up connections to the Beauchamps, Fitzwilliams, de Bourghs, and - heaven forfend if Miss Bingley should meet them - The Howards. My poor cousin, he does not deserve this.

"Elizabeth, even if it leaks out in Meryton what is going on, most of the ton will find it to be an amusing on dit - I can hear it now - 'Of course, such a beautiful woman with an old husband would take up with a handsome young militia officer! Would not you?' Lady Catherine and my sister will manage that gossip if it is necessary. But it will not leak. It cannot, I will not let it."

Elizabeth sighed. She was very tired and very worried. "Papa, before I leave to go to bed, do tell me how this scheme came about? Please say it was your idea and not Lady Catherine's?"

"It was both of ours. When it became obvious that I could no longer perform my duty with your mother, Lady Catherine started speaking of what we would have to do. She made the choice to give the living to Mr. Collins last year so that she could assess him as my potential heir and train him as necessary."

"She is very attentive to all the little details." Elizabeth wryly remarked. Bennet wryly nodded his head in response.

"By summer it was obvious that he was a man of little intelligence and mean understanding. While he is servile enough, he has been re-

sistant to learning anything of import. When Lady Catherine found
out that he could barely read, she called me to London and we made
a plan. She even brought her solicitor in to make sure the plan was as
watertight as could be."

"Dear Lord."

"Speaking of dears, it is my dear Lavinia who reminded us of her
son Wickham. He was at loose ends and rambling about in the stews
of London after his latest scheme to seduce an heiress did not come
to fruition. Sir Thurston Hurst had forcibly cut off all contact between Lady Hurst and her son, thus Lavinia was worried about what
would happen to him next. Lady Catherine felt that this would give
him a positive goal to work towards."

A harsh laugh bubbled unwanted from Elizabeth at the very idea
of the formidable Lady Catherine reforming a rake through an illicit
affair with her lover's wife. She held up her hand. "Do not tell me any
more tonight. I am going to bed."

Elizabeth stood, and before walking to the door said in a low
voice, "Papa, please make sure that Wickham does not blackmail you,
and that if Mama is increasing that she is protected. Furthermore, she
is trying to throw Mr. Collins at me. I will not marry the man."

"Elizabeth, you should know one more detail, a detail that Jane
found out tonight - but do keep it quiet."

Elizabeth, standing near the door, raised her eyebrow. "Yes, Papa?"

"Jane and your dowries, and Mary's if she finishes with a first at
Lorien, are twenty thousand pounds. You will not need to fear the
hedgerows, even if you choose not to marry."

Elizabeth's jaw dropped and in her eyes, which were tearing up,
Mr. Bennet could see a lack of comprehension due to the hour war-
ring with many questions. "Lizzy, it is now after 6 o'clock in the
morning, go to bed."

She walked back to the sofa and kissed her father on his cheek before taking leave of his study.

After Elizabeth's steps were no longer heard on the steps, Mr. Bennet said to himself, "Over my dead body will Mr. Collins marry any of my daughters. I will make sure he takes himself over to Lucas Lodge today."

9:37am, The same morning
Mr. Bennet's Study

Mr. Bennet slept nearly three hours on the study sofa after his early morning conversation with Elizabeth. His sleep had been disturbed by a fleeting set of dreams, nightmares actually, of Mr. Collins taking Lizzy off to Kent and burning Longbourn to the ground. Bennet sat up on the sofa as he heard a series of knocks to alert them that Hill was at the door. He quickly ran his hand through his hair and reached for his spectacles.

"Come in, Hill." It was not Mr. Hill, but Mrs. Hill.

"Sir, I have completed a thorough cleaning and airing of your chambers. Would you like a bath drawn?"

"Thank you, Hill. Yes, I would like to bathe. Also, can you have breakfast served for Mr. Collins and I at half ten?"

Mrs. Hill nodded. "Yes, sir."

"Please have the man woken up and let him know that his presence is necessary at breakfast. Also, if any of my daughters or my wife wishes to have breakfast before Mr. Collins' departs for Lucas Lodge, have them break their fast in the ladies' sitting room." He smiled ruefully. "I imagine that they will all sleep past noon or later."

Mrs. Hill curtseyed and took her leave. Mr. Bennet deposited the blanket on the sofa and put his shoes back on so that he could climb the stairs to his room and his bath.

10:30am, The same day
Longbourn's breakfast parlor

Mr. Bennet had arrived a quarter of an hour earlier to give himself enough time to drink a cup of coffee and eat a slice of game pasty before he spoke to his cousin. When Mr. Collins walked into the breakfast parlor, Bennet said to him, "Mr. Collins, please be seated and fill your plate. You are on time this morning, given how late we all were at the ball."

Mr. Collins sat across from his cousin and started to fill his plate with eggs, kippers, and bread. "I fancy myself prompt and..." Mr. Collins proceeded to chatter on about how aware he was of time and accuracy. He finished his speech with a quote. "As I always say, 'Early to bed, early to rise, makes a man, healthy, wealthy, and wise.'"

Mr. Bennet quipped, "I had not thought you a scholar of Mr. Franklin's life and writings."

Mr. Collins had swallowed half of the food on his plate with astonishing rapidity. "Who is Mr. Franklin?"

Mr. Bennet smiled over his second cup of coffee. "Mr. Benjamin Franklin was a renowned American author, printer, inventor, and diplomat." Collins grunted as he placed more kippers on his plate and then used his knife to put a whole small fish into his mouth.

"Mr. Collins, you have spoken much on extending an olive branch to my family. May I ask with whom did this idea originate?"

This question quite caught Collins out with the large sized kipper, uncut with any knife, half in and half out of his mouth. To save his cousin from choking or death by smoked kipper, Bennet signaled to the attending footman to help the man. Chalmers cheerfully beat Mr. Collins on the back. Collins was so surprised, that the fish was expelled back onto his plate. Chalmers, duty completed, returned to his place of attention.

Rather than excusing himself or apologizing for such outrageous table manners, Collins started to cut up his kippers in smaller pieces as he attempted to answer his cousin's question at length without saying a single word of sense. Collins made some noise about his noble and elegant patroness, his honored father, his own unease at the disagreement between his father and Cousin Bennet, olive branches, and his parishioners.

Bennet looked over his spectacles. He pinned Collins with a glare. "Cousin Collins, I have known the Lady Catherine de Bourgh for nigh on thirty years now, she would not suggest that you make an offer of marriage to one of my daughters. Please concisely answer where the idea originated."

Mr. Collins had dispatched his cut up kipper to its penultimate resting place, when he said, "Oh no, the idea was mine when my esteemed patroness informed me that I need to find a useful, sensible, and genteel wife for her sake. The Lady Catherine de Bourgh was quite emphatic that the rector of the Hunsford parish needs to set an example of matrimony to his parishioners. As I have also said, I have been uneasy at the disagreement between yourself..."

"Mr. Collins, let me be..."

"Cousin Bennet, I must tell you that the Lady Catherine de Bourgh, who is very conscious of station and rank, told me that I am not to attempt to court one of your handsome and amiable daughters, as they are quite above me. But upon arriving at Longbourn and speaking with Mrs. Bennet, I had hoped that you would accept my olive branch..."

"Mr. Collins, let me be quite clear, you will not court nor marry any of my daughters, regardless of what my wife may have offered to you. I am the head of my family, not Mrs. Bennet. It is I who will sign any and all marriage settlements."

A few bleats of protest issued forth from Mr. Collins. Mr. Bennet set down his empty coffee cup and stood. "Although, if you wish to pursue the matter and are willing to defer your suit for seven years from now. In the year Eighteen, my Lydia will have completed her

University degree and will have had her Season in Town and if you take the time to improve your mind and person then my Lydia may be persuaded to..."

Mr. Collins sputtered in horror, ejecting chewed bits of kippers out of his mouth. Mr. Bennet did not relent, "Cousin Collins, please attend my words. If seven years of waiting to possibly have your suit accepted is not desirable to you, then I recommend that after you have completed your breakfast that you walk to Lucas Lodge. Wherein you will find a clever, sensible gentlewoman to court - Miss Charlotte Lucas. She has appeared to be very amenable to your attentions this past week, she will make you a fine, genteel wife."

Mr. Bennet stood at the door, as Mr. Collins turned red in the face. "Moreover, I expect that you will take your dinner and supper at Lucas Lodge and that you will return to Kent no later than tomorrow afternoon." Mr. Bennet nodded at Chalmers and departed for his study.

Mr. Bennet napped in peace on his couch with an open book over his eyes until he heard his wife calling for Mrs. Hill and demanding to know where Lizzy and Mr. Collins were. He looked at his clock on the mantle, it proclaimed it was a quarter after two. *Well, time to remind Mrs. Bennet what the definition of discretion and secrecy is and how it is relevant to her behavior.*

2:15pm, The same day
  Jane's bedroom
  Longbourn Manor
  Elizabeth looked up from her sewing when she heard her mother's calls for herself and Mr. Collins. Lydia smirked.

Jane looked at both of them sternly and said, "Do not pay any attention to our mother's cries. You both must continue to sew, while I continue to embroider. If Lizzy and I are to depart for London next week, then we must make great haste these next few days on completing my Agincourt trousseau bed linens."

Jane turned her tambour over to make sure the embroidery threads were neat on the backside of the pillowcase she was stitching interlacing swords and shields on the hemline. "My mother will not think to look for us here. I extracted a promise from Mrs. Hill that she would not tell her where we are."

Lydia giggled. "Oh, Mistress Jane, are we permitted to talk quietly amongst ourselves while we toil away?"

Jane did not take well to being teased and did not look up from her rapid stitches as she replied. "Only if you are quiet and we get our work done before dinner, as the light from the window should still be good for another two hours, maybe less. Lydia and Lizzy, do make sure that your stitches are straight and even!"

Jane looked up just in time to see Elizabeth raising her eyebrow. "Lizzy, do watch your stitches - they are uneven - I can see them from here. I do not want to lose time picking them out and re-hemming the pillow cases."

When Jane picked up her chair and fine work to move closer to the window, Lizzy did her best to smother any creeping smile. Lydia saved Lizzy from further admonishments by talking about the ball last night.

"La! My dances after supper were a source of surprise! Papa actually danced with me and Mr. Darcy spoke at length while we danced!"

Elizabeth smiled at Lydia and replied, "I noticed that Mr. Darcy spoke most of the second dance of your set. What did you talk of?"

"The Quaker school that he recommended to Papa at Lucas Lodge. Mr. Darcy assured me that it was not all plain dress and silence, but challenging academics and tutors who would not be afraid of my cleverness nor threatened by my impertinence." Lydia giggled a bit too loud at this. A restless Jane rose from her seat and came to inspect Lydia's stitches. Lydia pulled the sheet she was hemming away from Jane's line of sight. "Jane, leave me be. I do best when I am not being so closely watched!"

All three young ladies stopped when they heard shouting coming from their mother's chambers. It was not their father shouting, but their mother. Most of the words were at odds with each other and they could hear their father speaking in a low, calm authoritative tone telling her to stop shouting and listen to him.

Lydia missed not a beat. "Mr. Darcy also assured me that if I were to take my studies of rhetoric, logic, and history seriously, that I would be able to study the law later. We devised a plan wherein I could fully prepare myself between school, university, and later law studies to be able to pass the bar when the time comes."

Jane had moved around behind Lydia's shoulder and was squinting to see how detailed Lydia's stitches were. Lydia turned again. "Lizzy, I do like Mr. Darcy. He may be high in the instep, but he did not mock my ideas and hopes. Instead, he encouraged me to learn to debate properly."

Jane turned her attention to Elizabeth's hemming. "Lizzy, you dropped a stitch here. Please attend to your work."

"Jane, please sit down with your work and let me attend mine. Worry not, we will be done with your bed clothes in time for your wedding." Elizabeth tried to smile reassuringly at Jane who remained agitated and unable to sit back down. "Jane, if Mr. Bingley said that he would visit before dinner to speak with you and Papa, he will be here. In the interim, sit back down and finish your swords and shields."

Elizabeth looked steadily at Lydia, "Not a word is to be breathed about Mr. Bingley to our mother before our father has time to announce the news."

"Lizzy, you have ears, as I do - right now they are still arguing about last night." Lydia walked over and pressed her ear to the wall. "Ghosts! Wooooooo...."

To distract Lydia, Elizabeth asked, "Has our father determined when you will go to Lincolnshire?"

Lydia pulled her ear off the wall and sat back down to her sewing. "I wish to go as soon as may be, as it is so dull here in Meryton now that the ball is over. But Papa and the school want me to come when the winter term starts after the new year. Thus, while you and Jane shop in London and dance your nights' away, have some thought for your suffering youngest sister trapped in Papa's study reading Latin!" Lydia assumed a slump and nearly fell off her chair, as she started to giggle again.

Before Jane could reprimand her for the third or fourth time, a knock was heard at the door. Jane ran to answer it. It was Mr. Hill.

"Miss Bennet, Mr. Bingley has arrived and your father has instructed you to meet with him in his study in 10 minutes." Hill departed. Jane patted her hair and dress with a look of panic in her eyes. Elizabeth and Lydia took control of the situation by placing Jane at her dressing table. Lydia repinned Jane's hair and Elizabeth put a few small silk flowers in her hair that matched the ribbon on Jane's dress. They draped her in her newest and prettiest sari shawl and pushed her out the door.

Lydia sat back down and gathered up her sewing. "Lizzy, remind me to only fall in love when I am old and sensible."

Elizabeth took her sewing back up and laughed at Lydia's joke.

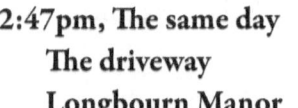

2:47pm, The same day
   The driveway
   Longbourn Manor

Mr. Charles Bingley's stomach was aflutter. He had been alter-nating, since he awoke just before noon, between extremes of long-ing for his angel and fluttering jitters of anxiety that he would not see his angel before he departed for London. It was less than two hours before the sun was due to set, but if he was to return on Friday by dinner time - as he promised Darcy and Hurst - then he must away to London this evening. It would give him tomorrow, Thursday, to ask the rector of his London parish to read the banns for his wed-ding and to visit his solicitor to have the marriage articles drawn up. He also hoped to have time to buy Jane a present at the jewelers. Per-haps they would have a jeweled angel pin or brooch. Most of all, he wished to buy a proper wedding ring for Jane, maybe he could find a sapphire that matched her eyes.

He handed his horse's reins to one of his two grooms who were riding with him. He looked up at the classical baroque splendor of Longbourn's facade. He regretted that his own father could not be here for this meeting with Mr. Bennet that would unite their fami-lies. His father would be so proud that he, Charles Swithenbank Bin-gley, would be marrying into an old English family who had been on their land for over five hundred years! He could hear the voice of his Bingley grandmother admonishing him that it was more important that he was marrying for love. *Yes, his dearest, loveliest Jane.* Oh, Bin-gley hoped that he would be given time to talk with her privately af-ter his meeting with her father.

Just as Bingley gathered enough resolve to knock on the grand entrance door, it opened. Mr. Hill greeted him and led him to the master's study. As he walked into the study, the beauty of his angel sitting demurely on the sofa took his breath away and he was stunned. A sharp rap on his shoulder blade startled him and a com-manding voice instructed him to breathe. Charles turned to his fu-ture father-in-law and bowed. "Mr. Bennet, Miss Bennet, I am hon-ored to be here..."

Jane rose and curtsied. "Mr. Bingley, thank you so very much for the lovely ball last..."

"Yes, yes, yes. Before you two love birds continue to coo at length to each other, I would like to go over a few matters of marriage business before Mr. Bingley departs for London." Mr. Bennet steered his eldest daughter back to her seat on the sofa and Mr. Bingley found himself sitting on a chair in front of his desk, whereupon Mr. Bennet sat down behind his desk and lifted up a sheet of foolscap with a list on it.

"Number one, last night we briefly discussed that both of you wish to marry before Christmas. Is this still the case, just nod for yes or no. Right, two yes nods. Excellent. Number two, may I suggest Monday, the 23rd of December? Does that date suit both of you?" Mr. Bennet checked off the first two items on his list that he received positive responses for. "Capital. Number three, do you wish to marry here at Jane's parish of Longbourn or Mr. Bingley's parish in London or do you wish to apply for a license to marry at your Aunt Beauchamp's drawing room?"

"Papa, Charles and I spoke more at length last night and I do so wish to marry here at the Longbourn parish church. Mama would be so very sad to give over all the planning of the wedding breakfast to my aunt. I do so very much wish for all of my family to be happy." Jane looked at her hands. "Papa, I do so desire to go to London for the weeks previous to visit with my Aunts and Uncles..."

"...As well as shop in London. Yes, my dear Jane, you and Elizabeth will still depart for London next week to stay with my sister and her family. Your mother will be able to manage planning the wedding breakfast without you here." Mr. Bennet smiled kindly at his daughter. "Mr. Bingley, if you would please have the banns read at your parish church and I will meet with Longbourn's rector tomorrow to have the banns read here."

Charles smiled brightly. He tried to keep his eyes and attention on Mr. Bennet, but they repeatedly drifted over to his beloved on the sofa. If only he could count the ways that she...

"Mr. Bingley, please attend my next point!" Charles sat up and turned his whole body towards the desk to keep his eyes from temptation.

"Right, the final number on my list is the details of the wedding settlement, last night I told you the amount of Miss Bennet's dowry and now I would like to have an idea of what you are planning on offering to her as a jointure in the settlement..."

Charles did his best to speak clearly on the points of the settlement that Darcy helped him craft before he left Netherfield that afternoon. He pulled the list out of his waistcoat pocket and gave it to Mr. Bennet. They then spoke for some minutes on the particulars, as Mr. Bennet made notes of their decisions on both of their lists. Finally, after what seemed an infinity but the mantle clock revealed to be less than a half hour had passed, Mr. Bennet stood, shook Charles' hand, and left him and Jane to a quarter of an hour of privacy.

"I will be in the library on the other side of that door. Please do not abuse my trust in both of you." Mr. Bennet bowed and walked into the library and lightly closed the door.

Both Jane and Charles jumped up and met with a kiss in the middle of the study. Many little, sweet endearments were uttered and light kisses bestowed as they held hands. Both bemoaned the two or more days before they would meet again.

When the quarter hour chimed, Charles with great difficulty left his lovely fiancée and mounted his horse with a large smile on his face. It was not until he had ridden nearly to Hertford that he wondered why he had not seen nor heard his future mother-in-law. *Odd that*, he thought before he encouraged his horses and his accompanying grooms to pick up the pace. It was cold and the sooner they reached London, the sooner he would return to his angel.

Chapter 11: Future Wedding Bells

5:42pm, Wed. Nov. 27, 1811
  The Butler's Pantry
  Longbourn Manor

China and glassware rattled in the basement butler's pantry as a shriek of pure joy reverberated throughout the whole of Longbourn Manor. Mr. Hill looked at Mrs. Hill with a raised eyebrow and wryly remarked, "I suppose Mr. Bennet has announced Miss Bennet's engagement to Mr. Bingley at dinner."

"Ah, Mr. Bingley, he is a fine young man. He will do quite nicely for Miss Bennet," Mrs. Hill said. "Mr. Hill, should we travel to Ramsgate or Brighton this summer for our holiday to the sea? I would so dearly love to see the Royal Pavilion in Brighton and walk on the beach."

"I was thinking that a trip to a seaside town in Essex may be a shorter distance to travel, Mrs. Hill."

"Essex! There is naught there but villages with a church and a few cottages. Nay, Mr. Hill! I say we..."

Mr. and Mrs. Hill's discussion was cut short by the glassware rattling in the hutch to the sound of screaming rage. Mr. Hill raised his eyebrow, "Mrs. Hill, you will be shortly called for. Take some of the apothecary's special sherry based tonic as a preventative with you."

Mrs. Hill sighed. As she collected the tonic and poured it into a rather large wine glass, she thought that promenading around the Prince Regent's Royal Pavilion in Brighton would be just the thing for her nerves. She then walked up the stairs and proceeded towards the sounds of anger emitting from the family dining room as

Chalmers was departing with trays from the first remove. Mrs. Hill gathered her courage and walked into the dining room.

5:44pm, Wed. Nov. 27, 1811
Billiards Room
Netherfield Park

A piercing shriek rent the air. Mr. Fitzwilliam Darcy stopped aiming at the cue ball and instead looked up at Mr. Hurst. "I suppose that is why you insisted that we play a game of billiards before dinner rather than waiting in the drawing room?"

"I suggest that you drink a bit more of your wine before we brave the dragon's lair." Hurst smiled at Darcy and took a long sip of his pre-dinner glass of wine. "All day my wife kept putting off telling her sister the news of Bingley's engagement to the delightful Miss Bennet. She knew it couldn't wait any longer and asked me to make sure that she had time to cool Caroline's temper before..."

Both of them looked up as Miss Bingley's voice carried halfway across the ground floor of the mansion, "I don't care if her dowry is as good as mine! That woman is not our cousin and all her connections are a lie! Charles can do much better!"

Hurst shook his head and motioned for Darcy to cue up his shot. "I hope you are not too hungry, as I believe we may be here for another game or two."

Another piercing scream rent the air and shouts of "It cannot be!" were heard by one and all at Netherfield Park.

A few minutes earlier
The Dining Room
Longbourn Manor

Another angry shriek accompanied the second with furious shouts of it cannot be. Mrs. Bennet's lovely peaches and cream complexion was mottled with fury.

"Why yes, Mrs. Bennet, it will be. You will remain at Longbourn and your two eldest daughters will travel to Town next week and stay with my sister, Lady Beauchamp." Mr. Bennet was firm, yet calm. He nearly lost his composure to laughter when he saw Mrs. Hill enter the dining room with a large glass of his wife's tonic unasked for. He did not begrudge the servants a peaceful evening. "We will discuss this later in our rooms, please cease your prattle on the subject now as it is a time of celebration of Jane's engagement."

Mr. Bennet stood and raised his wine glass. Mrs. Hill had passed the wine glass of sherry tonic to Mrs. Bennet. Jane and Elizabeth held up their glasses of wine, and Lydia made due with a glass of water.

Mr. Bennet spoke, "To my very lovely and intelligent daughter, Jane. May you always live in harmony with Mr. Bingley, may you always have more laughter than sorrow, and may you and Mr. Bingley be fruitful and multiply! Cheers!" All assembled clinked their glasses together and drank.

Mrs. Bennet drank deeply of her tonic several times and then began to list off the warehouses that Lady Beauchamp ought to take Jane to to complete her trousseau. She then fretted about the warehouses overcharging her sister-in-law on account of her being a great lady. Only if Mr. Bennet would allow Mrs. Bennet to go to Town, she would be able to get the best lace at the right price! She simply must be able to accompany Jane to any dinner parties and balls that Lady Beauchamp had arranged for the girls to attend. Just as her assertions, counter-assertions, and digressions were wearing on her family's nerves, Mrs. Hill came back into the dining room with a refill of Mrs. Bennet's tonic.

To Lydia's relief, Chalmers entered with the second course and placed the dishes on the table. Lydia distracted her mother by requesting her to pass the dishes or to fill her plate for her. Mr. Bennet smiled at Lydia. "I must not forget my second announcement of the evening. Our dear Lydia has been admitted into the Quaker's Preparatory School for Girls in Lincolnshire and will travel to start at the beginning of the winter term after Twelfth Night."

Before Mrs. Bennet could ask where Lincolnshire was and then complain about the great distance, Lydia launched into a speech about her excitement to study at such a revered school with many graduates who took firsts at Matlock College in Law and History. Her mother attempted to ask with a big wink why her favorite daughter would need a Law degree when she already had everything to capture a husband. Lydia then regaled the table with her story from last night's ball of discussing with Mr. Darcy her plans to become the first ever lady barrister in the whole of the United Kingdom.

Mr. Bennet questioned Lydia about her plan, while Mrs. Bennet complained that no man would marry a lady barrister and what was her dear Lydia doing dancing with that awful dour man. The second course of dinner was finished with laughter and warm conversation, particularly after Mrs. Bennet's tonic took effect wherein small giggles began to erupt at the most inappropriate times.

6:44pm, Wed. Nov. 27, 1811
   The Dining Room
   Netherfield Park

No giggles were erupting at the Netherfield Park dinner table. Caroline Bingley was attempting to hold court with tales of the savage inhabitants of Meryton wreaking havoc in their ballroom the night before. To her disappointment, Mr. Hurst and Mr. Darcy ignored her as they spoke of the prospects of hunting on the morrow and her sister was cutting up her vegetables very fine before chewing each bite very carefully.

"Louisa, you were gone from the ballroom much of the night, thus you ought to listen to what our brother allowed to occur by inviting such uncouth savages into our home!"

Louisa by now had minced every edible on her plate fine and was moving the food about. She refused to reply to her sister.

"Louisa! We must do something about Charles' engagement..."

Louisa looked up from her plate and firmly said to her sister, "No, Caroline, we must not. As I have already told you four times this evening, this is Charles' choice. It is a very good choice for Charles, and for the whole of our family. We shall not discuss how to stop him, instead we shall support him in his engagement and marriage to Miss Bennet."

From the other side of the table, Mr. Darcy opined, "Hurst, I dare say that if we go tomorrow afternoon an hour or so before sunset to the wood between Netherfield and the Old Rectory of Longbourn we should be able to shoot several braces of birds. Mr. Bennet gave us permission to shoot his birds this week, as they are overrunning the wood."

"Will we walk the two or three miles to the wood or ride? If we walk, we should leave here at half two." Hurst inquired.

"No! Will none of you listen to what I am telling you? We must stop Charles..." Caroline waved her wine glass about as she continued to drink deeply.

"Hurst, I do believe we ought to walk rather than ride, as we may find more birds along the path than if we ride." Darcy replied to Hurst as if Caroline had not spoken at all. A slight keening wail erupted out of the lady in question and the footman rushed over to refill her wine glass.

Mr. Hurst smiled tightly at the footman in thanks. Louisa continued to cut up the remaining food on her plate into smaller and smaller pieces. Mr. Darcy leaned back slightly and sipped his wine. All three of them missed Charles' cheerful presence.

8:32pm, Wed. Nov. 27, 1811
The Family Sitting Room
Longbourn Manor

"Mrs. Bennet," Mr. Bennet said in a firm, commanding tone as he stepped into the sitting room.

Elizabeth had come to his study to alert him that his wife was making his oldest daughter cry with her harsh complaints about being left at Longbourn while Jane and Elizabeth went to Town.

"Mrs. Bennet, please follow me upstairs to our sitting room. Now, if you please, not in an hour or two, not tomorrow - now." He held the door open.

His wife huffed in anger as she rose from her chair and waved her handkerchief at Jane, whose eyes were puffy and cheeks damp. Jane, Elizabeth, and Lydia had been stitching Jane's trousseau linens as Mrs. Bennet complained in a nonsensical fashion; her tonic was slowly wearing off. All three of his daughters looked at Mr. Bennet with relief. Mrs. Bennet stormed past him and up the stairs. Mr. Bennet smiled at his daughters and said, "There, there, Jane, wipe your tears. I will take care of your mother and soon you and Lizzy will be off to London."

He mounted the stairs even though it was hours before his usual bedtime - he felt weary. How many times did he need to remind Mrs. Bennet what the task was before her? He entered their shared sitting room to find that Mrs. Bennet had thrown herself onto the chaise lounge and was picking at her fingernails. He walked over to the fireplace mantle and turned to face her.

"Mrs. Bennet, do you wish to live in the hedgerows when I pass from this life?" She would not look up at him but started to pick off what appeared to be a piece of loose skin on the edge of her thumb-nail.

"Mrs. Bennet, you may very well travel with your daughters to London next week and stay at your brother's house as they reside for the month at my sister's house but then you will miss your liaisons with Mr. Wickham. The choice at hand is do you maximize your time with your new friend here at the Old Rectory and avoid the hedgerows after my death or do you go to London and assure your-self of the hedgerows?"

Mr. Bennet knew very well that his wife would not live in the hedgerows after his death, as he had saved money beyond her join-ture to assure a relatively comfortable situation if he should pass be-fore her. He would not remind her of this fact, as he needed the leverage to keep her on the straight and narrow. Well, as straight and narrow as conducting an affair with your husband's natural son with his permission could be. Mr. Bennet turned towards the fire so that she could not see him smiling at his own joke.

"At any time, Mrs. Bennet, the Militia could depart Meryton and then where would our plan be? Do you really wish to be replaced as mistress by Mr. Collins' wife? Or do you wish to live out your later years in the household of your son and his family here at Longbourn? Let me know your choice in the morning, as I bid you adieu for the evening." He then left the room and proceeded to his chambers.

He heard her rush up behind him and before he could close the door, she grabbed his arm. She agreed that she would stay in Mery-ton and requested that he arrange for Mr. Wickham to meet her on the morrow. After his wife departed his chambers for hers, he rang for Hill. He requested a hot bath, if it was not too much trouble this late, as he needed a good soak. Bennet felt all the weight of his machinations and he wished to wash them off.

11:49am

Thurs. Nov. 28, 1811

Longbourn's front steps

All of the residents of Longbourn were glad to see the back of Mr. Collin's rented post-chaise kicking up a small plume of dust as it receded down the drive. As the family stood out in the dry, cold sun, Lydia made a few rude noises and remarked, "Lord! Mr. Collins ate us out of breakfast this morning. I for one am glad not to be cooped up inside that small chaise with him!"

Before anyone could reprimand Lydia, Mrs. Bennet moved swiftly back into the house and lamented that Mr. Collins did not extend his promised olive branch to one of her girls. As she was warming to her topic and starting to berate her husband and Lizzy for interfering with her plans to marry Lizzy off to Mr. Collins by diverting him to Lucas Lodge and those artful Lucases, Jane and Elizabeth espied Charlotte Lucas walking towards Longbourn on a side path. Charlotte was beaming in the brisk morning sun, her breath making clouds before her as she walked.

"Look, Charlotte has come!" Elizabeth exclaimed. Jane and Elizabeth walked back out to meet her as the other family members retreated further into the warmth of the house.

Jane reached Charlotte first, "My dear Charlotte, are we to congratulate you on your future felicity in Kent?"

Charlotte smiled broadly and linked her arms with Jane and Elizabeth. "Yes! Jane, our planning has come to fruition: you are engaged to Mr. Bingley and I am, as of yesterday afternoon, engaged to your cousin, Mr. Collins..."

"Charlotte!" Elizabeth gasped, "He is such a man..."

"Eliza, I am not a romantic like you. I am seven and twenty with little dowry and fewer prospects in each new year. Unlike you, I do not expect to be in love before I marry a husband." Elizabeth looked to argue, so Charlotte gently squeezed her arm and kindly said, "Truly, Eliza, he is a respectable man, even if he is foolish and rough around the edges, with a living and a house of his own. Mr. Collins is in want of some domestic and social education, which I find that I can well supply him in exchange for a good situation: a home of my own and a few hens."

Elizabeth opened her mouth to further protest, when Jane quipped, "Why Charlotte, you can be the Hunsford henwife!"

"Indeed! In time, Mr. Collins will be hen pecked." Charlotte and Jane laughed with great vigor and not some small amount of relief.

A disconcerted Elizabeth attempted to push down her keen disappointment at the realization that they had both planned this outcome. She unlinked her arm from Charlotte's and opened the door of Longbourn. She did not relish the thought of her mother's diatribes on the subject. Jane and Charlotte continued upstairs to Jane's chamber to have a nice, long chat about their engagements and help formulate their plans. Elizabeth walked to the nearest footman and requested that tea be sent to her in the library, wherein she found Lydia studying and taking notes.

Elizabeth sat down where she would not be a distraction to Lydia and opened her new novel that she had left on a side table. Rather than reading, Elizabeth found herself sipping her tea and contemplating the surprise that Jane and Charlotte planned sometime in the past weeks to get engaged. Why would they plan it rather than let love take its course? Is it not better to allow yourself to have faith that Providence knows better than you? She picked back up her book, *Sense and Sensibility* by A Lady. Before this past month she would have aligned herself with sense - as she is a mathematician - or was Charlotte right and she had fallen in love with sensibility? To her further astonishment, Mr. Darcy kept creeping into her thoughts of love and future marriage.

3:30pm or thereabouts
  Thurs. Nov. 28, 1811
  On the path between Meryton & Longbourn
The militia's duties, trumped up as they are at this time of year while in their winter quarters, were over by noon allowing the officers to decamp to the public room at the Inn. Mr. George Wickham allowed himself two pints of ale nursed over three hours as well as purchasing some bread and cheese. When he received his note from Bennet requesting that he come at sunset - a full four hours early - to the Old Rectory, Wickham had high hopes that Mrs. Bennet would also feed him a fine dinner. The money she had palmed him two nights ago had already been spent to pay off his room and board balance with Mrs. Preece.

How he despised Mrs. Preece's rules and regulations! That woman would be more successful at running the militia regiment than Colonel Forster. Wickham couldn't decide if he despised Mrs. Preece's favored officer, the seemingly prim and pure Ensign Turner, or not. Wickham was rather astonished at Turner's ability to at all times appear prim, well-regulated with Mrs. Preece and his upper officers all the while Turner was a very dirty little bird behind closed doors. Wickham knew that he himself was a true proficient in charming people when he first met them, but he did not have Turner's ability to appear so very good and then be so very bad. Wickham found that he was not able to keep up the appearance of goodness over time, as he tended to slip up and lose the faith and trust of the people he had first charmed.

When Lady Catherine de Bourgh visited Pemberley during Wickham' boyhood, she would point out to him that he would need to be a man of his word and to stop telling so many little lies. More importantly, she would assert, he would need to be one man all the way through - a man of good, steady character. Lady Catherine would eviscerate Turner if she knew him. The thought made him smile.

As Wickham walked from the Inn towards the Old Rectory for this evening's rendezvous, he found himself thinking about Lady Catherine's advice. Was it possible for him to learn how to be a man of character? To be a man worthy of others' trust? To be a steady man who could achieve and keep that trust?

For years he had thought that being a man of good character was an accident of birth; if one was born to a good family and with an estate to inherit like Darcy, then being a man of your word and trustworthy was easy. But if one was born like Wickham, some man's natural son passed off as a steward's son, who would have to make his own way in the world if he wanted to attain the title of gentleman, then the prescriptions in the Scripture and moral teachings were useless. While his mother was of the lesser gentry, his father - old man Wickman - had been a solicitor and a steward. Wickham perceived as a young boy that he would need to charm, tell petty lies, and scratch his way into a better life if he did not want to be a steward.

Wickham wrapped his red coat closer and wished that he had brought his greatcoat. The brightness of the sun had tricked him into thinking it was warmer. The fields were plucked and empty, tilled waiting for spring. The trees and hedges were mostly bare with the exception of a few evergreens here and there. Wickham feared that he had reached the late autumn of his own life, even though he was only six and twenty. He berated himself as he walked. He should have studied harder at Cambridge rather than living a fast life. He should have taken the living at Kympton and then worked at becoming a good man and a good shepherd of the flock. He should have stayed at the Inns of the Court and actually studied the law. He should not have schemed with Mrs. Young to elope with Georgiana Darcy.

The lack of attention to his education and his taking the money in lieu of living were merely poor decisions made by a young man without a father's guidance, though his mother tried to warn him. But last summer's fiasco at Ramsgate was the straw that may have broken Wickham's proverbial back. His mother's new husband, Sir Thurston Hurst, made her break all contact with him. His godfather was dead, his godfather's son was more likely to challenge him to a duel over Georgiana then to help Wickham to figure out what to do next.

Wickman paused in his walk at a small stream to see if any fish were flitting about; it was too cold for even the fry to be darting about. He considered that a duel with Darcy would have solved all of Wickham's problems, as he would have never shot Darcy. How could he have been so stupid and so greedy to have so thoroughly destroyed his one good connection? He was fooling himself even now: a good connection? Nay, the one good friend of his childhood. Wickham kicked a stone out of the path and declared himself a fool.

What was he thinking even now? He was off to have a paid affair with a gentleman's wife? What would he do with the money if Mrs. Bennet gave birth to a son? If he had pissed away four thousand pounds in less than two or three years, did he think he could really save and make a good life on two thousand pounds? Wickham laughed at himself. He wouldn't even know where to start.

Then Wickham remembered what Turner told them in the public room at the Inn today. He was stepping out with one of the maids from Netherfield and they met up this morning. Wherein Turner's girl related that Miss Bingley not only had a dowry of twenty thousand pounds but was a wine sot to boot. According to Turner, the maid - Nan - told him that Miss Bingley got falling down drunk on wine and sherry nearly every night. Allegedly, last night she drank so much before and at dinner that she put a clean chamber pot on her head and walked into the drawing room after dinner trying to get Darcy to pay attention to her. Turner seemed to think that any of the officers who could get Miss Bingley drunk could compromise her and end up married to twenty thousand pounds.

Wickham would not lie to himself. He thought long and hard on the prospect as he nursed his second ale of the afternoon. Miss Bingley was a fine looking woman, if you liked them tall and spare with a flare for fashion, but she was rumored to be a shrew. He had not actually yet made the acquaintance of the lady himself, as he had been too busy with Mrs. Bennet to attend the ball two nights ago, but he had seen Miss Bingley out at the shops in Meryton once last week. The more he thought about it, the more he realized that the both of them could not live on the proceeds of her dowry as she appeared to be the type of woman who would overrun her allowance on clothes alone. No, it would be a disaster.

Wickham was by his estimation over halfway to the Old Rectory and the sun was close to setting. No, he must stay this course he had set himself on these past two weeks. Perhaps he could attend church on Sunday and make a habit of it. Perhaps the kindly old rector at the Longbourn Church could give him some advice on not how to start but how to continue to have good character over time, rather than just the appearance of it. Then he laughed at himself! What witchery did these woods and fields contain that he, George Wickham, was thinking of regular church attendance?!

Further into the woods that bordered Longbourn village and Netherfield, he could hear gunshots and voices. Hunters. Good thing that he was wearing his red coat, hopefully they would see him and not take him for a brace of pheasant in this half light.

Such maudlin thoughts for a man who is about to enjoy the delightful company of a beautiful woman! Snap out of it, George.

———— ◦◉◦ ————

4:00pm

Thurs. Nov. 28, 1811
The woods adjacent to the Old Rectory

"Hurst, the sun is nearly set and we will have less than a half hour before full dark. I think three brace of birds is sufficient. Let us hasten back to Netherfield." Mr. Darcy thought if necessary they could walk to Longbourn and ask for a torch to take with them on their walk back. Though the moon was nearly full and once the sun set, the moon should light their way nicely as the day had been clear and cold with no clouds.

Hurst assented and whistled to the dogs to follow them. The path out of the wood took them by the Old Rectory, where they saw a man walking up to the side door. They watched Lt. George Wickham extract a key from his pocket and let himself in. Hurst pointed and asked, "Darcy, is that not your old friend, Mr. Wickham, walking into the Old Rectory?"

While Hurst was a good four or five years older than Wickham, he had attended Cambridge and knew Wickham by reputation and from a few unsavory adventures with mutual friends in London. He did not like the man. Hurst stopped under the canopy of an old yew tree on the edge of the wood, he put out his hand to stop Darcy as well. Hurst then indicated that they should both be silent.

No more than three minutes after Mr. Wickham entered the Old Rectory, a woman wearing a dark cloak with its hood up walked into the Old Rectory's yard. An older servant followed her with a large basket. Hurst's eyebrow raised, "Is that not Longbourn's butler, Mr. Hill? And if I am not incorrect, that appears to be Mrs. Bennet entering the Old Rectory."

Darcy said nothing. The sun had set, dusk deepened as they waited. Hurst indicated that they should walk back. As they skirted the wood and walked on the path back to Netherfield, the moon's light filled their silence with enough light to see the path. When they could see the lights of Netherfield not more than a quarter mile ahead, Hurst slowed down his pace and stopped.

"Darcy, I do not think my nine and eighty year old grandfather really sired his new son with the new Lady Hurst. Has not Lady Hurst been an old friend of your Aunt Lady Catherine de Bourgh for many years?"

"Yes, since my childhood."

"Was not Mr. Bennet the vicar at Pemberley before he inherited Longbourn?"

"Yes, he was the vicar when I was a small child."

"Now that I have had time to think about it, do you remember when we had dinner at Longbourn a few weeks ago? After dinner, I studied the Bennet family painting in Mr. Bennet's study?"

Darcy did not reply to Hurst's inquiry.

"Darcy, I have a good memory for things I see. Mr. Bennet's older brother looks just like Mr. Wickham."

Darcy grunted in a non-reply.

Hurst continued to block the path and their dogs, anxious for their dinner, whined as they heeled at their masters' feet. "Darcy, my grandfather's letters this past year had great praise for the hospitality that Lady Catherine de Bourgh and Mr. Bennet showed him and Lady Hurst when they first went to London after their honeymoon. I think that Mr. Bennet fathered my new uncle."

With this pronouncement, Hurst unblocked the path and started walking towards a warm house and dinner. Darcy did not say a word. Just before they walked into the game room at the back of the house to hang the birds, Hurst said in a low voice, "I suppose I would be a great deal more worried about this if my wife had not allowed me back into her chamber two nights ago. Now, I have hope that we will anticipate the Hurst heir soon."

Darcy opened the door to the game room.

Hurst smiled and held up his brace of birds. "This was a good day of shooting, look at these fine birds."

Chapter 12: To London

Late Morning
Mon. Dec. 2, 1811
The London Road

Elizabeth was not quite sure what machinations her father was up to now, but she, Jane, and their maid were riding to London in Mr. Darcy's grand coach, as her father, Mr. Bingley, and Mr. Darcy rode alongside the carriage. The Hurst's carriage followed them. At the last change of horses at a coaching inn on the main London road, Miss Bingley was furious at Elizabeth and carried on in the private salon that Mr. Darcy had arranged for them to seek refreshment in. Elizabeth took care of what was necessary, drank a spot of hot tea, and followed her father out to the public room to avoid Miss Bingley's acid insults.

Elizabeth was quite sure that these travel arrangements were a collusion between her father, Mr. Bingley, and Mr. Darcy while they went out shooting this past Saturday morning, or perhaps this plan was concocted over after drinks at Saturday evening's engagement celebration dinner at Longbourn. Jane merely smiled as she watched Mr. Bingley ride outside of her window, and he frequently smiled back. Jane was so wrapped up in watching Mr. Bingley that Elizabeth had given up any attempts at conversation.

Elizabeth shifted her position on the fine, plush coach seats. She could see Mr. Darcy and her father quite clearly from her window, they were laughing. Mr. Darcy was quite handsome when he smiled. Elizabeth shifted in her seat again, as she began to wonder when Mr. Darcy went from proud and above his company to easily pleased and very nearly open and liberal in his manners.

This was the third time she had been in Mr. Darcy's company since the ball six days prior. The more he smiled at her, the more acidic Miss Bingley's comments became. Elizabeth mused that there was a direct correlation. She wondered if she could concoct a unified theory of Caroline Bingley using a portion of that direct correlation plus ostrich feathers dyed orange minus some algebraic equation solving for x wherein x involved wine consumption. Miss Bingley was not complex enough to warrant a derivative equation.

Elizabeth laughed at her own silliness. Mr. Darcy caught her eye and smiled at her. *Oh, I was not handsome enough to tempt the man in October, but now he is smiling at me. He is a riddle wrapped in a conundrum worthy of not only a derivative equation, but perhaps an integral one as well.* She laughed and through the window he smiled. Elizabeth raised her eyebrow at the man. He raised his back.

The Darcy coach and riders arrived at Beauchamp House in St. James' Square at a quarter to two. Lord and Lady Beauchamp were waiting to greet the Bennets, as well as Mr. Darcy and Mr. Bingley. Much to everyone's relief, the Hurst carriage had turned off on their own route a few streets earlier. Lady Elizabeth Bennet Beauchamp was glad to see her brother and her nieces. After a short greeting and well wishes, Mr. Bingley and Mr. Darcy departed on their horses. It was a bit more time for Mr. Darcy's coach to follow, as the ladies' trunks needed to be unloaded.

Elizabeth was vastly relieved to be in London at her Aunt's house. For many years, she heartily wished that her father's sister was her real mother and that the Bennets were only fostering her. She looked most like her Aunt Elizabeth and her departed Grandmother Bennet - so much so that in London people assumed that Elizabeth was Lady Beauchamp's daughter. They were of the same stature and figure, both had dark auburn brown hair - albeit Lady Beauchamp's was now shot with silver - and dark sea blue eyes. Most comforting of all, her London aunts, Lady Beauchamp and Mrs. Gardiner, understood her in a way that her mother did not.

On arrival at the guest chamber that she always stayed in, Elizabeth found two cheerfully wrapped parcels on the dressing table. Bewildered, she saw a note propped up against the parcels. Upon opening the note, she nearly burst into tears when she read:

Dearest Lizzy,

Please forgive me for ruining your new silk pelisse. I have asked our Aunt to have another one made for winter that matches, as close as can be, to the pelisse I ruined with my Agincourt knight embroidery. There is also a second one for spring that will be perfect for your morning calls during the Season.

I am grateful to Providence for your sisterly affection and fidelity, not just this past summer and autumn when I hated to be back in Meryton but also the eight years we attended school and then university together. Thank you for your friendship, I look forward to sharing this next stage of our lives together as I get married to Mr. Bingley and you have a divine and joyous Season in London.

Yrs. in love and sisterly affection always,

Jane

When she looked up from her note, Jane was standing shyly in the doorway. "Lizzy, do you forgive me? I am sorry I was so thoughtless."

"I do, Jane. I do." They embraced.

"Lizzy, you have not even opened your parcels!"

At Jane's encouragement, Elizabeth opened the top parcel and found an exact matching Chinese silk pelisse in a winter weight. She tried it on and it fit perfectly. She then opened the second package and found a lovely lighter weight silk pelisse in a jaunty spring apricot color trimmed with a subtle ivory lace at the cuffs and hemline. Jane made her try it on and it looked wonderful.

"Oh, Jane! Thank you!"

"No, Lizzy, you must not thank me but forgive me for the state I had worked myself into before Mr. Bingley asked for my hand. I was wrong."

"Jane, you are too good." They both laughed as they sat down and found that they were able to talk, at length, about what their true hopes were in a way that they had not been able to for a number of months. Just before they were called downstairs for tea, Jane started to tease Elizabeth about Mr. Darcy.

"Oh no, Jane, Mr. Darcy is only lightly flirting with me. Remember, I am only tolerable but not handsome enough to tempt him!" Elizabeth attempted to mimic his deep voice but failed, which sent both into laughter as they walked down the stairs to visit with their relations. Both were greatly relieved to be away from Longbourn and safely in London.

Tues. Dec. 3, 1811
   Lady Beauchamp's Sitting Room
   Beauchamp House
   London

After breakfast, Lord Beauchamp and Mr. Bennet decamped for his lordship's club, while the ladies moved upstairs to her ladyship's sitting room to strategize planning of Jane and Elizabeth's three weeks in London, as well as Jane's wedding. While Mrs. Bennet would have the pleasure of arranging the wedding breakfast for the morning of the 23rd of December at Longbourn, Lady Beauchamp and Mrs. Gardiner would arrange everything else in and from London.

To Jane's great delight as a future bride, everything else was her trousseau, shopping, looking through family heirlooms for which she would take with her to her new house, dinners, and a ball that the

Beauchamp's would hold to celebrate the engagement between their niece and Mr. Bingley. Jane and her Aunt had already exchanged letters with lists of what Jane currently had in her trousseau trunk and what she needed to obtain. Elizabeth was once again surprised that her sister's planning of her wedding pre-dated her meeting Mr. Bingley.

Her Aunt Beauchamp smiled and said, "Elizabeth, you must not be surprised. Many young women begin sewing for their trousseau when they are quite young. I imagine that many of the girls you went to school with were already working on theirs." Elizabeth nodded. "You and Jane, knowing you were to go on to university, did not spend your free time stitching but studying for your entrance exams. Then there is college life, too much to be done in too little time - even for heavily chaperoned young lady scholars."

Both Jane and Elizabeth laughed at their aunt's quip, who then winked at Elizabeth. "And if yesterday's short greetings were any indications, you, Miss Elizabeth Bennet, will not hold that name for long."

"Oh no, Aunt Elizabeth, Mr. Darcy is just flirting. He has been very careful to not raise any expectations."

"Oh, pish posh! I have known Fitzwilliam Darcy since he was in leading strings! If you will remember, Pemberley is less than three hours from Dove Dale estate and we were great friends with his parents. I have never seen him look at a woman the way his eyes followed your every move yesterday." Before Elizabeth could protest, her aunt said, "I will wager twenty pounds that you will be engaged to Mr. Darcy before the end of the season. Now, that is in the future, Jane has less than three weeks to complete her trousseau, so let us bring our attention to our lists." Aunt Beauchamp held up her lists and waved them about.

"Jane, as I promised, I have over on the sewing table three different place settings of silver and plates and goblets that have come to me from my mother and grandmother Bennet. My three sons have no need for such things, and Lady Judith brought her own to her marriage to Anthony." Aunt Beauchamp rose and led Jane and Elizabeth to look at the settings.

"Now the gilded shell and floral patterned china plates were my mother's; as you can see they are very apropos to her era of the late 1740s. The more sedate greco-roman key pattern china was purchased by my mother's mother as a wedding gift for me, but we rarely use it. And the simple but beautiful bone china with the gilded edges came with my grandmother Lady Phoebe Howard to her marriage. As you can see each set of silver matches. Which one will suit you to take to your new house, Jane?"

"Oh, Aunt, they are all so beautiful. I do love the shell and floral plate, it is a bit more ornate than one would like now but it was my grandmother's and I shall cherish it. Thank you for saving it." Jane was overcome with happiness. "Mr. Bingley's sister, Mrs. Hurst, has her mother's plate and silver. Miss Bingley has purchased new as she wanted the most modern place settings for her trousseau. I will be happy to have my grandmother's wedding plates and silver grace my table at dinners."

"Elizabeth, which of the two left would you like?"

"Aunt, I would like great-grandmother Phoebe's bone china with the gold rims. How have you kept a complete collection of plates and silver that are nearly one hundred years old?"

"Contrary to your mother's belief that I cannot find a good deal, I have one of our footmen scour the markets and other interesting little shops here and there to look for and purchase pieces out of the six dinner and tea sets that I have between London and Derbyshire. Thus, if a guest or a scullery maid breaks a piece, it is not a tragedy as I have replacements. You may even accuse me of being artful as when we have not been able to find a replacement, your Uncle Gardiner has a man with a bone china pottery in the midlands who is able to

recreate pieces for me. I have a full thirty place settings for each set."
Aunt Beauchamp was quite pleased to confess her methods. "Which
is six more settings than I can seat in the long dining room at Dove
Dale."

Elizabeth then asked, "But what about my other three sisters?
Should they not have an opportunity to choose? Or will you save
them for Andrew and Augustus' future wives?"

Aunt Beauchamp shook her head. "Andrew is too busy with
Wellington to marry. You heard last night that Augustus has been
made a Captain in the Navy. He is on leave while they find a seawor-
thy ship for him, so he will turn up here sooner or later. He claims
he won't marry until Napoleon has been routed." Both Elizabeth and
Jane laughed at their Aunt's description of her two youngest sons.
"Your sister Mary has already declared that she does not want any of
these heirlooms for a dinner party, as she plans to marry an Oxford
theologian and any fine dining they will do will be done in the college's dining halls. Kitty saw the place settings recently and declared
she would like to buy new. Do you think Lydia would like the greek
style key pattern, now that she plans to be a grand London barrister?"

Jane agreed. "I do think Lydia will like it. She has grown up into a
rather wonderful young lady this autumn. I hate to say it, but I think
getting expelled from school was good for her."

"Then I will save it for her. Jane, would you like the ornate tea
and coffee set that goes with the floral and shell pattern?" Jane nodded. "I imagine that we should also have your Aunt Gardiner take
us to some of the warehouses near your uncle's so that we can also
find a nice silver tea and coffee service in a modern pattern as well.
Speaking of which, I have asked Mrs. Gardiner if we may visit those
warehouses tomorrow after breakfast and look at what the drapers
on Gracechurch Street have in the way of silks. The prices will be
much better than on Bond Street."

As the planning session continued, Elizabeth ceased to be surprised at each decision her Aunt asked Jane to make; she also asked for and noted Elizabeth's preferences. "Not only do we have to prepare you for the Season, but we should also be preparing your trousseau trunk as well."

By the time tea was brought up, each day of the next two weeks was completely planned out and it appeared that as Jane started having her wedding clothes made, Elizabeth would be visiting the modiste for her upcoming Season. Elizabeth was not shocked but surprised to hear that her father had asked his sister to outfit Elizabeth not just for the Season but also for her future marriage. It was all happening a bit too fast for Elizabeth's tastes, but it was better to get it over with than spend all of January and February fretting over it. Aunt Beauchamp told them that they would worry about their presentation gowns in January after Twelfth Night and after Jane returned from her wedding trip.

"Aunt, we have not spoken of the wedding trip at any length, but Charles and I would like to take the time between Christmas and Twelfth Night to ourselves and then travel to his relations in Yorkshire after the Season."

"Jane, whatever you do, don't spend those two weeks after your wedding at Netherfield Park, as our mother will invade your privacy each and every day if you do," Aunt Beauchamp said with a mocking seriousness. Elizabeth laughed at the look of horror on her sister's face. All three ladies laughed at the very idea.

"Your father's good friend, Lady Catherine, will be holding a dinner party in your honor, Jane, this Friday evening for a select group of family. The engagement ball will be held here on Thursday the Twelfth of December. We have much to accomplish, as well as some strategic social calls to make - mostly to our extended relations." Aunt Beauchamp's face lit up with a rather energetic smile. She then hugged both of them, "For many years, I lamented my lack

of a daughter. Now I have you two. I hope you are excited, as I am to
be launching both of you lovely ladies into society!"

Late afternoon
    Thurs. Dec. 5, 1811
    A dark corner at a Gentlemen's Club
    Mayfair, London

Colonel Fitzwilliam was sitting in a dark corner at the club his
father had belonged to for years nursing a brand new grudge with
a glass of not-so-great brandy. The day had dawned quite fair for
Colonel Fitzwilliam. He had joined his father and his cousin Bennet
at Tattersall's with the newly commissioned Captain Horatio Denny
of the Horse Guards to help Denny pick out the best horse possible
within his price range. All four men had a delightful time inspecting
the horses, participating in the auction, and enjoying each other's
company. His father and Mr. Bennet surprised Denny by purchasing
him a fine charger.

It was a grand morning until he ran into some friend's of Bingley
and Hurst's on his way back from Tattersall's in Hyde Park corner.
These gentlemen were gossiping about Bingley's engagement and
wanted to know if it was true that his cousin, Miss Bennet, really was
an angel. The Colonel opined that while Bingley's Miss Bennet was
a classic beauty, it was her next sister, Miss Elizabeth, who was the
true gem of the family. One of Bingley's idiot friends then joked that
for a twenty thousand pound dowry combined with a classical beauty in one woman who was also said to be an angel there would be
no complaints from him. Everyone laughed at this on-dit except the
Colonel.

Hours and not a few drinks later, the Colonel was in no shape
to return home for dinner. He had some thinking and planning to
do. Why would his cousin Bennet outright lie about Miss Eliza-

beth's dowry? What he told Bingley's friends was true, of all the Bennet daughters, Miss Elizabeth was the true gem. Bennet had already turned down the Colonel's suit once and now Miss Elizabeth was to come out into society.

If he was honest with himself, he was not in love with his cousin Elizabeth, as he had rarely been in company with her these last four years. No, it was the fact that she was several cuts above the usual young lady that various mothers were foisting off on him in terms of her beauty, her mind, and now her potential dowry. Miss Elizabeth Bennet would be the sort of woman a man with any intelligence would want to come home to, not stay at his club drinking through dinner.

What did Bennet see in him, that would make his cousin lie about Miss Elizabeth's true dowry? Was it that he had attempted to negotiate the dowry up to thirty thousand? Why he, the son of an Earl, could not possibly live on a penny less than the interest from a thirty thousand pound dowry on top of the proceeds of his half-pay and the rents from the small estate he inherited from his grandmother. Why did Bennet outright lie in October and say that Miss Elizabeth's dowry was only five thousand?

Did not Bennet wish for a closer connection to the Earl of Matlock? Hmmph!

The Colonel glared at his nearly empty glass.

The hour before dinner
　Fri., Dec. 6, 1811
　The de Bourgh Townhouse
　Mayfair, London
"When did little Auggie Beauchamp grow into such a round, firm rear? I must go over and compliment him at once!" Not that Captain Augustus Beauchamp had grown much taller since the last

time any of the party had seen him, but he had filled out. Any thoughts of the superiority of the first circles of London over the vulgar and savage inhabitants of Meryton vanished in an instance when Mr. Fitzwilliam Darcy's youngest and tallest Fitzwilliam cousin, Lt. Howard Fitzwilliam of His Majesty's Royal Navy made the loud declaration at the entrance of his Aunt Catherine's drawing room.

Darcy's young sister, Miss Georgiana Darcy, was agape at the spectacle their cousin had just created. Darcy sighed and led Georgiana further into the drawing room full of relations assembled to celebrate Miss Jane Bennet's engagement to Mr. Charles Bingley.

The youngest son of the Beauchamp family was standing with his back to the drawing room doors talking to a resplendently overdressed Miss Bingley, who had been fawning under the attentions of such a handsome naval officer who was also the son of a prominent Derbyshire baron. In a moment, Darcy determined that Lt. Fitzwilliam and the Darcys were the last to arrive. Darcy could see that three Beauchamps, three Bennets, all the Fitzwilliams, both the Bingleys, both the Hursts, the de Bourghs, and a couple that he assumed were the Gardiners were in attendance and that other than the aforementioned Miss Bingley and Captain Beauchamp, the whole of the room had turned towards the entrance and the rather loud Lt. Howard Fitzwilliam.

Darcy's cousin Lady Helena Fitzwilliam, closest to the door, sighed and told her younger brother to keep it to himself. Lord Lindon, the eldest of the Fitzwilliam siblings, walked over to his youngest sibling and clapped him on the back. "Howie, it has been some time. When did the tide wash you up? Walk over with me and I will re-introduce you to Miss Bingley and Captain Beauchamp."

Lady Catherine came forward and ushered Darcy and Georgiana over to greet the Beauchamps, the Bennets, and the Gardiners. As Georgiana shyly extended her hand to Miss Bennet and Miss Elizabeth, Darcy found himself shaking the hands of Lord Beauchamp and Mr. Gardiner. Lord and Lady Beauchamp moved over to greet Georgiana, Darcy found himself facing a very pretty and elegant Miss Elizabeth.

Upon arriving to his London home earlier in the week, Darcy had a long talking to himself—wherein he determined that as delightful, clever, and perfect as Miss Elizabeth Bennet was –he could not court nor marry her due to the situation of her mother's family, the total want of propriety betrayed by her mother and youngest sister, and even on occasion by her father. Not on occasion, Mr. Bennet had proven himself a mastermind in scheming new improprieties. Darcy had determined that for the sake of his sister, the Darcy name, and the larger Fitzwilliam clan, that he could not and would not succumb to Miss Elizabeth's charms. Until now.

Darcy listened as the whole room erupted into levels of noise that would have made fifty Mrs. Bennet's and Mrs. Philips' proud. To his horror, it was his relations - the honorable, noble Fitzwilliams and de Bourghs who were creating the most of the clamor. Before him, quiet and smiling was Miss Elizabeth who was everything lovely. Darcy smiled, took her hand, and raised it to his lips as more tumult appeared in the form of Colonel Fitzwilliam.

"Now, Darcy, keep your hands and lips off Miss Elizabeth who I have singled out as the companion of my future life!" Darcy could be excused for first thinking that his favorite cousin was teasing him, but less than a second of looking into the Colonel's eyes, he could see that the Colonel was very serious.

Miss Elizabeth lowered her hand and gasped at the Colonel, "You are too hasty, Sir! Neither we, nor our families, have any such agreement between us and nor shall they."

Darcy was too astounded to speak, but in turn was astonished at how fast the Colonel switched from defender of his alleged claim of the lady to all that was amiable and charming to the lady. Miss Elizabeth stepped back and turned to draw in her aunt to defuse the tension, "Mr. Darcy and Colonel Fitzwilliam, have you met my aunt, Mrs. Gardiner?"

At the sound of a bubbling giggle, Darcy looked up to see that his youngest Fitzwilliam cousin was now flirting with Miss Bingley while his hand was patting Captain Beauchamp's rear. On the other side of the room, he could hear his Aunt Catherine exclaiming to anyone who would listen that she had planned the engagement of Darcy to her daughter Anne from their cradles and now Anne had ruined it all by entering into a courtship with some Cambridge scholar from a no-name country squire's family in Scotland - all the while Anne and Mr. Turing stood before her, Lady Helena, and the Hursts. From another corner, Darcy saw Lord Lindon pound Bingley on the back proclaiming him a lucky man to secure the affections of his cousin, Miss Bennet, and if Bingley didn't watch it he, Lord Lindon, would steal her out from under his nose. Bingley looked rather panicked as Lord Lindon brayed in laughter and winked at Miss Bennet as he stared down at her bosom.

Before a word could escape Darcy, Elizabeth expertly changed the subject. "Mr. Darcy, my aunt Gardiner spent some time in her youth in Lambton."

As Darcy was formulating a reply, the Colonel started expounding on the many beauties of Derbyshire to Elizabeth and Mrs. Gardiner. In a work of a moment, Lord Matlock, his father came over to claim the Colonel for another conversation. Darcy, to his relief, was left to quietly converse with the two ladies until dinner was announced. Darcy offered his arm to escort Miss Elizabeth into the dining room as she tilted her head up to him with a welcoming smile gracing her face.

After Mr. Darcy helped Elizabeth into her seat in the large formal dining room and sat down across from her, she could only laugh, to herself, at Lady Catherine's antics to rearrange the seating at the dinner table with all of its leaves extended to suit her notion of rank, good conversation, and family members not sitting next to or across from each other. Given that nearly everyone at the dinner was related to each other, with the exception of the Bingleys and the Gardiners - of whom Lady Catherine now knew to be related to each other - it took over 10 minutes of sitting, standing, moving, and sitting again before the first course and soup could be served. Miss Darcy, Mr. Bingley, Captain Beauchamp, Jane, and Lord Lindon were moved up to three times.

Eventually, Elizabeth found herself sitting between her cousin Anne de Bourgh and her cousin Lord Lindon with Mr. Darcy remaining opposite from her; her uncle Gardiner was opposite Anne, next to Mr. Darcy, which allowed for a delightful dinner conversation on how theoretical mathematics could be applied to business and trade.

Anne's beau, Mr. Turing, argued for a more pure mathematical approach to the funds and stock exchange. Mr. Gardiner and Mr. Darcy were appalled. Anne and Elizabeth argued for a more level approach wherein newer mathematical theories would be applied in small controlled situations. Lady Catherine, three seats away at the head of the table, had to shush them several times when the debate got too heated. Although, she was not able to shush the uproar at the foot of the table wherein her son, Lewis, was presiding over the young Fitzwilliams, Lady and Captain Beauchamp, and Miss Bingley. Elizabeth observed that Sir Lewis was in no way prepared for a tipsy Miss Bingley.

As dinner progressed, Lord Lindon attempted to lighten the mathematics versus business debate by making arguments for increased canals and road infrastructure to be made by floating equal shares between investors and the government wherein half the dividends would go to the investors and half to an education fund so that all young people would have an equal state funded education up to age 16.

This did not lighten the debate as Mr. Gardiner then asked who would invest in such a pool. Lord Lindon argued that farming hands, maids, and factory workers all needed to know how to read and write and do their sums. Eventually, Mrs. Gardiner on his other side was able to get him to speak to her about the trial school he had set up in Matlock. From there Mrs. Gardiner and Lord Lindon spoke on the glories of Derbyshire through the whole of the second course, much to the relief of those within the hearing range of Lord Lindon's booming voice - which was the whole of the table and the servants in the rooms surrounding the dining room.

Each time Mr. Darcy would challenge one of Elizabeth's assertions with a smile or a grin, Elizabeth would raise a brow at him. Across the table and down on the other end, she would occasionally see - to her amusement - Colonel Fitzwilliam leaning around Miss Bingley to wink at her. She was relieved that the Colonel was so far down the table, as before dinner she had felt a bit trapped by his aggressive flirting. Earlier that day, her father had warned her that while the Colonel was an amiable relation who was well liked in London, the truth of the matter was the man was a fortune hunter. Mr. Bennet had assured Elizabeth that he could not approve of a man who sought Elizabeth's fortune before her mind and character.

More laughter and delightful conversation as the third course was served, Elizabeth found herself smiling more at Mr. Darcy. And to her surprise she found him smiling in return. She would be honest with herself and admit that she was warming to the man. His manners had improved these past weeks and much to her dismay- in light of her previous prejudice - she was beginning to find his clever mind and wide knowledge of the world refreshing and enchanting.

Towards the end of the third course, Lady Catherine called for all wine glasses to be refilled and she rose to propose a toast. "I would like to thank all of you in joining me to celebrate and toast to the engagement of the accomplished Miss Jane Bennet to the estimable Mr. Charles Bingley. Before we toast, I would like all of us to reflect on the wonders of a university education for both sexes and how a shared bachelor's degree in military history has been the means to unite this young couple before us..."

While Lady Catherine expounded on the need for persons of elevated rank to be equal in consequence and education prior to marriage, as well as her thoughts on the advancement of females in the professions, most of the table had to have their glasses refilled before the toast was actually made in honor of Miss Jane Bennet and Mr. Charles Bingley's future felicity. To Colonel Fitzwilliam's mild horror, Miss Bingley drank two full glasses of wine in the five or so minutes it took his Aunt Catherine to get to the point. Not much later, he could feel a finger tracing up his thigh and it was not his own...

Chapter 13 : Of Swords and Scabbards

---⟨∾⟩---

Thurs. Dec. 12, 1811, 7:48pm
Beauchamp House
London

Miss Jane Bennet sat at her dressing table as her Aunt Beauchamp's abigail put the final touches on her hair. After a final smoothing of a wayward curl, she dusted Jane's nose and forehead with a little powder. Jane profusely thanked the maid, who departed leaving Jane alone with her nerves.

Jane waited for the door to click shut before leaning in to inspect her appearance. To her surprise, she found that she was as lovely as her mother frequently proclaimed her to be and hopefully she could be as elegant as her Aunt Beauchamp this evening. Jane's fears of exposure at tonight's engagement ball had increased over the course of the past week's trousseau shopping and walking in Hyde Park during the fashionable hour with Charles. Each encounter with one of the overly friendly young men from her Oxford days did not end in the disaster of exposure that she feared.

Much to Jane's subdued surprise, each young man was terribly sad to find out she was engaged to be married before her first Season in London, they would then compliment Charles on his good fortune. Instead of questioning Jane on why so many enthusiastic young men knew her, Charles became more and more convinced that he had made the right decision to ask her to marry him after such a short acquaintance before his angel was stolen away from him during the upcoming Season. As the news of her engagement spread amongst the Oxford set, Charles' pleasure increased and Jane's fear of exposure grew out of proportion to the reality of the young men's courtesy to her.

Jane found herself in tears yesterday afternoon upon returning home from the latest shopping expedition. Aunt Beauchamp followed Jane into her room and with the application of tea, small cakes, and well placed questions, pried the whole story out of Jane. As Jane expressed her terror at Charles discovering her wanton past, Aunt Beauchamp firmly told her, "Jane, after seeing your Mr. Bingley puff up in the pleasure that he won the prize all the Oxford men desired, you need not worry. Men like it when other men admire their wives."

Jane had burst into more tears, "Aunt, they did not merely admire, they kissed and touched!"

"Pish posh! Who has not kissed a few or more frogs before choosing one's prince? Besides, practice does add to one's proficiencies." Aunt Beauchamp smiled and winked at her, "Jane, the more you worry the more trouble you will create for yourself. Relax and enjoy this season of your life"

Her aunt's lack of shock or condemnation at her full confession soothed Jane's worries. Additionally, Lizzy had reminded her this afternoon that tonight's engagement ball would mostly be extended family, their grown children, and more than a few of friends thereof. These assurances calmed her.

Jane smiled at her reflection and rose to join her family in a drawing room adjacent to the entrance to the house. Guests would be arriving soon and she would be at the top of the receiving line standing next to her Charles.

Thurs. Dec. 12, 1811, 8:18pm
  The Ballroom
  Beauchamp House

London

The duties of the receiving line were left to the aegis of her father, Jane, Mr. Bingley and Lord and Lady Beauchamp, allowing Miss Elizabeth to wait in the ballroom in the pleasant company of her cousin Captain Augustus Beauchamp, her younger sister Kitty, and the Gardiners as the gaily plumed and very elegant guests arrived. Upon entrance of the Fitzwilliam family, particularly Colonel Fitzwilliam and his younger brother, Lieutenant Fitzwilliam, her cousin Augustus attempted to hide behind her out of the line of sight of the ballroom entrance.

"Cousins Elizabeth and Kitty, I do not want you to think that I lack courage, but Lt. Fitzwilliam is so forceful and looming." Augustus looked about for his escape and he bowed to the ladies. "Please do excuse me."

Elizabeth turned around to look at his retreating back in astonishment as he walked to and bent over the hand of Miss Bingley. She heard a soft sigh from her sister Kitty.

"Our cousin is ever so handsome in his naval uniform." While Kitty was not out to London society until she completed her studies, she was allowed to attend family dinners and in this case her oldest sister's engagement ball. Kitty was to stay by Aunt and Uncle Gardiner's side all evening and only dance with family members, unless her father or her uncle both approved of the dance partner. Given that the ball was mostly extended family of both the future bride and groom, as well as a few particular friends, Elizabeth had great hopes that Kitty would enjoy herself this night.

Elizabeth laughed, "Kitty, do not repine our handsome cousin flitting about and flirting; there are many more fish out in the sea than just our relations. We both have plenty of time in which to meet and dance with handsome young men."

Kitty smiled, "I know, but I can still admire how handsome cousin Auggie has become. Look over there at the Colonel in his regimentals! He is looking for someone."

"Kitty, shush! Do not draw his attention!" Elizabeth hissed, but it was too late. Kitty's animation drew Colonel Fitzwilliam's eye to their party.

"Why ever not? The tall, naval lieutenant next to him is ever so handsome!" Kitty happily waved at both of the Fitzwilliam brothers.

"Kitty!" Elizabeth and Aunt Gardiner both remonstrated at Kitty's forwardness. Elizabeth groaned. Aunt Gardiner whispered to Kitty, "First warning, on the second we will withdraw and depart. You know the rules, we have discussed them at length."

"Miss Elizabeth! Mr. and Mrs. Gardiner!" The Colonel boomed as he bowed and took Elizabeth's hand to kiss it. Mr. Gardiner introduced Miss Kitty Bennet to both gentlemen. Kitty beamed and gushed her happiness at the introduction to the Fitzwilliam brothers. The Colonel acknowledged Miss Kitty with a courtly bow, as his brother inquired, "Where is Auggie?"

The Lieutenant answered his own question when he espied Captain Beauchamp flirting with Miss Bingley not more than ten feet away. "How delightful! Auggie and Caro are just over there." Without a by-your-leave, Lt. Fitzwilliam departed to commence his flirtations.

"He didn't even ask for a dance," Kitty unhappily sighed.

"Miss Kitty, would you do me the honor of a dance this evening?" The Colonel asked. "And Miss Elizabeth, do say you have the supper dance available?"

"Yes! I will dance with you!" Kitty happily rapped the Colonel's arm with her fan. "Which dance would you like? I have the first and the second available."

"Colonel Fitzwilliam, my dance card is quite full. If you wish, I have the fourth available." Elizabeth replied. He need not know, that she worked most of her male relations this week to make sure that her dance card was full and she would not be trapped by this most determined flirt of a man at the supper or last dance. Mr. Darcy had surprised her greatly by requesting the supper and last dances via a note yesterday afternoon. She remained rather baffled by that man's vacillating behavior, but she much preferred his aloof diffidence and occasional quiet courting to the Colonel's rather determined flirting.

The Colonel gave the appearance of gentleman-like responses, though his jaw and shoulders were set in harsh lines. "Miss Kitty, I will take the first if your chaperone will allow it." He made a quick bow towards the Gardiners. "And Miss Elizabeth, I would be honored to take the fourth."

Elizabeth doubted the sincerity of his honored reply and braced herself. Since the dinner party at Lady Catherine de Bourgh's last week, the Colonel's courtly, yet overly bold, flirtatious manner had begun to grate on her nerves. He had accomplished the feat of replacing Mr. Darcy out of the position of the second to the last man she would ever marry. The last man was Mr. Collins, who would soon be out of the running altogether.

Miss Caroline Bingley stood towards the rear of the crowded ballroom sipping a glass of wine; if anyone had asked it was only her second glass of wine of the day. The truth of the matter was it was really her third or fourth, possibly fifth, as her first alleged glass of wine was in truth in a pint mug full to the brim that she drank in totality as her ladies' maid prepared for her the ball.

It was her mother who introduced Caroline to taking a small glass of watered down wine to calm her nerves. After her good mother died, Louisa married that rude sot, and then her particular friend Miss Fenimore married and departed the country possibly for life, the small glass of wine gradually grew larger as Caroline faced a greater exposure to society alone. Caroline's private anxieties grew faster than she could consume a calming glass of wine most days and nights. If asked, she could not describe what she was anxious about, merely that she was.

Caroline supposed that she should blame her own driving ambition to move into the highest circles, and yet here she was at a ball hosted by the Lord and Lady Beauchamp of the ancient Derbyshire barony and leaders of the ton. The private ball that was celebrating the engagement of her brother to a niece of that very same family.

The enormity of this step up for the whole of the Bingley family did not give her the intense feelings of joy, relief, and power she had craved ever since she received her first slight and cut for being the mere daughter of a tradesman - no, instead a wave of acute anxiety washed over her this afternoon with great tremblings and fear. The only relief was to be found in a large ale flagon full of wine.

Now as she stood in this ballroom surrounded by the glittering members of the haute ton, on the verge of joining their ranks by dint of her brother's marriage, she was disgusted with herself. Disgusted with her nerves and how large her anxious feelings had grown. Ashamed at the amount of wine she drank daily to calm those nerves. Disgusted with her behavior, be it drunk or sober. Disgusted that for the past two months she had resisted her brother's attachment to a very sweet girl. And that she, Caroline Bingley - the granddaughter of an Irish tinker, had resisted admitting to herself that her chance at attaching herself to Mr. Darcy was diminishing rapidly and by her own fault.

She told herself repeatedly that she must use the opportunity of her brother's marriage to spread her wings past her brother's friend, who - if her eyes and instinct proved correct - would very soon be also attaching himself to the Bennet family.

Caroline sighed as she looked into her empty wine glass and told herself that she must not have another - while she was not swaying or slurring, yet - she knew she was at the line of no return. She turned to a servant and requested a glass of light punch with no brandy. From her vantage point, she could see Captain Beauchamp speaking to his cousins and the Gardiners. She caught his eye and smiled. He winked at her.

She blushed and looked towards the ballroom doors. She could see that Colonel and Lieutenant Fitzwilliam had entered with members of their family behind them. She smiled to herself and reflected that all three military men were younger sons of prominent, powerful noble families whose eldest brothers' had not yet married nor had produced any sons. *There may yet be hope.*

Hope was a powerful incentive fuelling Caroline's ambitions. She considered that Captain Beauchamp was the handsomest of the three, albeit shorter than her by a few inches, and - most importantly - he had as a naval officer had won the larger fortune in prize money and the best future earning potential. Caroline nearly laughed loudly while musing that she would not be her father's daughter if she did not make her plans without some attention to future profits.

To her pleasure, Captain Beauchamp left Miss Elizabeth's company to join hers and then Lt. Fitzwilliam soon joined their small party. Both gentlemen regaled her with amusing and, in Lt. Fitzwilliam's case - titillating, stories of naval life on the high seas. After both men made her laugh enough to forget her determination for no more drinking, Caroline was holding a new glass of wine as she espied the entrance of Mr. Darcy into the ballroom.

While she did not love nor even admire his taciturn disposition, she would make one last attempt to capture Mr. Darcy and his estate Pemberley for herself, before she capitulated and left the field open to Miss Elizabeth.

The naughty Lt. Fitzwilliam shocked her out of her revelry with a brush of his hand along her waist and down her hip to her rear! As she turned to admonish the rogue, he winked and licked his lips.

Oh, my.

After Mr. Bennet had dispatched his duties to dance the first two sets with his two eldest daughters but before the third dance set of the evening ended, he was determined to investigate the card room to see who was losing because they had no ability to count cards. In the hallway, he was approached by the Beauchamps' first footman, Headon. The footman drew Mr. Bennet aside and stated that he was given, first, a note to the "lovely Miss B" from Bennet's cousin Colonel Fitzwilliam.

Mr. Bennet raised his eyebrow, opened the note to read that his cousin, the Colonel, was requesting the lovely Miss B. to meet him in the shell alcove in the library on the second floor.

"Sir, the Colonel very specifically requested that the note was only to be delivered to Miss Elizabeth before the fourth set."

"What about this second note?" Bennet pointed at the other note in Headon's hand with a large curlicue "F" grandly written on the visible portion.

"Oh, this one is from Mr. Bingley's sister. Miss Bingley said this note was only to be delivered, discreetly, to Mr. Darcy."

Mr. Bennet smirked, "Hand it to me, my good man, we must uncover all stratagems to make sure that the library will not be overrun with illicit affairs!"

As he turned over the missive, Mr. Bennet laughed lightly at finding that the note addressed to "F" was remarkably similar to the Colonel's. Miss Bingley's note requested that "F" meet "Miss B" in the library during the fourth set. A plan hatched in the wink of an eye. He smiled at Headon and looked at his pocket watch.

"Headon, be quick about it before the next set starts and give the note entitled 'The Lovely Miss B' to Miss Bingley. Then give the note titled "F" to Colonel Fitzwilliam. Make sure you use due diligence that neither party sees you handing the notes to the other. With any luck, during the fourth set Miss Bingley and the Colonel will keep each other occupied in the library alcove."

Colonel Fitzwilliam patrolled the edge of the ballroom holding two glasses of wine while waiting for the Beauchamps' footman to return to him. Much to his relief, the Beauchamps' footman promptly delivered a note addressed with a large curlicue 'F' to him. He thanked the man and asked him to hold one of his glasses of wine while he read the note. A large grin spread over his countenance as he tucked the note safely into his coat pocket. The Colonel retrieved his glass of wine from the footman and resumed his pacing as it was too early in the third set to remove to the library. He scanned the dancers to see if he could catch Miss Elizabeth Bennet's eye. When he did, he winked at her as she danced down the line with one of Bingley's milksop friends.

To the Colonel's joy, Miss Elizabeth raised her eyebrow as she turned back down the line. He was delighted that she acknowledged their plan with both a note and a saucy gesture. *She is such a woman! I can't cool my heels down here any longer. I will wait in the library before the fourth set is to start so that we are not seen leaving the ballroom at the same time. This plan must succeed!*

The Colonel found himself sitting in the dark library alcove drinking his two glasses of wine wondering when the third set would be over. He did not wish to compromise his cousin's daughter, but he did not see another option as she had been resisting his advances and paying attention to Darcy's. Fitzwilliam was very surprised this past week or so to see his reserved cousin Darcy actually exerting himself to pay obvious attentions to a woman. Not any woman, but the woman that the Colonel himself had picked as the partner of his future life over a year ago.

Colonel Fitzwilliam did not see himself as a bad man, nor even a rake or schemer on par with Mr. Wickham, but merely a man greatly constrained by the norms of his time and society. He had, as second son, eagerly joined His Majesty's Army, as neither the Church nor law would have suited him. He had gone with Wellesley to India, then to Egypt with a new regiment, before joining the newly minted Viscount Wellington in Portugal and Spain. He had loved India, but India had not loved him back - he was certainly favored by the good Lord above for living through the first bout of malaria and the subsequent bouts of recurring fevers and chills. Egypt was just plain hot and he greatly rejoiced when Nelson won the Battle of the Nile, mostly so he could return home. He mused that Spain was a true delight when one wasn't getting shot at.

He was not only proud of his service in the Army during a time of war - it had made him into a man - but he would also be happy to return to the field if he was called to do so in the future. He wasn't sure if he was pleased that his family had called in political favors to have him posted in London this past year and a half. Although, the cool, damp air of England had a calming effect on his health - of which he attributed the tonic medicine of Peruvian Bark readily available in London greatly helped quell the fevers as well.

As he drained the first glass of wine and safely stored the empty glass under the chaise lounge he was sitting on, his mind rebelled against the constraints he now faced. Between his current pay, his future half-pay, a small inheritance from his mother's family, as well as the future part of his mother's settlement when she passed, he would absolutely need to marry with a mind to a good dowry if he did not wish to be the poor relation always fobbing himself and his future family off on his brother, Lindon, or on Darcy, or his mother's Howard relations.

This half-cocked plan was not just to secure a woman with a good dowry, but to secure a woman with a university education in mathematics, whose father had brought his estate back from the grave into prosperity, and furthermore - a woman with a very prosperous uncle in trade. It was Miss Elizabeth's clever mind and her connections in money making that the Colonel sought. Darcy simply could not appreciate this aspect of the lovely Miss Elizabeth, as his cousin was disgustingly good with turning a small amount of capital into a good investment.

He admitted to himself that he did like the thrill of the chase, whether it be hunting, at war, or in negotiations. If society were not so rigid about rank and consequence, he would enjoy a profession as a trader at the Exchange or as a high level export merchant like Mr. Gardiner. As it stood, the second son of an Earl must marry with some mind to money if he was to remain in his rank and still be a gentleman. *I am not a fortune hunter, nor am I resentful of my status as a second son - no - I am merely prudent.* Or so he told himself.

This past month, the Colonel had reflected a great deal on how his cousin Bennet was able to resurrect Longbourn's fortunes after his brother's dissolute bankruptcy of said estate. What the Colonel didn't apprehend was, where had his cousin gotten the seed money to start his investments? When this was all over he planned on asking Bennet exactly how he accomplished such a feat.

He had finished off the second glass of wine, and had safely stored the glass under the chaise next to the first so that it would not be knocked over nor broken when he saw a crack of dim light as the library door opened. He softly called, "I am over here, my love..."

A few minutes before the beginning of the fourth set, Miss Elizabeth Bennet conducted a cursory scan of the ballroom and did not see Colonel Fitzwilliam. She was relieved as the set started and the Colonel did not come to claim his dance with her. As she considered her options now that her set was free, Mr. Darcy approached with two glasses of punch.

"Miss Elizabeth, would you like a glass of punch?" She smiled at him and happily sipped the punch as they discussed the ball, where her partner for the fourth disappeared to, and then books. Both were delighted to have time to simply enjoy each other's company while others danced.

Their tête-à-tête was interrupted near the end of the fourth set when Lt. Fitzwilliam strolled over to them and inquired if anyone had seen his brother the Colonel or the delightful Miss Bingley.

"Caroline! What are you doing? Stop it now!" Charles Bingley held up a full candelabra over the entwined bodies of his, allegedly, maiden sister and a man in a half on and half off red coat ensconced on a chaise lounge in a rather dreadful, old fashioned shell alcove in the Beauchamps' library. Hands and mouths were everywhere with various bits of clothing divested about the chaise lounge, although much to Bingley's relief, it was not Caroline's clothing. Bingley had been alerted surreptitiously at the end of the dance set by his future father-in-law that there was mischief afoot in the library. Even now, Mr. Bennet closed the door to the library and lent another brace of candles to light the scene.

"I am kissing Mr. Darcy! He must marry me now." Miss Caroline Bingley slurred, her eyes squinting to make out where her brother was standing.

"Caroline, open your eyes and look at the man you have been kissing," Charles ground out. Caroline ignored her brother and continued to kiss her version of Mr. Darcy as she grabbed his rear to pull him closer to her.

Mr. Bennet chimed in to the other member of the entwined couple, "Colonel Fitzwilliam, whatever are you doing?"

The Colonel looked up at his cousin, of whom there were currently two or three Mr. Bennets and four or five candelabras dancing before him. "Cousin Bennet, I am trying to convince your daughter to marry me!"

Bennet laughed softly as to not alert others outside the library to their presence, "I have more than my fair share of daughters, Cousin, but I can assure you that Miss Caroline Bingley is not of my get."

The Colonel attempted to take in this information, until he was diverted by the young lady's breasts in his plain view were in dire need of his mouth's attention. As he started to kiss what was revealed by the low neckline of her ball gown, Mr. Bingley coughed loudly to get their attention once more.

"Caroline, how could you ruin my engagement ball with this behavior? I thought we discussed that you cannot continue drinking and wantonly kissing strangers at balls without ruining the whole family with scandal!"

Caroline pushed off the man who was so delightfully kissing her and tried to stand by herself while waving at the Colonel, "This is Mr. Darsh-cy, not the Colonel. See Mr. Darsh-cy."

Charles cried out, "Caroline! I will not stand for anymore of this nonsense! That is Mr. Darcy's cousin, Colonel Fitzwilliam. Look! Open your eyes! This is not Miss Fenimore who you were caught kissing and more repeatedly at seminary! This is not the groom at our Aunt's stables in Scarborough nor one of the footmen at Hurst's townhouse! This is Colonel Fitzwilliam!"

Caroline startled and fell back down on the chaise, landing in a heap on Colonel Fitzwilliam's lap. "Miss Fenimore, I loved her. She was the best kisser and she really knew how to..."

The Colonel's brain cleared of wine and lust to come to attention, "Truly? Indeed! May I watch you kiss Miss Fenimore?"

Caroline tried to slap him and missed, the force of attempted slap drove her off the chaise and onto a heap on the floor. "I loved her! She betrayed me. She married that...that... dish-grace of a man!"

Charles was furious and would do whatever he could to get his sister out of this room without a scandal attached to the Bingley name. He would not fall for either of their schemes. "No, Colonel Fitzwilliam, you may not watch. Miss Fenimore has married and moved with her husband to the East Indies." At the sight of Caroline in a heap on the floor, her ball gown mussed beyond current repair, Charles sighed as he leaned over to pick her up. "Caroline, how am I to get you out of here and safely home before the supper set which is to start soon. I am to dance with my beloved Jane and there is to be a toast at supper. I don't have time..."

The Colonel stood up and looked at his cousin and Mr. Bingley in surprise, "Wait! Aren't you going to demand that I marry Miss Bingley?"

Mr. Bingley looked at the Colonel blankly as he attempted to hold up a crumpled Miss Bingley who was whispering Miss Fenimore's Christian name with great longing.

Mr. Bennet leaned in to Charles to say in low tone, "Bingley, don't fall for his plea for thirty thousand pounds."

With that tip, Mr. Bennet walked out of the library and motioned to Headon waiting outside the entry. Whereupon he suggested that the trusted footman take Mr. and Miss Bingley to a guest room on the fourth floor and have Miss Bingley watched so that she would not escape before the ball was over. Bennet walked back into the library to help Mr. Bingley escort his nearly unconscious sister to the guest room.

Colonel Fitzwilliam was stunned by the turn of events. Mr. Bingley had left his brace of candles on the side table next to the chaise lounge, which cast a clear light on the departing men with Miss Bingley. "Wait! She compromised me! I will need to discuss the settlement with you..."

After Mr. Bennet helped Mr. Bingley settle Miss Bingley into a guest room, wherein the young lady promptly fell into a deep drink induced sleep, he returned to the library alcove to make sure his cousin had returned downstairs to the ballroom. Upon arrival in the library, Bennet found the Colonel sitting on the chaise lounge with his head in his hands.

Bennet walked up and lightly touched the Colonel on his shoulder, "Come now, cousin, we should both return downstairs."

The Colonel looked up, put his hands in his lap. "How did you do it?"

Bennet was surprised. "Do what? Know you were here in the library with a young lady? The staff, of course."

"No, not that. How did you get the original capital to restore the Bennet family fortunes?"

A deep laughter erupted from Mr. Bennet. "Oh, my friend, the 1780s were a very different time. Do you wish for capital to invest?"

"I suppose by this time any right thinking father in London will not accede to my request of a thirty thousand pound dowry." The Colonel rose and started to pace. "Once this infernal war is over, how will I live in polite society if I don't start investing wisely as you did, on top of marrying with a mind to a good dowry. Will you help me?"

"Is that why you wanted to marry Elizabeth? To have access to my experience?" Bennet asked. Fitzwilliam nodded. "If you have some ready money, then come to call early next week before I depart for Longbourn and I will arrange for you to discuss the matter with myself and Mr. Gardiner."

Colonel agreed to the plan. Before they departed, Bennet turned to his cousin and asked, "I suppose it is too radical to ask if after the war you would be willing to be an active partner in an import / export business with a good man like Mr. Gardiner?"

Fitzwilliam sighed. "I would be a great deal more happy and content in my life if I could use my talents in such a way, but my family and society would never accept such a radical idea. Imagine the son of a prominent Earl going into Trade? Never!"

Bennet clapped his hand on his cousin's back as they exited the library. "Beware, life has a way of turning nevers into reality. In the meantime, do leave off with the Bingleys."

Mr. Charles Bingley made it back to the Beauchamps' ballroom in time to claim his angel for the supper set. They lined up next to Darcy and Miss Elizabeth, the back of Charles' brain that was not occupied with the vision of loveliness that was Miss Jane Bennet wondered whatever was Darcy about. He did not have time to think of it as the dance with his fiancee consumed his every thought and all of his feelings. As they danced, his sister's recent debacle was also erased from his mind. He was truly glad to have won Jane's hand and heart.

Supper was everything that Charles could have ever envisioned his engagement supper to be, if he had ever taken the time to envision such a thing. It was more what Caroline had longed for, but she was dead to the world two stories above him - so he was determined to enjoy every moment of congratulations from two Earls, a Duke, and several other peers of some sort for her. Jane was radiant with happiness by the time that Mr. Bennet and Lord Beauchamp toasted to their future union, and Charles' natural ebullience had reasserted itself.

Once the supper and entertainment was over and the dancing had recommenced, Charles found Colonel Fitzwilliam following him out of the dining area and back into the ballroom. Everywhere where Charles went, the Colonel was soon to follow. Charles walked down a hallway past the card room and turned around just as the Colonel was about to run into him.

"Colonel Fitzwilliam, it is obvious you wish me to speak to you, so I will." Charles drew the two of them further down the hallway towards the servants' door and in a low voice said, "I will have no rumors or scandals come from tonight's misadventures. Do not speak of my sister's dowry nor a compromise, she was insensate with drink and was convinced you were Darcy. Let us not bring embarrassment upon either of our houses by speaking of this."

The Colonel started to say something when Charles cut him off, "No, you have nothing to say that I wish to hear. Furthermore, your comment about the former Miss Fenimore, now thoroughly married to a director of the East India Company in Madras, was uncalled for and I should call you out for that." The Colonel merely smirked at this.

"Do not make light of my sister and her particular friend. Caroline has had a difficult time since my mother passed. She does not need to marry a man who is merely after her dowry."

The Colonel attempted to defend himself but Charles would not hear of it. "Cease! This is over. You will not marry my sister, please go find another mark. And warn that roguish younger brother of yours to steer clear of my sister as well! I have nothing more to say to you, as I wish to think kindly of you and forget what happened this evening."

Charles left a deflated Colonel Fitzwilliam in the hallway as he returned to watch his beloved dance with her relations and a few of their friends, before he would claim her for the last set of the night.

Monday, December 23, 1811
   Netherfield Park,
   Meryton, Hertfordshire

Much to Colonel Fitzwilliam's dismay, the only settlement and marriage contracts that were finalized and signed the day after the Beauchamps' ball were those between Miss Jane Bennet and Mr. Charles Bingley. A little less than two weeks later at eight o'clock in the morning, on the eve of Christmas Eve, the two were joined in holy matrimony before their closest friends and family at the Longbourn village church.

The wedding breakfast was a great delight to all and sundry, even to the newlyweds who were overwhelmed with happiness to share their joy with those they loved. The only two people who did not enjoy the breakfast were Miss Bingley - hungover - and Mrs. Bennet, who was beside herself with tremblings and flutterings at the thought of a daughter well married and was nauseated by the smell of food and the guests' perfume. Mrs. Bennet, all the while nearly ecstatic with happiness at the prospect of what these signs might mean, had spent the previous three mornings kneeling over her chamber pot before rising to dress and organize for the grand event. The morning of the wedding, she had no time for such luxuries as she had a wedding breakfast to conduct.

By the time that Jane and Charles found themselves happily tucked away into the warmth of their shared chamber at Netherfield Park, both dressed in their best nightwear, even though it was not yet half three in the afternoon. They sat shyly on the embroidered Agincourt bed linens, when Jane made a most unusual request of her newly wedded husband.

Upon hearing her request, Charles laughed and could not deny her. She moved to the spot she was most comfortable on and they both giggled.

The morning after their wedding night, before they removed to their sitting room for a private breakfast, Jane asked her maid to please not change the bed linens and that the said linens were under no circumstances to be treated or laundered in such a way that the blood stains were removed. Mrs. Bingley's new lady's maid was rather astonished until she took a good look at the bed coverlet and realized that the new blood stains were perfectly placed to render complete realism to the embroidered battle scene.

Chapter 14 : In the Fullness of May

---❦---

Monday, December 23, 1811
   After the Wedding Breakfast
   Meryton, Hertfordshire

Mr. George Wickham had greatly enjoyed the wedding breakfast that the divine Mrs. Bennet had thrown for the newly minted Mr. and Mrs. Bingley. It appeared as if all of Meryton was here. The food was not only plentiful but delicious, the drink flowed, and the company was delightful - well - as long as he made sure that he was never in the same room with his old friend Fitzwilliam Darcy at the same time. To his best ability, Wickham had done his utmost to make sure that Darcy never saw him at the wedding breakfast.

The few times that Wickham had glimpsed Darcy in the crush of revelers in the reception rooms of Longbourn, he had bemusedly noted that Darcy was much too fixated on staring at Miss Elizabeth to even detect his presence at the party.

The militia officers mostly stayed near the food and drink during the course of the breakfast and only broke their ranks to flirt with various local ladies. Wickham had noted early in the day that Mr. Philips was keeping watch on him, thus he stayed with his fellows and only occasionally winked at a pretty lady who happened by.

Much to his amusement Miss Mariah Lucas, egged on by Miss Lydia and Miss Kitty Bennet, attempted to flirt with him and Mr. Saunderson - only to be foiled by her stuttering as her natural shyness asserted itself. Miss Lydia was a handful, Wickham had thought it best that she was to return to school after Twelfth Night. If he was honest, he saw too much of himself in her at that age as she was at an age where she was standing on the fulcrum. He felt oddly like an older brother worrying if she would pick the right path.

As he walked into the back door of the boarding house, he felt curiously content. It was not merely the bodily pleasures of excellent food and drink, nor was it the company of a most handsome and insatiable woman this past month, no - as he settled before the fire in his room at Mrs. Preece's - he felt at home here in Meryton amongst the people and the land in a way that he had not since he had been ejected from Pemberley after his godfather's death. If he remained honest with himself, he had not felt this content even before then, perhaps not since he was fifteen and made his first set of poor choices after he yielded to temptations he knew that he should not yield to at Eton that led him to his current path.

Perhaps, here in Meryton, he could become a better man. He did not think he had the fortitude to become a man of good character if he remained in the militia - there were just too many temptations. Perhaps he could remain here in Meryton and build a life here. The question that he had posed to himself over the course of the past month is would he be able to change his path in life by his own efforts and strength of will?

In the meantime, it was two days until Christmas and he had a full two and twenty pounds of money in hand safely hidden - his mother had secretly sent him a letter with two five pound notes in it on top of the monies that Mrs. Bennet had given him - and he had not a care in the world. He had one niggling thought at the back of his consciousness, a small concern that his seed would take too soon and he would be cut off from his fun with Mrs. Bennet, which then would be the end of his weekly pin money. He pushed such thoughts away as he drifted to sleep under the warmth of the drink consumed earlier and the heat emanating from the fireplace.

Thurs., April 2, 1812
  Late afternoon,
  The Drive at Longbourn
  Meryton, Hertfordshire

It had been a long week at Rosings Park. Normally Mr. Bennet would not have left his wife alone at Longbourn to attend Lady Catherine at her estate for Easter, but this year the good Lady had invited her nephews and his daughter Elizabeth to spend two weeks at Rosings. Bennet only agreed to the scheme if Elizabeth was only to spend one week and be chaperoned by himself.

His sister, Lady Beauchamp, had kept a regular twice weekly correspondence with himself and Mrs. Bennet on how Elizabeth's season in Town was progressing. It was through these letters that he knew that Mr. Darcy's regard had increased to the point that his sister and others felt that the young man was about to come to the point. There was Bennet's cousin, Colonel Fitzwilliam still nosing about. For all of his connections with Lady Catherine, he did not trust her to make one last attempt to throw her daughter, Miss de Bourgh, at Mr. Darcy and thus leaving Elizabeth open for the Colonel's machinations.

Off to Rosings Park Bennet had gone with a slightly reluctant Elizabeth in tow. He knew that his daughter would be delighted to visit with her friend Charlotte, the new Mrs. Collins, at Hunsford even if that exposed both of them to his cousin Collins' nonsensical conversation. Much as he had feared, Lady Catherine's schemes caused some distress to Miss de Bourgh, Miss de Bourgh's fiancee - Mr. Turing, and to Elizabeth. The diverting part of it all, as Bennet saw it, was Lady Catherine's behavior had forced Mr. Darcy into action, albeit poorly planned and executed action.

On Easter Monday, Bennet had risen early to ride the palings and through the grove, only to discover his daughter disputing with Mr. Darcy under a large ash tree about his arrogance and his selfish disdain for the feelings of others. After listening to them both, it appeared that Mr. Darcy was attempting to win the honor of the worst proposal of the year.

Later that day, Bennet called both of them into the library at Rosings and was able to mediate a discussion that revealed Elizabeth feared that Mr. Darcy only accepted her due to her noble relations in town and would reject the parts of her family who were in trade and her life in Meryton. Bennet was able to tease out of the young man that he did not perform well in front of others which led him to erect a mask of disdain and self-protection in large gatherings.

The late afternoon discussion in the Rosings library concluded in Mr. Darcy and Elizabeth agreeing to a formal courtship for the next six weeks. They promised that they would meet chaperoned at the Beauchamps' or Gardiners' homes or at the various events of the season, rather than alone out on walks. Both agreed to forgive the other for past mistakes, check their own prejudices, and take the time to expose and investigate each other's character with the goal of determining at the end of the time period if they wished to marry or not. While Elizabeth was still in a fit of pique due to Darcy's rather insulting proposal, she agreed to her father's scheme. Bennet knew that the stoic young man would be delighted to be given the opportunity to prove himself to Elizabeth.

The long carriage ride home was nearly over as it had just crossed the first boundary marker into Longbourn, Bennet hoped that Darcy would take the time to reflect upon his arrogance and check it before he damaged his suit with Elizabeth beyond repair. Bennet chuckled to himself. *Ah, young love, all the opportunities in the world to fall over oneself and trip oneself as one attempts to court one's beloved. What is Mrs. Collins' appropriate proverb on love? Something about being a fool in love?*

The spring-new grass and blossoming orchards on Longbourn's land was striking as the carriage passed into the park's drive. Bennet loved this land deeply and hoped that more than just lambs, calves, and litters of piglets would be born to Longbourn this year. Before he departed for Easter at Rosings, Mrs. Bennet had all the signs that she was with child but the babe had not yet quickened. He had promised his wife that with the exception of attending Elizabeth and Jane's Presentation ball at the Beauchamps' on the last day of April, that he would remain at Longbourn until after her confinement.

Mrs. Bennet had previously expressed her desire to have a grand dinner party on May day inviting all of the four and twenty families in the area to celebrate their four and twentieth wedding anniversary as well as their future child. Bennet was not sure if he was spry enough at six and fifty to be traveling to London for Jane and Elizabeth's ball on May Eve and then to travel directly back for a large party at Longbourn the following evening. The very idea gave him a strong desire to nap. He made a note to discuss a later date for the dinner with his wife.

The carriage came to a stop before the entrance to Longbourn and Mr. Bennet was greatly surprised to find his wife, already great with child, running out the doors and down the staircase to greet him. As he descended from the carriage, Mrs. Bennet was bouncing with ebullience on her toes.

"There must be consequential news you want to tell me, and I have no objection to hearing it." Mr. Bennet said to Mrs. Bennet as he kissed her cheek.

Her news did not surprise him, the babe had quickened in the week he was away. She could feel the babe move within her womb. Her joy transferred to him, all weariness fled from his mind and body. In that moment - in front of the servants and grooms - he gently picked up Mrs. Bennet and twirled her around as they both rejoiced with laughter.

Sat., May 2, 1812
   Early Evening
   Longbourn Manor

"How ever did they fit all of Hertford and surrounds four and twenty families for a sit down dinner in here?" Mrs. Long asked Lady Lucas as they took their tea, while servants removed the dining tables and rearranged chairs after the celebratory meal.

"Amelia, you know as well as I do, that Longbourn manor was designed over a hundred years ago to entertain well over one hundred and twenty people. Your eyes, as well as mine, can see that they have opened every set of double doors on the ground floor - with the exception of the library and Mr. Bennet's study - to make room for the tables and chairs." Lady Lucas spitefully replied

"Euphemia Anne Potter Lucas! That is not what I was asking and you know it." Mrs. Long sniped back.

Lady Lucas merely raised both of her eyebrows in surprise that the friend of her youth from the Meryton Dame School would use her full Christian name in polite company. "Amelia Gertrude Johnstone Long!"

The two ladies stared at each other. Mrs. Long broke the impasse by whispering over her teacup, "L-a-d-y Lucas, you well know what I meant to ask. If you must, what I wish to know is why did Mrs. Bennet want all of us to hear her boasting of the future heir..."

Lady Lucas' countenance took on a sour expression. "There is no way to know if Mrs. Bennet will have a boy. After five daughters, it is most likely that the sixth Bennet child will also be a daughter. Besides, my Charlotte may have some news on that score as well."

Mrs. Long persisted. "What I was saying, before you interrupted, is that did she gather all of four and twenty families just to have it cast abroad her good fortune to be increasing so late in life and to have her two eldest daughters lately presented to the Queen."

"That is why she had this dinner. Mind you, Amelia, do not forget that Mr. Darcy asked Miss Eliza - pardon, Miss Bennet - to marry him at her presentation ball." Lady Lucas then proceeded to mimic Mrs. Bennet's boasts of the evening. "They are to marry on St. John's Day in June here at Longbourn. Mrs. Bingley is living in a grand townhouse in Mayfair. Miss Mary Bennet is soon to be engaged, after she completes her degree at Oxford. I can hear her even now boasting two rooms away that the baby will be a boy. Will the good news from Mrs. Bennet never cease?"

Mrs. Long in a fine imitation of Mrs. Bennet whispered, "God has been so very good to us!"

Both ladies humphed quite loudly. Mrs. Long, who had two nieces to marry off - neither of whom attended school nor university nor were they particularly handsome, found her tea tasted sour.

George Wickham, who sat in a dark corner in the vicinity of and listening to Lady Lucas and Mrs. Long mock Mrs. Bennet, groaned. He was still hungover. He had been hungover for some days, though he wasn't sure how many days. What was clear is that he had made a fine hash of his life—again.

He received his initial agreed upon two hundred pounds from Mr. Bennet a few weeks ago upon the quickening of the babe. As fast as he received it was as fast as it whirled out of his pockets. In defense of his attempts to redeem himself, he was proud to admit that he used some of the monies to pay off his debts of honor to his fellow militia officers. He was not proud to admit that he had paid none of his debts to the Meryton tradesmen before he went off on his spree to London last week. Militia was to depart in two days time to Brighton for the summer encampment.

Even his worst self knew that he could not leave Meryton on Monday without paying the shopkeepers of the town as Mr. Bennet and Mr. Philips would find out ere long. If he wanted that two thousand pound payout when the child came of age, if it was a boy and broke the entail, then he would have to come up to scratch. There would be no escaping his debts this time and no Darcy to pay up for his misdeeds.

Before his departure to London, Mrs. Preece demanded all of the room and board to be paid through to the Militia's removal to the southern coast. Wickham acknowledged that for all of Mrs. Preece's niggardly ways, she was a clever woman.

He had the time of his life in London for four days. At first he was up and had won nearly nine hundred pounds off of some wastrel of a viscount at one of Madame Vernay's gambling dens. That was before one of Madame's most lovely and skilled associates had plied him with fine brandies and in a wink of an eye - he was down on his luck.

What was wrong with him that he could not have left with his winnings? Why did he think he could win more? The greater question is, knowing what the woman was about, why did he drink more and allow himself to be seduced? He returned from his jaunt with just enough cash left to pay Mrs. Preece and have a meal at the Inn with his fellow officers yesterday evening.

The free small beer at the Inn made no dent in his self-disgust, let alone the worst hangover of his life. And there was no one he could blame but himself this time.

Now as he listened to the two matrons gossip about the Bennet family, he knew that he had to take action lest he fall into penury before his arrival in Brighton. Not that he wished to depart with the Militia. The closer the removal date came, the more that Wickham ached to have a different life. A life where he had a family, a secure profession, and a home. A home in a town like Meryton. No, to be honest, he wanted to live here in Meryton.

He groaned again. Dinner was attempting to revisit his mouth and the sour stench emitting from his mouth was revolting. The only thing he could comfort himself with was that at least he had not lost the family lands at the gambling tables as his rumored natural father had done. There had to be some hope, something that he could do to relieve his present discomfort.

He hastily rose and walked immediately to the water closet, wherein he lost the contents of his stomach. He lost count of the number of times he retched. Finally, when all that came up was bile, he wiped his mouth with his sleeve.

Good Lord, what have I done with myself? How have I fallen so? With this thought, George Wickham fell into a stupor next to the chamber pot.

Once the dinner guests had quit Longbourn and the mistress had retired to her chambers, a satisfied Mr. Bennet retreated to his book-room for a bit of reading and a small pour of port before bed. He had not fully settled himself into his seat and opened his book when Mr. Hill knocked and entered.

"Sir, Mr. Wickham has been discovered in the withdrawing room asleep next to the chamber pot."

"I beg your pardon?" Mr. Bennet sat up straight. "Mr. Wickham was not even drinking or drunk at the dinner this evening nor afterwards, unlike the other militia officers. He may have been alone in a corner, perhaps - but not drunk. Why would he sleep next to..."

Mr. Bennet rose and followed Mr. Hill. Upon perusal of the small room wherein a sour smelling Mr. Wickham slumbered on, Mr. Bennet proclaimed, "Oh, for heaven's sake! Mr. Hill, if the man cannot be roused, then have him installed in a guest chamber and lock the door. I will deal with him in the morning."

Mr. Hill and two of the footmen picked a slack Mr. Wickham up, as an exasperated Mr. Bennet returned to his port and book.

Sun. May 3, 1812
Early Afternoon
Longbourn Manor

An hour before departing for church, Mr. Bennet asked Mr. Hill if their guest had woken up. At Mr. Hill's negative response, Bennet requested that Hill keep their guest in his room until the family had returned from church. Hill bowed.

When Mr. and Mrs. Bennet returned from the Sunday service and dinner at Lucas Lodge, Mr. Hill informed an astonished Mr. Bennet that their guest was still asleep.

Mr. Bennet waited for Mrs. Bennet walk into the family sitting room to enjoy the full west sun, when he instructed Mr. Hill. "Please send coffee, nourishment, and hot water up to the guest room. Pound on the door to rouse its inhabitant, if you must. Tell him that I will come speak to him at two o'clock prompt. He is not to leave the room until then." Bennet scrubbed at his face and looked Mr. Hill in the eyes, "I realize that the last half year has been quite irregular; thank you, Mr. Hill, for your discretion."

Two minutes before the two o'clock prompt, Mr. Bennet ascended all four sets of stairs to reach the under the eaves guest and servants quarters floor of the manor house. On arrival at the door of the guest room in question, he dismissed the footman to return downstairs and he knocked. A rusty "Come in." was heard.

When Bennet opened the door, he found a rumpled young man bent over on the bed with his elbows on his knees and his hands in his hair. Mr. Wickham did not stand, nor did he bow, instead he remained as he was - silently.

The coffee and pastries were untouched, so was the steaming pitcher of hot water on the wash basin counter top. Bennet said not a word as he poured a cup of coffee for himself and one for Wickham. He handed one to the man and sat in a wooden chair as he sipped his coffee, waiting.

Wickham sipped his black coffee and tried to speak. "Sir, um..." His eyes were bloodshot, his countenance rough with flaky skin and stubble. "I don't know where to start, other than thank you for not tossing me out last night."

Bennet stared directly and firmly at him, "Why don't you start at the beginning, but keep it brief."

Wickham took a long drink of the coffee, straightened up, and said, "I had hoped to reform, the best I could, but I fell. Hard."

"That much is obvious."

"I don't want to stay in the Militia nor do I wish to go to Brighton." At Bennet's disbelieving stare, Wickham quickly finished, "I know myself; if I go to Brighton, I will remain as I am - a wastrel. I find that for the first time in years, maybe ever, that I feel at home here in Meryton. These past months, I have reflected on what I could do as a profession to stay here and build a life. Instead of moving forward, against my best efforts I sauntered backward into my own destruction, yet again."

"Do you mean to tell me that you have already spent, in full, the two hundred pounds that you received less than three weeks ago?" Bennet's voice was harsh as his eyes beheld the young man.

Rather than reply, Wickham got up and poured more coffee from himself and offered more to Mr. Bennet, who declined. This was not the charming, gentleman-like young man who had arrived to the flutter of many hearts in November, but instead here was a broken man who looked years older than his true age.

Wickham sat back down. "Sir, I know that I should not be for-given, but may I have an advance so that I might pay off my debts to the tradesman in Meryton?"

"What the hell did you do with the two hundred pounds? Gam-ble it away in London?" Bennet's ire had run over.

Wickham looked at him beseechingly. "Only in part. I swear on my..."

"Do not swear on your good father's grave! Do not swear on your mother or grandmother or even on your good word - as you have none! How could you!" Bennet stood and thrust the chair away. "I do not want to hear a single excuse. I do not desire to hear of any ac-counts of gambling hells in London and how you were up before you were down! Did you honestly think that they make their money by letting you win? Are you truly that stupid?"

A furious Bennet now loomed over Wickham. "Do not bring Lady Luck into this discussion at all. From what Philips and I dis-covered last week after we canvassed Meryton's tradesmen and your landlady," a groan emitted from Wickham at this last statement but Bennet was not deterred, "you owe a total of one hundred and fifteen pounds, which leaves five and eighty left of which to support yourself on until the summer quarter starts! That is more than sufficient funds! Most people will never make more than eighty pounds per annum for the whole of their lives! How can you waste more than twice that amount in less than half a month?"

Wickham resumed his bent over pose with his head in his hands as Bennet began to pace the small guest room. "Truly, Mr. Wickham, how many young men of six and twenty have had every opportunity to improve their lot in life as you have? How many men can say they attended Cambridge? To study the law after they turned down a liv-ing - of which many curates wait twenty years to finally obtain even half of such a living? Do tell? If my two youngest daughters can be the silliest young women in all of England on occasion, you must be the stupidest young man in all of England every day!"

Mr. Bennet caught himself. "No, I have unduly insulted Lydia and Kitty, please forgive me. Now you on the other hand are a wastrel! Is this how you wish to conduct the rest of your life - however short it will be when the drink, debauchery, and creditors' strong men catch up with you?"

A small "no" wafted up from the nearly folded up Mr. Wickham.

"I won't ask how you burnt through two hundred pounds in less than a month, when one can start their bets at a gambling hell at that amount or higher. That is how my brother nearly destroyed this family, I will not have you destroy it further."

Wickham groaned again. Bennet stopped and stood still.

"I should throw you out of here and let you shift for yourself. But I will not." Bennet then waited until Wickham looked up. "Do you know why?"

Wickham shook his head.

"When we first met at the Philips' card party, I let you think that your natural father was my brother. He is not. No, he is not. I am." Bennet sat back down, this time next to his son on the bed. "I will not go into the full details now, but you are my natural son. I will not allow you to destroy yourself. I could not stop my brother, I was too young and had no idea where to start, but now I am older and I have an idea. Though this idea, mad scheme - really, relies completely on your willingness to truly change."

To both men's surprise, Wickham began to cry – wracked with sobs that shook his whole body

"Come now," Patting about his waistcoat, Mr. Bennet pulled out a clean handkerchief and handed it to Wickham. He then got up and poured another cup of coffee for both of them, as he waited for Wickham to regain his composure. "While I cannot recognize you as my son to all and sundry, there are other ways I can help you as a father would. I promised your dear mother last autumn that I would make a man of good character out of you. I cannot fail her and you must not fail yourself."

Before Bennet let Wickham in on this new idea of his, he passed the young man the plate of apricot pastries. "Have some food and wash your face before the water becomes completely tepid. When you are ready, come meet me in my study and we will discuss how you can set your life to rights."

Sun. May 3, 1812
4:04pm
Longbourn Parish Church

George Wickham stumbled out of Mr. Bennet's study in an acute tumult of mind. His legs walked him over to the Longbourn parish church, wherein he sat down on a back pew and started to tremble.

Before long, he was kneeling in the pew, crying, and praying. Beseeching the God that he had long turned away from for help and the strength to become a better man so that he might accomplish this next set of tasks that Mr. Bennet proposed less than an hour ago.

When the storm had passed and the tears ceased, Wickham found himself filled with new resolve and a peace that passed his present understanding. As he returned to sitting on the pew, he glimpsed the elderly clergyman who held the living of the parish standing behind the pews waiting.

"Sir, I am sorry! I did not hear you enter."

"Mr. Wickham, you are very welcome to pray for as long as you wish, but when you are ready, please do come and join me in the Rectory's library for dinner. My cook has outdone herself this afternoon."

Wickham quickly considered his options: the rumored delicious cooking of the parson's cook which along with it came this long winded old scholar or the plain and rather terrible fare at Mrs. Preece's that also included her harsh lectures. He stood and graciously accepted the parson's offer.

"Are you very certain that you came to be in Meryton quite by chance?"

"Are you implying it was by Providence?" Wickham asked, as he wondered if wine would be served with the soup.

"Perhaps providence in the form of Mr. Bennet," replied the Right Reverend Samuel E. Johnstone, D.Div. Christ Church College, Oxford, the holder of the living for Longbourn and Netherfield; as well as a few smaller livings in Hertfordshire and Berkshire that were within the giftings of the various Long and Johnstone families and the author of not a few theology books. One should not forget to mention, also, the owner of the second largest library in this part of the county next to Mr. Bennet.

"No, a Mr. Denny," a weary Wickham answered, beginning to regret joining the old man for dinner, "formerly of the ___ Militia told me about the open position in the Militia this November past when I was still residing in London."

The first course of Sunday dinner at the rectory was exquisite. It was both delicious and torture, as Wickham's mind and emotions were not up to debating theology with the old scholar.

"Mr. Wickham, I may be old but my eyes can still see." The old man, wearing his more than seventy years lightly, looked up and down at the drooping, still wretched young man whom he had found kneeling in a back pew sobbing not a half of an hour ago. "What my eyes see is that you are the very vision of the current Mr. Bennet's older brother - who was a mere fourteen years old when I came to be a curate in this parish after I had been ordained."

Wickham's shoulders slumped further as the old man poured both of them a glass of wine. "That I have been told..."

"You are a natural son of the family."

"Yes."

"What I apprehend from the tale you just told me, our Mr. Bennet - who may be your natural uncle - or father - has made you an offer that would help you to turn your life around and make a man out of you. A man of good character and fine reputation."

"Yes."

"The very same Mr. Bennet who has spent the past thirty years reversing the fortunes of the family and taking good care of those under his purview, including myself - even if in a slightly distracted fashion?"

"Yes, he told me that if I resign from the ____ Militia this evening he will take me tomorrow to sign on as a clerk to Mr. Philips' law practice. Furthermore, I will have to sign a contract that I will forswear all gambling, profligacy, licentiousness, as well as immoderate partaking of drink. Upon the completion of my law studies, of which I started in the Inn of Court in London some five years ago, and clerkship with Mr. Philips - Mr. Bennet will sign over the deed to the Longbourn Old Rectory and some acres of land so that I might start my own family."

"That is a very fair deal. Do you not have faith that the Lord God Almighty will give you the fortitude to avoid temptation and become a better man?"

Wickham looked down at his soup and said, "What I have no faith in is in my own strength of will and my ability to eschew dissipation."

Mr. Johnstone lifted his glass, "I suggest that we make a toast to the efficacy of salvation to propitiate, justify, and sanctify you."

With a whiff of mischief buoying up his spirits, Wickham added, "And to my being filled with Sophia, the Holy Ghost, so that I might walk out my renewed faith."

"Oh dear, you have been listening to Lady Catherine de Bourgh..."

"Since I was six years old she has been telling me about salvation through Christ Jesus and the ability to live a life of obedience in Christ is given to us by Sophia, the Holy Ghost."

"Yes and Mrs. Wollstonecraft while you are at it." The parson stopped himself from laughing and grew serious. "Mr. Wickham, let us rationally review the facts."

"Are you not going to tell me that I need to repent, turn around, and be filled with the Holy Ghost?"

"What do you take me for a fire and brimstone Evangelical? Sir! This is the Church of England you entered into to have your crisis of conscience, and at my dinner table we use our sense and our minds to reason out God's truth."

"By all means, let us reason together." Wickham truly smiled for the first time in days. *I think I may like this old scholar after all.*

Johnstone laughed at this quip and raised his glass to clink it with Wickham's.

------ ◦◈◦ ------

Chapter 15: It is a Boy!

------ ◦◈◦ ------

Fri. August 28, 1812
    1:30am
    Longbourn Manor
    Meryton, Hertfordshire

"Papa," a tired Mrs. Darcy called to her father from the entrance to his study. "There is a very young gentleman upstairs who wishes to meet you."

A dozing Mr. Bennet woke and stood up immediately, "A son! Elizabeth, are you sure it is a boy?"

Elizabeth laughed. "Yes, Papa, I saw all that was necessary to identify the baby as a boy while Mrs. Hill bathed him."

Elizabeth smiled at her weary but ebullient father, who was surrounded by her husband, Mr. Bingley, and Mr. Philips. Rather than drinking too much brandy, the gentlemen appeared to have been playing backgammon and napping.

Mr. Bennet did a small jig of joy on the carpet before running out of the study and up the stairs, much to the delight of Mr. Bingley and the others gathered to await the birth.

Mr. Philips roused himself up off the sofa and walked over to the window to look out. "Hmmm, while all congratulations are in order, there is enough of a moon out that Mrs. Philips and I can return safely to our own beds tonight. Elizabeth, can you please ask your aunt to prepare herself to leave, while I get the grooms to ready the carriage."

Elizabeth smiled and walked over to her husband, who was beating Mr. Bingley at backgammon. "Charles, Jane wishes to stay here tonight and asks that you remain with her."

Charles Bingley looked up from his five remaining pieces on the board. "Certainly, I will let Darcy beat me another round or two and I will join Jane when she is ready in her former chamber."

Darcy smiled at his wife and stood to lightly embrace her. "Elizabeth, please give my every compliment to your mother. I will await down here in case your father wishes to display the infant. I am very pleased for your parents."

Elizabeth laughed, "My mother will receive every compliment, praise, and congratulation, as is her due after giving birth to Longbourn's heir. Now, I must return upstairs to see if I am needed for anything more than heralding the birth."

When she entered her mother's chambers, Elizabeth beheld a scene that made her heart glad - her mother was giggling and her enchanted father was holding the baby wrapped up in swaddling as her sister Jane and Aunt Philips stood nearby.

As Mr. Bennet stroked the infant's cheek - all of his hopes contained in one tiny person, he praised his wife, "Mrs. Bennet, I thank you very much for such a fine son. He is truly a handsome little fellow, all his fingers and toes are present, and such a full head of dark hair!"

He leaned down and kissed a very pleased Mrs. Bennet on her cap.

Mr. Bennet would not give up the baby when asked, thus Mrs. Philips gurgled nonsense to the infant as she chucked his chin. As Mrs. Bennet fell asleep, her sister continued to overflow with praise to her sister on the birth of a son! A son after five daughters - how good God has been to the whole of the family.

After much to do, Elizabeth ushered her Aunt downstairs to an impatient Mr. Philip as the foyer clock chimed half two in the morning.

Fri. August 28, 1812
    Early Afternoon
    Mr. Philips' Law Office
    Meryton, Hertfordshire

Mr. Bennet's joy knew no bounds as he entered into Mr. Philips' law office. A clerk told him that Mr. Philips and Mr. Wickham were awaiting him in the former man's office. As Bennet walked into the enclosed office, both men rose, and to Mr. Wickham's surprise - after the clerk closed the door - Mr. Bennet embraced him.

"My dear Mr. Wickham, I do not know how I can thank you. The lad is a fine hearty boy, I am beyond pleased." Bennet embraced Wickham a second time and pounded on the younger man's back as he thanked him.

"Yes, Bennet, you are pleased. I would be even more pleased if you would sit down and we can conduct our business." Rather than being insulted by Philips' mock dour statement, Bennet bounded over to embrace his brother-in-law as well who attempted unsuccessfully to ward the man off.

"Philips, you cannot deny my joy at this moment. It has been five and twenty years since I left my parish in Derbyshire to clean up my older brother's mess and as of early this morning all my hard work is not for naught. As of today, there is a fruition that gives hope that a Bennet and not a Collins will inherit Longbourn when I die!" Mr. Bennet waved his hand away as he said, "Yes, the young Thomas - for that is what we have named him - could yet still perish of some horrible childhood illness, but all five of my girls survived various fevers and the like - so shall he."

Bennet sat down in the previously indicated chair with a large grin on his face. Mr. Philips shook his head as he attempted to wipe a smile from his own countenance. "I see you have been infected by your son-in-law Bingley's customary enthusiasm, if you keep this attitude we will not know where our Mr. Bennet has gone off to."

"Philips, you can stop teasing me. Shall we get down to matters of business?"

Mr. Philips pulled an envelope out of a locked drawer in his desk. "Mr. Wickham, per your first contract with Mr. Bennet, I present you with a bank cheque for one thousand pounds. When and if, the young Bennet reaches the age of his majority and is able to break the entail at the Court of Chancery, you will be presented with another cheque for one thousand pounds."

Mr. Wickham looked at the proffered envelope as if it were a poisonous snake and would not take the extended cheque. "Sirs, rather than accept the full amount, I would greatly prefer to have the monies put into the funds, via a trust wherein I cannot access the principal, that will collect interest. Four months of improvement is not long enough to resist the temptation to spend it all."

A quieted Mr. Bennet looked at Wickham, "To be sure, it would be very prudent to put the monies into a trust that is invested in the funds. Would you like to have Mr. Philips set up such a trust?"

"Yes, I would. It would be best not only for me but for my future." Mr. Philips' eyebrows rose in some surprise at Mr. Wickham's response.

"Mr. Wickham, I am very pleased to help you in this matter." Mr. Philips retracted his arm and put the envelope with the bank cheque back into his locked drawer whereupon he turned the key and pocketed it. "In fact, while Mr. Bennet is here, I would like to commend you on your apprenticeship, further law studies, and professional comportment in this law office the past four months."

Philips stood up and shook Mr. Wickham's hand. "Furthermore, given the bachelor's degree you have from Cambridge, the three years you studied at the Inns of Court in London - although you were not called to the bar - and now the months studying and thoroughly going over common law cases, I would like to recommend you to the solicitor's exam when it is next held."

Mr. Philips held up his hand to keep either Wickham or Bennet from speaking. "To that end, I would like to offer you a place as a partner in this business once you pass your solicitors exam and have practiced as a solicitor of good standing and repute for at least two years. You have an intelligence and quickness about you that none of the other clerks nor apprentices exhibit. Would you like to pledge yourself to this course of profession?"

Mr. Wickham contained the ebullience welling up in his breast and said, "Yes, sir, I would be very honored to work hard and prove myself in this practice." He extended his hand to Mr. Philips and both men shook.

"As I discussed with Mr. Bennet last evening, I would like to extend this practice beyond the common country attorney and solicitor tasks of wills, deeds, contracts, and occasional man of business for landowners to a full Common Law and Chancery Court solicitor practice so that our clients do not have to search for a London solicitor when the need to go to Court arises. A man of your cleverness and willingness, as well as previous experience studying at the Inns of Court, would be just the man to eventually make partner. As Philips and Wickham, we can expand our business quite profitably for all. What say you, Wickham?"

"Yes! I agree." Mr. Wickham bowed in his agreement.

"Of course, per our previous two contracts, I will detail out each task you are to complete and what is expected of you. Moreover, Mr. Wickham, I will expect you to continue to be a man of sterling character, above reproach in every part of your life if you are to eventually be my partner in law."

Philips once again extended his hand and Wickham shook it firmly.

"I must have my share of this discussion," Mr. Bennet laughingly inserted himself into the conversation. "Mr. Wickham, I would like to compliment you on the speed and thoroughness that you have applied yourself to the studies of common law and solicitor apprenticeship these past four months under Mr. Philips, who is quite convinced that you are ready to start practicing as an attorney. To that end, I would like to reward you by fulfilling my part of the May contract."

Bennet smiled and extracted a key from his pocket, whereupon he handed it to Wickham. "Here is the key to the Old Rectory.

A QUIVER FULL, OR HOW MR. DARCY WILL NOT SIT ON THAT SOFA AGAIN!

227

When you make full partner in this business, I will deed the property to you. In the meantime, the Old Rectory is yours to live in, along with three hundred pounds per annum from the rents on the tenanted land to pay for a few servants, a cook, and a groom in the stables."

"Sir, I am very honored! Thank you." Mr. Wickham looked down at the key, which was much more than just a key to a door to a house where he could live. It was a key to his future life as a gentleman - perhaps his future life as a respectable attorney with his own home. "But I do not have a horse for a groom to care for."

"Oh, ye of little faith." Mr. Bennet laughed, "Please join myself and Mr. Philips outside." Bennet opened the door and walked through the main part of the solicitor's office to the front door. Mr. Philips and Wickham followed him outside.

Upon opening the door to Meryton's high street, Wickham saw a prime phaeton with two perfectly matched bays awaiting. A young groom, who he recognized from Longbourn's stable, was holding the pair of horses' heads. Wickham's jaw dropped and tears collected in his eye as he beheld the deep burgundy and black phaeton. "Sir?"

Bennet came up and clapped him on the back. "The Old Rectory is nearly four miles from this office, I cannot have you late to your work every day, can I?"

To both of the older men's surprise, on a public street in front of all of Meryton, Mr. Wickham embraced both Mr. Bennet and Mr. Philips. "Thank you for giving me another chance. I promise I will be the best man I can be."

Fri. Aug. 28, 1812
5:27pm
Dining Room, Longbourn
Mr. Fitzwilliam Darcy found himself bereft of his wife, who was seated next to her father quite far from himself, at the rather boister-

ous celebration dinner at Longbourn. All of the Bennet daughters, as well as Darcy and Bingley, plus the Philipses, George Wickham, and Mr. Johnstone the vicar were present. While he did sleep well, as well as a newly wedded man ever sleeps, after he beat Bingley at backgammon a number of times into the early morning, he spent most of the day feeling a bit foggy.

Instead of his beloved wife seated next to him, Darcy was seated with Miss Lydia on his right, Mr. Johnstone on his left, Wickham directly across from him. As Mrs. Bennet was upstairs in confinement, so Mrs. Bingley had taken the foot of the table and was directing the meal. Miss Lydia had started a debate, as was her wont, and Mr. Wickham and Mr. Johnstone were keeping up their parts. Darcy preferred to listen to their various points on the war in the Peninsula and what Wellington ought to do next rather than join the debate.

As he ate, he enjoyed listening to the snippets of conversation that floated past the debaters. Mrs. Bingley, Miss Kitty, and Miss Mary were discussing the differences in experiences between Miss Kitty's London arts school and Miss Mary's theological studies at Lorien College, Oxford. Mrs. Philips was bending Bingley's ear about the joys of a son and heir, Bingley was kind enough to listen and ask pertinent questions. Darcy's wife, Elizabeth, who was seated next to her father at the head of the table, and Mr. Philips were deep in a discussion on matters of law and the recent assassination of Britain's Prime Minister, Mr. Perceval.

If he had his druthers, Mr. Darcy would not be at this table but somewhere up in the Scottish Highlands in a small croft alone with his wife, roasting fish and game over an open fire and enjoying newly married solitude. Alas and alack, that was not his fate. They had only the first two weeks after their wedding alone together, before they were obligated to take their wedding tour to visit various Darcy and Fitzwilliam relatives culminating in hosting the delightful Gardiners as well as various Bennets, Beauchamps, and de Bourghs for the first few weeks of August at Pemberley. He was in awe of his wife's ability to host a party at a home she had only just arrived at herself. It was a flash of a moment before they had to return to Longbourn for Mrs. Bennet's confinement.

Darcy would have preferred to stay at Netherfield with the Bingleys but Mr. and Mrs. Bennet insisted that they must stay at Longbourn. Here he was. He consoled himself with the fact that once Mrs. Bennet and little Thomas Bennet were churched that he and Elizabeth could return to Pemberley for the autumn. Alone, together.

As he was ruminating on the wondrous joy that was Elizabeth Darcy, he saw his wife and all the other ladies rise to remove to the drawing room. The footmen removed the plates and second course, while Mr. Bennet brought out his best brandy for the gentlemen.

Several toasts were proposed by Bingley, Mr. Philips, and a rather lengthy one on the joys of a quiver full of children by Mr. Johnstone. Darcy duly raised a toast of his own to the continuation of the Bennet line at Longbourn for many more generations. After the first glass of brandy, a second was poured and the gentlemen moved seats to have new conversations. Darcy found himself at the foot of the table with his old friend and nemesis, George Wickham.

At first both men remained quiet as they sipped their brandies, to their astonishment it was Darcy who broke the silence.

"I must know," Darcy asked in a low tone of voice, "how are you getting on?"

"Well. I am sure you have heard from your wife that I am now a full clerk at Mr. Philips' office and taking the exam to qualify as a solicitor to the common law courts in the autumn."

"George, may I call you George?" Darcy asked tentatively. Wickham nodded. "Both of our fathers would be very proud of you right now."

Darcy extended his hand. Before Wickham would take it, he asked, "Fitz, are you proud of me or are you withholding your approval until I can further prove myself?"

Darcy continued to extend his hand and looked Wickham in the eye, "I am proud of the steps you have taken this year to improve yourself and your situation."

Wickham nodded again and shook Darcy's hand. "It has not been easy. I have made so many bad choices this past decade that I have to think and rethink again on each new good choice, however small it may be." Wickham dipped his head at the three older gentlemen at the head of the table. "Without their guidance and a not a few lectures from Mr. Bennet, Mr. Johnstone, and Mr. Philips I would not be here tonight nor in my current employment."

Wickham lifted his glass and Darcy clinked it. "Truly, Fitz, it has been very hard to stay on the straight and narrow. For a long time, I worried that I would never reach the true status of a gentleman by my wits and charm alone. Now I worry that I can retain the status of middling solicitor with an improving character by dint of hard work and much toil. Don't tell me it will get easier with time to make a decision for right and good; I know it and feel it down to my bones each and every time I figure out how to not saunter downwards."

Darcy laughed. "George, can I ask one question of the past that has plagued me these few months?" At Wickham's assent, Darcy inquired, "When you came back to me in the year Ten and asked for the Kympton living because the law had not been profitable - what did you exactly mean by that?"

Wickham cleared his throat and took a long sip of Bennet's excellent brandy. He did not gulp it, as he did not want to waste what would be his second and last glass of brandy. "Frankly, Fitz, you may not know this but after you gave me the three thousand pounds in lieu of the living, I - in fact and in deed - commenced on the study of the law at the Inns of Court for three years. After the three years of study and dinners were completed, I was not called to the bar."

Darcy was astonished. "You completed the full three year course of the study of the law after Cambridge and you were not called to the bar? I was under the impression that..."

Wickham interrupted him, "That I lied to you and did not study the law at all but merely lived a life of vice and dissipation? No, I was told that as the son of a steward that I had not the connections to have one of the judges call me to the bar."

"Why did you not call on me so that I could ask my great-uncle the judge to call you to the bar?"

"Pride, anger, and pride again." Wickham looked about and leaned in. "I desired to do it of my own merit, not with the help of the Darcy family."

"Thus, when the money was all gone, you came to me to ask for the Kympton living but why did not say anything more than that the study of the law was unprofitable?"

"Do not mistake me, Fitz, I did gamble and whore my way through the three years of law studies, I was no saint."

Darcy stared at Wickham, he did not want to break this fragile peace between them but he also wanted to know...

"Fitz, I was full of pride and schemes of my own future exaltation." Wickham lowered his head and took a deep breath, then he whispered, "Please forgive me for my grave sins against you and Miss Darcy last summer. I was deeply in debt and was more than a fool - it was a malicious action which I have no excuse for."

Rather than address the Ramsgate incident, Darcy asked again, "You studied the full course of law at the Inns and were not admitted to the bar and that is what you meant when..."

"Yes. If you can't forgive me now for Ramsgate, please file it away for a later time when I have continued to build my good reputation and character. I have been meeting weekly with Mr. Johnstone and it

has been very profitable for my program of improvement and refor-
mation."

Darcy raised an eyebrow and took the last sip from his brandy
glass. "What do you want from your future life?"

"I want a family, a home, and a community to be a part of. I have
the beginnings of a home in the Old Rectory, the start of a community at the law office as well as the Longbourn church, and the four
and twenty families here in the Meryton area. Eventually, I hope -
Lord willing - that I will be blessed with a family." Wickham said
earnestly.

"George, I pray that you can achieve this future life. Do not back-
slide into your previous life."

"I try not to look too far into the future, but take each day as I
may and try to live it to the best of my ability."

Darcy extended his hand again. "That is the best any of us can
do."

Wickham extended his hand and they shook. Both heard sounds
of the piano playing a song and the sweet sound of the ladies singing.

Wickham stood and asked all the gentlemen, "What are we doing sitting in here when there is music and delightful company to be
had in the drawing room?"

Same evening, somewhat later
Longbourn Manor

A slightly tipsy and deliriously happy Mr. Bennet left the party
early to visit with his new heir and to see if his wife was well. As he
entered her rooms, he saw the baby asleep in a bassinet next to Mrs.
Bennet's bed and the lady herself in slumber. He tiptoed into the
room and sat lightly on the edge of the bed to peer at his grandson,
or his son as the world would know him. Little Thomas was perfect,

from his translucent eyelids, to his dark lashes, to his little nose, and the shock of hair extending out in all directions from his head.

As Mr. Bennet reached out to tuck the blanket more firmly under Thomas, his wife awoke. From her position on the bed, she asked, "Is he not the most perfect boy you have ever beheld, Mr. Bennet?"

"Yes, he is. I am in awe of him."

"Mr. Bennet, I am deeply happy to have given birth to a son. I feel a peace that I have not felt in the four and twenty years since Jane was born." Mrs. Bennet began to cry tears of joy. She then whispered, "I feel a deep joy. Thank you for arranging for his birth."

Bennet looked at his wife with a gentle gaze. "Francine, I feel a sense of peace and joy that I have not felt in years as well." He picked up her hand and tenderly kissed her soft palm. "I wish to give you a gift. What would you most like to celebrate the birth of your son? A parure of diamonds or rubies?"

"Mr. Bennet, I am very tired of talking and not being heard." Her eyes drooped as she struggled to stay awake. "The only gift I want is for you to listen to me when I speak, to really take the time to hear me."

"Oh, Francine, I apologize. Please have patience with me. I promise I will do my best to listen and hear you." Bennet was not sure if she heard his promise, as she was now asleep, thus he returned to admiring little Thomas and how perfect he was.

On the morrow, he would have to send a letter to Mr. Collins to announce his heir's birth before Lady Lucas sent one. For now, he was content, full of joy, and at peace with his life and marriage. The Bennets would continue at Longbourn, as they had since the year of our Lord Twelve Hundred and Sixty Three.

Perhaps, next year he could convince Mrs. Bennet and Mr. Wickham to try for a spare...

Chapter 16 - The Epilogue

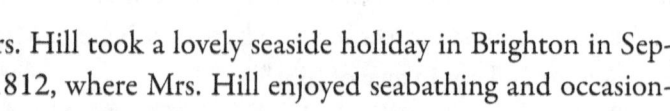

Mr. and Mrs. Hill took a lovely seaside holiday in Brighton in September of 1812, where Mrs. Hill enjoyed seabathing and occasionally ogling young officers in their red coats. Mr. Hill found himself sunburnt across his nose for the first time since he went into service at age twelve. It was a wonderfully relaxing two weeks.

To the great astonishment of the fine folk of Meryton, in late 1813 at the grand age of one and forty, Mrs. Bennet delivered another son to a delighted Mr. Bennet. After Mrs. Bennet confessed to Mr. Bennet that she believed both sons had been conceived upon his favorite reading chair, with some measure of chagrin he gifted it to her. She had it installed in the family sitting room, and she would sigh happily every time she sat on it. Life was busy at Longbourn as the voices of two young boys and the pitter patter of little feet could be heard running down the halls, even with all of their daughters either married or finishing up at school.

Mr. Philips made Mr. Wickham a full partner in the solicitor business in October 1814. By the time Wellington had rid Europe of Bonaparte the second time, Mr. Wickham had over £2000 in the funds, a good attorney position and much to the surprise of all, made an offer of marriage to Miss Elinor Beauchamp - a woman worthy of being pleased. What no one, with the exception of the Longbourn vicar, could figure out was how Mr. Wickham was able to court a young lady who lived in Derbyshire while he firmly resided in Meryton.

Little did they know, but Mr. Johnstone discovered during one of their weekly meetings that Mr. Wickham had long admired Miss Beauchamp, whose father was the rector after Mr. Bennet and a second cousin to the Beauchamps. Longbourn's vicar encouraged Wickham to not lose this chance to win a lady worth being called wife. It was a rather mysterious courtship that included letters between the two vicars arranging for the two young people to make a match of it.

In the Autumn of 1833, much to the delight of all parties Mr. Wickham prepared and successfully represented to the Courts of Chancery the case of "Bennet and Bennet" to break the Longbourn entail.

Over the years, Mr. and Mrs. Wickham had three sons and one daughter of their own and increased the Old Rectory's tenanted lands as they purchased more of the farmland adjacent to the Old Rectory that was not a part of the Longbourn nor Netherfield estates. By the time the Wickham boys were ready to go to school and after Mr. Philips retired, the family had nearly 2,500 acres and £3000 per annum between rents, as well as Mr. Wickham's now ownership of the Meryton and surrounds solicitor business. In the end, Wickham's combination of tenant rents, law income, and interest from investments gave him an income a tad hair larger than Bingley's. By his middle years, George Wickham was very satisfied that he had lived a worthy life as a husband, solicitor, and member of the Meryton community.

Genetics, not yet discovered, unfortunately overcame any good intentions and foxglove tisane drinking on Mr. Hurst's part. In 1813, at age 33, he died quietly on the sofa after dinner one night of a heart attack. After her time of mourning was over, Louisa met through the Gardiners a fine, handsome, sociable, and very rich tradesman - a Mr. M.C. Malvern, and married him, much to Miss Bingley's horror. In a spark of coincidence, Mr. Malvern was a first cousin twice removed from Mr. Hurst's grandfather. They had a number of children, of which, Louisa's daughter, Frederica, would go on to marry the Hurst heir - Sir Thurston Hurst, III. Louisa Bingley Hurst Malvern lived a long and happy life with a delightful man who brushed his teeth daily without having been asked to do so.

Colonel Fitzwilliam tried various stratagems post-Waterloo to create a new life for himself to no avail. In early 1817, after the year of no summer & terrible harvest, he decided to follow his cousin Bennet's suggestions and threw society's restrictions to the wind. He went into business with Mr. Gardiner as his import/export negotiator in the East Indies. Before he departed in late 1817, he made one last attempt to convince the newly sober Miss Bingley to marry him before he left for India. Much to his surprise, she accepted.

In the East Indies, the good Colonel made quite a bit of money in the silk and cotton trade for himself, the Gardiners, and their investors - various Bennets, Bingleys, and Darcys. Caroline and the former Miss Fenimore, who had just lost her husband, were reunited in early 1818. The Colonel, Caroline, and the former Miss Fenimore remained happy and relatively sober as a nice threesome until they all died in their old age, or in the Colonel's case of a particularly acute attack of gout, malaria and dengue fever when he was sixty-nine years old. The Colonel left a great deal of money to his descendants, more than his brother Lord Lindon as Earl of Matlock left to his. Once the steamers were in force, a bit after 1837, The Darcys made the trip from UK to Egypt, over land some odd miles, and then a steamer boat from Suez to Madras, India, and visited the Fitzwilliams several times. The Bingleys were only as adventurous to have made the long voyage once.

To everyone's surprise, with the exception of Mr. Darcy, Lydia graduated from Matlock College, Cambridge, with a Bachelor's in Literature & Rhetoric in 1817. She married one of the de Bourgh cousins, a barrister, in 1818 after her season in Town with the Beauchamps. The newly wedded couple lived in London and she helped him craft his rhetorical arguments and read all his law books. Eventually as times changed, after bearing two children, she shocked everyone by applying to the Bar and passing. de Bourgh and de

Bourgh barristers were formidable and nearly unbeatable in the 1830s-1850s.

Mr. Collins, defrocked as heir to Longbourn by the birth of young master Thomas Bennet and never able to sire children with his wife, served as parson at Hunsford for another seven years until he was convinced that the Lord was calling him to the mission field. Charlotte and Lady Catherine de Bourgh were not quite sure about this calling and encouraged him to go on a trial trip while Charlotte remained in Hunsford.

Mr. Collins departed in 1819 for a two year mission in West Africa and never returned, nor was he ever heard from again even by the other Missionaries with whom he had arrived with in Freetown. After not hearing a peep from the man after three years, Lady Catherine gave Charlotte a nice cottage plus a few acres of land adjacent to Hunsford and hired a new vicar. After Mr. Collins was declared legally dead, Charlotte - at the grand age of 51 - remarried a local widowed squire. They enjoyed his grandchildren and lived quite happily near Seven Oaks until she passed away.

Anne de Bourgh married her scholar, Baltazar Chapman Turing, Ph.D., in the autumn of 1812 and they both remained in Cambridge and achieved full professorships. Lord Matlock bestowed a mathematics professorship on Anne that was the first full professorship given to a woman at Cambridge. By the time of Anne's death in the 1870s, there were four chairs bestowed to lady scholars at Matlock College and it produced many fine, young scientists, doctors, lawyers, and mathematicians amongst its young lady graduates through the course of the 19th and 20th centuries.

The young Sir Lewis de Bourgh obliquely fulfilled his mother's desire to unite Rosings and Pemberley when he married his cousin, Miss Georgiana Darcy, two years after her debut. Lewis and Georgie gave Lady Catherine many grandchildren to coo over. Life was good at Rosings Park. Strangely, at least to the younger generation, none of the de Bourgh offspring were allowed to marry any of the Darcy offspring.

Mrs. Bennet passed away in 1823, age 51, of a fever that swept Hertfordshire - which she insisted was a cold. Her last words were, "No one dies of a trifling cold!"

The widowed mother of Mr. Wickham, Lady Lavinia Wickham Hurst and Mr. Bennet married in 1824 and together finished raising the Bennet boys and Hurst son. They enjoyed all of their Bennet and Wickham grandchildren. Mr. Bennet's felicity increased every year, as he was now married to his one true love and they were raising their sons together.

Even after paying out dowries for all five of his very accomplished daughters and breaking the entail on the Longbourn estate, Mr. Bennet continued saving and investing and eventually he bought back all the lands that his brother and great-great grandfather lost. Longbourn was inherited by his first son, Netherfield by his second son with farmlands reapportioned to make Longbourn the larger estate, and the Old Rectory by the Wickhams.

Sir Thurston Hurst, III, grew up to be a fine young man who inherited both a thriving estate and a large amount of money that had prudently been invested in the Funds - as managed by Mr. Bennet. He was a tee-totaller who only liked to eat plain food, was a great walker, and he loved the Lord. Young Thurston married Louisa Bingley Hurst Malvern's daughter, Frederica, by her second husband and they had a quiver full of children.

And what of Charles and Jane Bingley? They had six children, all girls, until at last a boy was born on Jane's fortieth birthday. Due to Mr. & Mrs. Bingley's passion for medieval history and battles, they first decorated Netherfield, and then after Bingley sold it to Mr. Bennet - an estate in Derbyshire in medieval battle decor. As a family they enjoyed taking their holidays to visit famous battle sites, including Agincourt.

They had enough children and relations to do re-enactments of great medieval battles - very popular with all the Darcy, de Bourgh, Beauchamp, and Wickham children. The Bingleys' youngest, plainest and only brown haired daughter went on to marry a friend from Oxford, who was the heir to a dukedom that included a Scottish castle, wherein the Battle of Bannockburn was re-enacted every September during the hunting season by the next generation.

Until she passed away in 1839 at 91 years of age, Lady Catherine de Bourgh continued to visit with Mr. Bennet - much to the embarrassment of Mr. Darcy, although Elizabeth did understand Lady Catherine's need for comfort and a good argument. Mr. Bennet passed in 1846. He was survived by his wife, Mrs. Lavinia Wickham Hurst Bennet, who lived to the ripe old age of 97.

And what of the Darcys? Mr. Fitzwilliam Darcy and Mrs. Elizabeth Bennet Darcy enjoyed a long and fruitful marriage, of which the first few years were spent traveling around the British Isles until the first of an assortment of girls and boys were born. Darcy and Elizabeth as a couple greatly enjoyed reading, loving, and a good roaring debate. Once they launched the oldest three of their children off to university, they felt free to start traveling to the Continent, Egypt, and eventually to the East Indies. Luckily for the Darcys, their eldest daughter was a dab hand at estate management and their second son inherited the Bennet knack for mathematics and investing. The first son was too busy avoiding matchmaking mamas and randy widows, as well as skirting the edges of ballrooms, to become accomplished at much more than evasion, stony silence, and staring out of windows. Not a single one of them married one of their numerous cousins.

Longbourn, Netherfield, and the Old Rectory lands were kept in the Bennet/Wickham family until 1987, when it was sold to a real estate developer who built a semi-detached housing estate with parks and a school on the Hatfield rail line into London's Kings Cross. Strangely enough, the developer was a man named Thomas de

Bourgh who hailed from a commuter town called Hunsford in Kent. The Netherfield mansion house was then restored and turned into a hotel and conference center that catered to corporate training on the weekdays and romantic breaks on the weekend.

Don't miss out!

Visit the website below and you can sign up to receive emails whenever Jenifer Hanen publishes a new book. There's no charge and no obligation.

https://books2read.com/r/B-A-IASAC-YZDCE

BOOKS 2 READ

Connecting independent readers to independent writers.

About the Author

Jenifer Hanen, aka Ms. Jen, is a writer, photographer, and web designer. She enjoys humor, Regency and historical fiction, living in the mountains, and all things web.

Read more at https://www.msjen.com.

www.ingramcontent.com/pod-product-compliance
Lightning Source LLC
Chambersburg PA
CBHW020637260626
47157CB00008B/2791